I PROMISE YOU

Wall Street Journal Bestselling Author
ILSA MADDEN-MILLS

I Promise You
Copyright © 2020 by Ilsa Madden-Mills
Cover Designer: Letitia Hasser, RBA Designs
Photographer: Wander Aguiar
Model: Kaz
Editor: C Marie and Rebecca, Fairest Reviews Editing
Proof Reader: Deaton Author Services

IMM Publishing
ISBN: 9798694398961

Copyright Law:

If you are reading this book and did not purchase it, this book has been pirated and you are stealing. Please delete it from your device and support the author by purchasing a legal copy. All rights reserved. Without limiting the rights under copyright reserved above, no part of this publication may be reproduced, stored in or introduced into a retrieval system, or transmitted in any form, or by any means (electronic, mechanical, photocopying, recording, or otherwise) without the prior written permission of the above copyright owner of this book or publisher.

This is a work of fiction. Names, characters, places, brands, media, and incidents are either the product of the author's imagination or are used fictitiously. The author acknowledges the trademarked statue and trademark owners of various products referenced in this work of fiction, which have been used without permission. The publication/use of these trademarks is not authorized, associated with, or sponsored by the trademark owners.

First Edition October 2020

TABLE OF CONTENTS

Prologue	---------------------------------	1
Chapter 1	---------------------------------	13
Chapter 2	---------------------------------	24
Chapter 3	---------------------------------	39
Chapter 4	---------------------------------	48
Chapter 5	---------------------------------	65
Chapter 6	---------------------------------	79
Chapter 7	---------------------------------	87
Chapter 8	---------------------------------	99
Chapter 9	---------------------------------	116
Chapter 10	--------------------------------	123
Chapter 11	--------------------------------	132
Chapter 12	--------------------------------	154
Chapter 13	--------------------------------	179
Chapter 14	--------------------------------	193
Chapter 15	--------------------------------	210
Chapter 16	--------------------------------	219
Chapter 17	--------------------------------	243
Chapter 18	--------------------------------	259
Chapter 19	--------------------------------	265
Chapter 20	--------------------------------	273
Chapter 21	--------------------------------	285
Chapter 22	--------------------------------	299
Chapter 23	--------------------------------	304
Chapter 24	--------------------------------	317
Chapter 25	--------------------------------	332
Chapter 26	--------------------------------	345
Chapter 27	--------------------------------	352
Chapter 28	--------------------------------	363
Chapter 29	--------------------------------	367
Chapter 30	--------------------------------	371
Epilogue	----------------------------------	378

I PROMISE YOU PLAYLIST

Check out the below link to hear the music that inspired I Promise You!

http://bit.ly/IpromiseYou

DEDICATION

This book is for all the girls in the world who believe in the power of destiny and true love.

PROLOGUE

Dillon

There's a universal truth at Waylon University: the first girl you kiss freshman year at the annual bonfire party is the one you'll never forget. She'll crawl under your skin and make her way into your heart. She'll spark a passion so fierce you'll burn the world down to possess her.

You might even put a ring on it.

But...

As in all things with fate, the caveat is timing. That kiss can go horribly wrong. She might not want you. She might run in the opposite direction.

And because you kissed, you are screwed.

Supposedly.

The ridiculous legend—*the warning*—swirls around in my head as I saunter around the crackling fire, my eyes surveying the party in the meadow. The September night is crisp with autumn, the scent of leaves and smoke from the fire wafting in the air. The crowd of students is thick and mostly drunk, some headed to the barn for games, others dancing as a band plays on a stage. My gaze snags on a couple as they sit under a giant oak tree and make out. Here's some truth: I'm kissing no one tonight. I'm not the superstitious sort, but I'll admit to a good sense of self-preservation.

Sorority girls follow me as I shoulder my way through the crush of people. I shake off an insistent blonde in a Theta jersey who's been tailing me since I got here.

"Not tonight, sweetheart," I tell her with a lazy smile when she latches onto my arm again. She's hot, all long legs and big tits. "Find me tomorrow." After this legend crap is null and void.

"Sure, baby. Call me. I stuck my digits in your back pocket."

Of course she did.

She gives me a blinding smile, strokes my arm, and flounces off.

Some of the guys from the team call my name, motioning me over as they stand next to a keg. I head that way and am almost there when—

Wait.

I stop and my body tenses when I see *her*.

This girl.

I do a double take.

What the...

An unseen hand strokes down my spine.

She dances alone in the midst of a crowd. Flickering light from the nearby fire glitters over her body, half of her in a dusky shadow, the other draped in glowing illumination. Tanned, slender legs bend as she twirls in a short red mini skirt and black military boots. Swinging her hips, she holds her long hair up as she sways. There's a dandelion tattoo on her nape.

A silver piercing in her belly button glints under the lights. Closing her eyes, she undulates her body in a hypnotic body roll, her arms stretched toward the sky as she moves to the bass of the guitar.

Her face is heart-shaped with high cheekbones, her lips bee-stung full. Dark eyebrows frame eyes with a slight tilt at the corners. Her breasts are small but pert as they push against a white crop top with suspenders that snap to her skirt. "Not my type," I murmur to myself, taking in her petite frame.

"Get over here, rookie!" comes from one of the guys, and I wave them off, still watching the babe. From a few feet away, a dude with a red Solo cup in his hand also checks her out. His buddies slap him on the back, urging him on. He takes a deep swig of his drink, hands it off to a friend, and pushes his way through the throng toward her. Dancing behind her, he grabs her hips and leans into her. She shoves him away, and I smile. That's right, sweetheart. Be you. Dance alone.

Or not, I muse.

Screw that legend. It can't be real, and my type or not, I'd like a taste of her.

I maneuver her way, moving through the crowd—

"Dillon! Let's go, man. The guys are asking for you," comes from Blaze as he grabs my shoulder and drags me to the group of football players. He hands me a beer and grins broadly. He's a sophomore, and we just met at summer camp. I have a good feeling about him; in fact, the whole team is like a dream come true. I know I'm not the best player—yet—but it's the happiest I've been since my brother died.

"We're gonna get a group together to enter the rope pull contest. Those Kappa guys are built like tractors, but we can take 'em. You in?" He pops an eyebrow at me.

"Mhmm," I reply, my gaze back to the girl as yet another guy approaches her. She's like a damn magnet. She gives him a withering glare then prances off and settles closer to the stage. *Off limits*, her body language declares.

Vicious girl.

She knows what she wants, and it isn't those guys.

"I thought this kid was focused. He looks dazed," Ryker murmurs. He snaps his fingers in my face. "Freshman, get your eyes off the girl."

"Done," I say, looking at him. Ryker's our starting quarterback, and I have a ton of respect for him.

Ryker chuckles. "It's your first bonfire, but don't be fooled. Remember: if you see a girl you like—"

"Run as if there's a three-hundred-pound linebacker on your ass. Don't engage. Do not get leg-shackled," I repeat, recalling the warnings the upperclassmen gave us at their dorm room before we piled into cars and drove to the party.

A deep laugh comes from Maverick, another sophomore and our best defensive player. "No joke. There's weird juju in this part of the woods."

I let my gaze drift back to her. "Meh, she looks harmless to me." And what would be wrong with talking to her? Getting a name and number? "Starting to think you tell all the freshmen that so you guys can pick out the hot girls for yourselves."

Maverick looks at me, and whatever he sees on my face makes him smirk. "Let me tell you a story, kid. I kissed a girl freshman year at this party, and the next time I saw her, she was dating our kicker. Weird, man, just strange how she's always in my head. I'm telling you, don't get sucked in. Not worth the headache."

"Uh-huh. Sounds like she found something better." I grin.

Maverick barks out a laugh. "Tell him, Blaze."

"The legend got me by my balls last year, man," Blaze

says ruefully as he shakes his head. "I kissed this chick and we ended up in the loft of the barn making out hot and heavy. Poof. She disappears on me. You see a girl with pink hair, call me."

"Sure." I'm barely listening, my eyes darting back to the dancing girl, trying to be covert but also not really caring what they think right now.

Ryker guffaws. "Kid, you're wearing a hungry look. If you wanna go talk to the girl, go on—"

"Says the guy who hasn't kissed anyone at the bonfire," Maverick interrupts tersely.

Ryker laughs, waving him off. "But as the legend says, it will come back to haunt you, Dillon, somehow, someday. Wiccans used to live on this land, and they specialized in love spells. The ground we're standing on is where they lived, where they did their sacrifices. Some say they're buried in the woods—"

Someone snorts in the background, and I roll my eyes. "Seriously? Come on. There's no legend, is there? This is a prank and you pull it on all the freshmen."

Maverick mimics dusting his hands off. "Alright, why don't you test it and we'll find out? Just remember, once you kiss her, it's branded on your heart, some kind of soulmate thing."

"I call bullshit," I say on a scoff.

He nods. "Swear. Go to the library on campus. It's in the history books about Magnolia. They called themselves the Daughters of Venus. You know who Venus is, right? Roman goddess of love, desire, and fertility."

Unease curls in my gut. If these guys aren't kidding... "Venus?"

Maverick nods. "Read it after what happened to me freshman year."

"But the legend itself isn't in these books? Just the history of the wiccans?" I need specifics. I really want to go talk to this girl.

Maverick raises a brow. "The legend is superstition based on personal experiences. Do you really want to question hundreds of stories from former Waylon students? It's believed the legend only applies to your first bonfire or to a freshman, so technically the upperclassmen who've been here before can kiss anyone without getting hexed, but who knows what's really true." His broad shoulders shrug. "I avoid all girls at the bonfire now."

The seriousness of his tone gets to me.

Okay, I lied before. I *am* superstitious. Athletes generally are. Sawyer, another freshman, likes to eat a piece of the grass before he takes the field. If it's turf, he kisses it. Other guys do similar things. And me? Before every game and at halftime, I kiss the tops of my hands as I walk out of the tunnel. It started my senior year in high school, a silent greeting sent up to my brother in heaven. The tradition brought me a prep school state championship. Some scoff at athletes performing repetitive tasks before they play, but it gives me a measure of control and confidence that I'm going to have a kickass game. My motto is, *if you believe your ritual gives you a topnotch performance, then why not do it?*

Ryker laughs. "Stop messing with him, Mav."

"I'm not!" he replies. "Delaney..." He grimaces. "She's everywhere I turn—with another guy..." He takes a swig of his beer.

I don't know this Delaney, but judging by his face, she got under his skin... "Alright, you convinced me." I pull out the phone number the Theta tucked in my pocket, crumble it up, and toss it in the fire. It's extreme, but hey, I'm leery of all and any repercussions from the legend. Sure, I want to meet a nice girl someday in the future, but not my freshman year. Plus, Maverick and Blaze's stories don't have happy endings.

Blaze slaps me on the back. "Smart. Wait out the curse. Don't even talk to a girl tonight."

An hour later, I've had a couple of beers and leave to grab another round for us when I see her again, still dancing. Damn. Isn't she tired? I stop and stare as she dips down then snaps back up as she slings her hair. She moves like a pro. Stripper? Nah. She's too young and fresh looking. Maybe a dance major...

My fascination from earlier resurfaces, intensifying tenfold. I've imagined her before, like in a fantasy. The slope of her bare shoulder, the dimple at the base of her spine, the weight of her breasts in my hands—

Impossible. I've never seen this girl before tonight.

It's the beer talking.

Yet...

Another lingering look at her and my skin hums, the beat of the nearby speakers pounding, syncing with the thrumming rhythm of my heart. I swallow thickly and nerves fly at me, the same way I feel as I look down a football field with the ball in my hands. Barely aware of what I'm doing, I set my drink on the ground and walk her way. I'm behind her in ten seconds, wondering what the hell is happening.

Don't even talk to a girl chimes in my head, but I ignore it. I can't resist the temptation. What's wrong with just having a little conversation?

The wind rustles through the trees, carrying her scent to me, something tart and fruity.

"Hey," I say softly.

She doesn't hear me.

"Hey!" I call.

She turns to me, her lips curled in a smile, and my stomach does a weird flip. An errant thought flies through my head—*Wish I could see the color of her eyes*—yet I don't need the light to see the teasing quality of her smile.

Ah, I get it. She's beautiful. She's used to guys coming up to her. Right.

But I'm different. I'm the one she's been waiting on.

Her hair is a rich mahogany color, intermingled with pops of copper and pale honey, and long, the soft ends brushing her mid-back. I picture my hands sliding through those strands as I spread them out on my pillow. I see her sleep-glazed eyes looking at me when she wakes in the morning—

Whoa... That's just insane.

"Hey?" Her voice is husky and low as she tilts her head, eyes peering deep into mine. The hairs on my arms rise, goosebumps erupting as instinct kicks in.

I pick you whispers through the right side of my brain while simultaneously my left side yells *Danger, danger.*

I kick the negative thought down as I lean down, my big hands awkward as I cup her face and brush my lips against hers softly. It's barely anything.

Holy shit, what have you done my brain yells.

She lets out a startled sound as we pull apart.

That's it, I tell myself, just a little taste and I'm not going to take it any further, but I do, ignoring that voice as I go in and slant my mouth across hers again. My tongue twines with hers, crushing her soft, pillowy lips under mine. She tastes like cherries, rich and sweet. There's a moment when she hesitates, then she melts into me, a whimpering sound coming from the back of her throat as she parts those luscious lips. Her hair blows around us, caressing my face, tickling my cheeks. The universe tilts, shifts, and spins off in a new direction.

The kiss burns a hole right through me and blood rushes to my groin. I'm in over my head—*Who cares?*—and I groan, deepening our connection. My hands slide down her cheeks, her throat, then to her arms at her sides. Our joined breaths mingling, I trace my thumbs over the rapid pulse in her wrists. My head swims with images of her body draped on top of me, her fingers tracing my heart as she counts the beats of *my* pulse—

A cry comes from her as she breaks away. "Jerk! Don't do that."

"You liked it, babe."

"What? No."

"I'm Dillon."

"Um, I don't care. Step away."

"What's your name? You got a number?" Dillon McQueen does not give up easily. When he sees what he wants, he goes after it. He also sometimes talks about himself in the third person. "Are you a freshman? I play football. Quarterback." Usually that's enough to catch a girl's interest.

She shakes her head, looking almost surprised as she touches her lips briefly. I think she mutters *pigskin-toting Casanova*. Then, she flips around.

"No, wait! Don't go!" I say, reaching out for her, but

she's gone, daring one look over her shoulder as she disappears into the crowd of people.

I take off after her, navigating through the throng, jostling into dancers. One of them, a big barrel-chested guy, shoves at me when I bump into him. I fall on my ass. Heart pounding, I scramble back up, dirt and grass on me as I dart through the crowd and look around. My height gives me a decent vantage point, but she's vanished.

Off in the distance, the football guys hoot my name, then chant *Venus* over and over.

Well, hell.

Legend 1, Dillon 0.

1

Serena

Three years later

A tall, ripped man wearing the tightest black leather pants I've ever seen struts into the Piggly Wiggly Saturday night.

Admittedly, I've never seen a dude in leather pants, so perhaps there might be some tighter, somewhere.

Why is his dress shirt unbuttoned?

My God, he is cut.

More importantly, where on *earth* did he come from? He's obviously not one of the laid-back locals here in Magnolia, Mississippi. They wear flannels and jeans or Waylon University apparel.

I tug my earbuds out, cutting off "Girl on Fire" by

Alicia Keys. True, it's my theme song, but this can't be missed.

I watch as an entourage of three women float through the sliding glass doors with him like pretty made-up dolls, each one long-legged and busty. They're also all wearing some form of cowhide.

One of the girls, a platinum-haired beauty in a red leather mini skirt and platform heels, trails behind him, adjusting his white dress shirt as it billows around his trim hips, giving a peek of tattoos and washboard abs with defined hills and valleys.

The brunette—dang, she looks like a tall Mila Kunis—wears a purple-fringed suede vest, skinny jeans, and strappy stilettos as she holds his hand and preens.

A willowy redhead with double Ds flanks his left side, her hand on his shoulder playing with the ends of his golden brown hair as it curls from underneath his ball cap. Her honest-to-God black and white cow-printed mini-dress looks amazing, as if it came straight from a New York runway.

His hat creates a slice of diagonal shadow on his chiseled face, giving me half a view of one bladed cheekbone and part of a full, pouty mouth. Dark stubble covers his diamond-cut jawline, and a pair of expensive silver-mirrored aviators shield his gaze. A golden belt buckle as big as a dessert plate glimmers at his waist.

There are so many sensory details hitting me at once

that my mind spins and my fingers twitch to write. *Serena Jensen uncovers secret leather cult inside the Piggly Wiggly. Someone call PETA.*

Wondering if they're even real—it's been a long week—I close my eyes and reopen them. Still there.

My spidey sense is screaming athlete judging by his muscular build and his height, around six foot, four inches. The man is practically towering, a veritable wall. Footballer, most likely—and not a Southern boy, because they wouldn't be caught dead in those pants. At least not in Magnolia, Mississippi. Maybe Memphis, just two hours away.

"Must be a full moon or a banging party," I muse aloud to a crate of seedless green grapes. They nod their agreement, silently reminding me that only weird people talk to inanimate objects.

"Just tired," I tell them as I pick up a bunch, put them in a plastic bag, and tie them off. I worked a catering job for the university last night, and I'm beat.

The man and his harem move farther inside the store, and a regretful pang washes over me. I didn't always spend my weekends at the grocery. The parties off campus used to be my favorite, especially the bonfire. Crisp fall weather, local bands, and macho games—there's nothing more entertaining than watching D1 jocks playing tug-of-war over a mud pit. I sigh. The last college party I went to was the bonfire my junior year.

I'm not that girl anymore. I work and study. I rarely go out just for fun. Nana says it's because I'm an Aquarius and we internalize heartbreak, taking longer to recover. My birth sign also means I'm offbeat and peculiar. True.

Mr. Hot Pants stops at the flower center, and the girls pause with him in sync, six eyes riveted to him, bodies on alert, anticipating what he'll do next. Maybe buy some supermarket roses for them?

Snapping a finger, he murmurs something I can't hear, and the blonde rushes to tug a piece of paper out of her purse. She drops it in his grasp then strokes his cheek before settling back into her position behind him, all of it graceful and mesmerizing—as if they've done this particular dance before. He whips off the sunglasses and tucks them handle side down inside the pocket of his dress shirt. Staring down at the paper, he smirks, and I think he mouths, *Oreos*.

Next to him, the girls await instruction like well-trained greyhounds. They stand patiently as his phone rings and he answers it, talks, and laughs at whoever is there then tucks the phone into the pocket of his pants. His thighs are muscled and thick, bulging against the leather. His stomach is sun-kissed and hard as iron. And, he's a leftie. "*A nice one*," I murmur to the grapes as the outline of his crotch draws my eyes. It's been a while, and a girl can look, okay? Just don't touch.

The moving around with his phone forces the

brunette to lose her hold on his hand, and the redhead jostles to his right side and elbows the brunette—*ouch, that looked like it hurt!*—then pounces to grasp his hand.

Chaos ensues.

"It's my turn, Bambi! You snooze, you lose!" exclaims the redhead with glee.

"Listen here, Ashley—" snaps Mila/Bambi.

"Can't we get what we need and leave without arguing?" grouses the blonde.

"Girls, please," comes his deep voice. "No fighting. The number-one rule: all of you get along or I'm not doing this."

Rules?

Oh, oh, he's *precious*.

The sexy beast emits a lopsided smile that's somehow perfect, an aw-shucks attitude blended with an air of confidence that only comes from a man who's had women at his feet since he was born. "You're all beautiful, sweethearts. Breathtaking, the cream of the crop, and, yes, any man would be lucky to have you on his arm." He tucks his list away. "But, I'm a lot. Being with me is hard, and really, I'm not worthy of any of you."

"You are!" they exclaim.

Is he?

"Wicked, wicked boy," I murmur under my breath. I take in the muscular chest, those rippling muscles. "Hmm. I'd turn you into a centaur if I wrote about you."

I sneak a bit closer to them, easing behind a display of Little Debbie cakes. I'm not really spying, not truly, just curious. It's the writer in me; I get ideas from the strangest occurrences.

He rocks on his heels, seeming to think for a moment as he gazes at the girls. "Fine, if you insist, you must know that I like a girl who loves the game as much as I do."

"We do," they say ardently.

He puts his hands on his hips, paces around for several moments in deep thought. "I know you love the game, but my girl also needs a good grasp on my stats—even how fast I run the forty-yard dash."

"4.7 seconds," declares Mila/Bambi, giving the other girls triumphant looks. "One of the fastest in the league for a quarterback."

He blinks. "But... I know this is a new thing, so don't get pissed, but she needs to know the running back, tight end, and wide receiver's stats too. I know, I know, I see it on your faces—something new. Thing is, in the end, stats help me with my game, and you do want me to play pro, right? Make the big money?"

"But, Dillon, I already know your stats." Mila/Bambi rattles off percentages and phrases: *total plays, passing attempts, completions, yards rushing...* It's like Greek to me, and I get lost during her Ted Talk.

"Why are you giving us new requirements?" the blonde demands.

"Because football is a game of numbers. My girl, maybe the love of my life"—he places his hand over his heart—"will live and breathe numbers...for the whole offense."

"That's eleven players!" she replies.

He nods. "A complete analysis for the past three years will work."

His announcement goes over like a lead balloon as the girls glower and give each other baleful looks, maybe fearing one of the others already has these strange stats in her back pocket?

He continues, "If that's too much, I totally get it if you want to drop out. My loss."

"We can do it!" Mila/Bambi and the redhead say.

A worried expression flits over his face, quickly hidden. "Are you sure? You'll have to talk to coaches and assistants to get the numbers and then make an Excel spreadsheet. Are any of you a statistics major?"

They admit they aren't.

"Well, that's just too bad," he murmurs. "This is going to be a lot of work. I don't think you have the time to commit to it. You have classes and your own personal lives." He sighs—extravagantly—his muscled chest wilting, his shoulders slumping as if they've just told him his puppy died. He appears so despondent, I half-expect him to wipe a tear from his eye.

My eyes narrow. He's a faker.

"It sounds easy enough. I'm pre-med with a 4.0," Mila/Bambi declares, and I stifle a sound of surprise. Jersey chasers for the win, I say! Beautiful, intelligent women can fawn over athletes all they want. I'm a believer in women following their own path, and if she's in some sort of competition to win this guy's favor, well, who am I to judge?

Once, I was like her, and I would have moved heaven and earth for a certain musician. I made myself available the moment he called, skipping classes to go to every gig within a four-hour drive of Magnolia. I treasured each moment we shared together, rolling them over in my heart like little jewels, certain he loved me. Newsflash: he didn't. Not the way I needed. I wasn't technically a "groupie" because he called me his girlfriend, but it was a very thin line. Part of his appeal *was* the music.

"I'm pre-law, and there's no doubt I can do it," quips the blonde with a mulish look on her face. "Though I personally hate math."

"Dillon, Babycakes, I can switch my major to statistics," offers the redhead as she poses in her cow-print dress.

I bite back my giggle at the flash of fear that flits over his face before he covers it up with that disarming, sexy, oh-so-slow smile. "Nah, no need for that, Ashley. You're a senior—too late to be changing majors. You've got a whole future in..." He purses his lips, thinking.

"Music. I texted you a video of me singing Taylor Swift's 'Lover' last week. Remember? I said it reminded me of us."

"Um, yeah." Another long-suffering exhalation as he stares at the floor for several tense moments then looks up at them. "Truthfully, I'm asking too much for just a date with me. I know you ladies signed up for this tradition we have between the team and the Thetas, and I'm the prize"—he winces—"but maybe you should move on to Sawyer or Troy and convince them to do it. They're gonna be superstars, and I'm going to be focused on winning games. This contest won't lead to a relationship—"

Ashley tosses her red hair and lifts her chin. "The football players voted *you* as the prize, not Sawyer or Troy, and you agreed in May. We can't change it and you can't back out now. It's not fair. We've been at your beck and call since summer camp."

His face flattens. "Yes, I'm aware of your presence everywhere I turn."

She smiles sweetly, her nails trailing over his muscled forearm. "We'll get to work on the stats, and you'll choose the winner before the dance." Ashley inspects the other girls, and they nod their assent then look back at him.

He thinks for a moment then plants his hands on his hips, calling attention to long, tan fingers and his taut six-pack. A long, gusty exhale comes from him. "Son of a nutcracker, alright. Until then, no arguing, no name-calling, and no sneaking into my room at night, feel me?"

They nod and he seems to find his equilibrium, then murmurs something as he touches each girl, a stroke of his hand there, a cheek kiss for another, an ass pat for the next.

A bubble of laughter escapes me, but it goes unheard as Patsy Cline sings on the PA system, crooning about being crazy about a man. Seems appropriate.

I pause, nearly dropping the mango in my hand. Wait a minute... *Son of a nutcracker?* I know that! Where's it from? It sounded odd coming from him. It's not a Southern saying—wait, yes! *Buddy the Elf!*

I grab my phone from my purse. Dang, this is so perfect! Just what I need for the photo/video bingo challenge we have going in the journalism grad department. It's going to be hard to top someone's pic of Professor Whitley getting his bum attacked by a goose on the quad yesterday (excellent for the *Animal Attack on Campus* category), but a woman-wrangling athlete quoting Buddy checks the *Likes to Quote Will Ferrell* box. Gah, I just might win!

Normally, I wouldn't be so motivated to win the pool, but the prize is five hundred dollars and this girl needs new tires. Not only that, my poor car is falling apart, overhead lights winking off and on, the motor sputtering at every stop sign and red light. I'm driving on a prayer. The newspaper isn't paying me for the internship, and my catering jobs are scarce. It would be nice to have extra money and not worry about depleting my meager savings.

Scrambling around in my purse, I finally find my phone and yank it out, only I stumble over a crate of pumpkins—*Why are they out in August?*—and my cell flies out of my hand, landing under the refrigerated fish section ten feet away. Dashing over, I bend down, butt in the air, *I don't care*, and snag it. Phone clasped tightly, I jerk up to my feet—*Success!*—but Mr. Hot Pants and his entourage have vanished.

I blow out a breath.

Shoot.

Then I smile.

2

Serena

"Where are the blasted Oreos?" I say loudly enough to get his attention. My hands plant on my hips (just like his did earlier) as I check then re-check the shelves. "Usually, they're next to the Nutter Butters," I tell the strawberries in my cart. It's sad that my friends are either produce or my family.

"You missed out," says a deep male voice behind me. "So good, right? They're my favorite. I mix up how I eat them. The first bite, I nibble, then the next one I take my time, separate the wafer from the white cream, and lick it off."

I realize two things at once. One, he said *lick*, which is gross, and, two, he isn't flirting with me, not when his voice screams *boredom*.

Fine. I don't want him to flirt with me.

Nana likes to say, *Serena, you don't like to start trouble, yet somehow it's always there when you arrive.* Might get that as a tattoo, but first, a long sigh comes from my chest as I prepare to annoy Mr. Hot Pants enough to say *son of a nutcracker*. The fighter inside of me, the one who's been hurt and trampled by another pretty boy, is roaring to rip him apart, to be cold as ice and let him know I am unaffected by his hot guy aura, but the other side of me is pissed I'm wearing a coffee-stained, holey Four Dragons band shirt and baggy camo pants that make me look like I'm ready for a deer hunt. I admit, lately my sense of style has gone downhill, slammed into some rocks, and rolled right off a cliff.

My thick hair has a slight frizz to it (thank you, humidity) and is scraped back in an unflattering low ponytail. My vented straw cowboy hat is old and worn, though rakish and a bit sexy in a former life. In my early days at Waylon, I wore it with a little red bikini and heeled flip-flops as I sunned at the lake with my sorority sisters. Now, it just covers bedhead. My oversized glasses are smudged from bumping my index finger into them, and there's still a pillow crease on my cheek from my late nap.

So. Honestly, I don't care. The day I start caring about what some jock thinks about my appearance is the day I quit. I've learned the hard way that the only person I should ever try to impress is me. My days of craving the attention of some womanizer are over!

I set my phone to record video. As surreptitiously as possible, I cant it in his direction as I turn. Visions of my ten-year-old Highlander tuned up with new tires dance in my head.

From my five-four height, I look up at him.

Well.

There's no need to charm this guy. His girls are tall. I am not.

This close, about six feet apart, his beauty is pretty much a physical assault to my senses, rich and heady, vibrating with intense masculinity. He's breathtakingly beautiful, that chiseled face, the divine body, all with an air of smoldering sexiness.

Should be illegal to be that attractive.

I check my heart rate: not even a skip. I'm entirely unaffected.

At some point, he's moved his cap, and it's on backward, small tufts of brown, almost blond hair shooting from the adjustable band on his forehead. His cheekbones flash under the fluorescent lights, and his bad-boy stubble is thick and dark. I wonder if he has to shave every day to keep that shadow at bay. Framed by thick curly lashes, his eyes are a turbulent turquoise, an ocean of color. They're serene, yet hinting at a tendency to be stormy. Interesting. He seemed lackadaisical earlier, not a ripple or wave in sight, but here I sense a man whose edges are frayed. The writer in me smells discontent.

Aw, is it hard to be surrounded by pretty girls who are vying for you?

His nose is a blade, straight and Romanesque, and his neck isn't brawny or thick like some footballers, but strong, the hollows sculpted and molded as if those of a statue in a museum. He reminds me of an erotic Michelangelo's David. And his chest—ugh, man, why don't you button that up? I can almost see nip! My weakness is tattoos, and his dance over his chest, enticing me. Maybe if I just touched that one little rose—

Stop, Serena.

I keep my eyes on his face, refusing to feast.

He flicks his gaze at me in an uninterested way. *Nope, not a pretty girl*, his attitude insinuates. He turns his attention to the shelf.

I watch him for longer than is polite, letting him feel the weight of my scrutiny then giving up when he doesn't notice. I settle for counting the twenty packages of Oreos in his cart. Pig.

He darts his eyes back at me with a questioning glance.

Oh, oh! He was the last one to speak and he's waiting for me to gush over him!

My index finger adjusts my white glasses. "Did you know it takes 59 minutes to bake an Oreo?"

"Mmm, fascinating." He reaches around me to grab a package of Nutter Butters.

Just what I expected—I don't register in his world.

I grab a Nutter Butter package—he won't get all of those—and my arm brushes against his. Not one tingle.

"Each Oreo wafer is baked for exactly 290.6 seconds at a temperature of 400 degrees Fahrenheit on the top and 300 below," I say. "That's very precise cooking."

"Um, yeah." He checks the watch on his wrist, an expensive diving one, then looks around me, probably searching for his harem. On his other wrist is a wide leather cuff with a glittering quartz stone in the center. It looks worn and doesn't quite fit with my perception of him. Maybe a memento? Whatever.

"And the whole Double Stuf Oreo thing? Total lie," I muse. "They're only 1.86 times bigger than a regular one. Very annoying advertising gimmick. I mean, if it says double stuffed, it should be. Wonder if I should contact the Better Business Bureau? On the other hand, I doubt it would do any good. Enough Oreos have been sold to wrap around the world 481 times."

He moves down the aisle to grab chocolate chip cookies. "I get it, you love Oreos. Sorry I took them all. They're on sale, five dollars off if you buy ten. At that price, they're practically free. Everybody loves free cookies, and we're having a party. Leather and Cookies is the theme, and before you ask—yeah, it was my idea."

"Creative." I follow him, accidentally on purpose bumping his cart with mine.

His head comes up and he frowns at me as those emotional—*yes, emotional*—blue-green eyes flash over my face, lingering on my hat, bouncing off the hole in my shirt, taking in my black and green camo pants then landing on my shiny red Doc Martens, my only claim to fashion. Taking his time, he makes his way back up to my face, which I keep composed, but okay, it's hard. Being the center of that attention for these few seconds is a little disconcerting, but nothing I can't handle. I'm invincible to his hotness! I am woman!

"Each Oreo has 90 ridges around the perimeter—"

"Perimeter?" He shakes his head as if waking from a bad dream.

"—and National Oreo Day is March 6. Sadly, most people don't know. I usually celebrate by deep frying them inside a crescent roll. Delicious."

He blinks. "Look, fine, you want a package of my Oreos—I get it. Normally, I'd be sweet—*I am sweet*—but I promised my team I'd bring enough back for everyone. I've got forty people at my house. You understand, right?" There's the barest hint of hesitation on his face, as if he's close to just giving them to me. Maybe he feels sorry for the plain girl—but then his phone chimes and he forgets about me, his fingers flurrying with a text.

As he wanders down the aisle, I follow him, keeping

our carts side by side. It's hard because I have to dodge a display of bagged peanuts, but I manage. Also, my legs are shorter than his, and he walks fast.

"A study in 2013 said Oreos are as addictive as cocaine. If I had to pick something to be addicted to, a cookie isn't bad. My little sister loves them so much. She's so adorable."

His phone forgotten, he swivels his head in my direction, squinting as they sweep over me again, lingering on my hat. A pained expression flashes on his face, as if it hurts to gaze at me. It's the hat, I know. Horrid.

"Sister? How old?"

"Four. Just precious." Seventeen, hellion—just like I was.

"Oreos were my brother's favorite. He used to crumble them up in a glass of milk. Rather gross." A faint smile flickers on his lips.

"Nice. Just give me a pack of cookies and I'll be on my way."

A wary silence settles between us, a crackling in the air. A strange expression spreads across his features, and he lowers his lashes, shielding his gaze. "Do I know you?"

"No."

"You look familiar."

"Do I?"

"You go to Waylon?"

"Doesn't everyone?" No way he knows me. I don't

keep up with sports or attend undergrad classes. Since most of my friends have graduated and moved away, I tend to keep to myself. Maybe he's seen me in the library, but somehow I have a hard time envisioning this man in the stacks. He'd just have one of his girls study for him.

"You always answer a question with a question?" he asks.

"Is this a trick?"

"Do you know who I am?"

My lips twitch. "Oh, yeah. Totally. David. You play lacrosse."

He rocks on his heels. "Wrong. If you knew who I was... Well, I might have given you one of my packages of Oreos."

I let my gaze drift over him lazily. "My bad. Daniel."

"No."

"Oops. Dexter, tell me, how does the new lacrosse season look? Think we'll beat Leland University this year? Or Whitman? I heard Hawthorne really kicked your ass last year."

A flush rises on his cheeks, and if I had to guess, I'd say annoyance is starting to build inside him. Is it weird that I like sparring with him? Yes. Definitely.

He moves down the aisle.

I follow, and his gaze sharpens as it darts over to me. "Are you stalking me?"

"Hello, there's only one aisle. Do people actually stalk you? What on earth for?"

"Girls follow me everywhere. I'm used to it, but you're kind of strange, and if I need to call security…" He shrugs broad shoulders.

Ugh! I sputter as indignation rises, mixing with my insane and, yes, irrational need to needle the jock. This was supposed to be about getting the video, but now I just want to push his buttons. Maybe it's because he reminds me of my ex and his entourage.

"I just want the Oreos," I snap.

He picks up a bag of M&M's, throws them in his cart, and moves ahead of me. "Huh, I bet Walmart is still open."

I resist the urge to stamp my foot. "That's on the other side of town. I still need to finish my shopping then go visit my nana at the nursing home. You know what her favorite cookie is?"

"Oreos, I wager," he drawls. "Poor Nana. If only you'd asked nicer, maybe batted those lashes at me, I might have been willing—"

"Dillon! Which beer did you want? There isn't much to choose from," calls Ashley from the other end of the aisle as she holds up a six-pack of Bud Light in one hand and Michelob in the other. She poses against the end cap, and I arch my brow. It really is a pretty cow dress. It's super tight, but I've worn just as clingy, although I didn't look as good as she does.

He smiles broadly at her, the effect lighting up his face, and it's such a different expression than he was giving me that my ire rises higher. "Nah, sweetheart, none of that piss. Get the Fat Tire—it's all I drink."

"Flat Tire, right," she says.

"No—Fat Tire," he replies.

She huffs and glares at the other girls. "I told y'all this wasn't right!" She smiles for Mr. Hot Pants. "Got it, Babycakes! I'll get them all just for you!"

She blows him kisses, barely sparing me a glance, then disappears down another aisle, and when I pivot back around, he's moved closer to me. The scent of him hits me, assailing my senses, the smell of leather (of course) mixed with earthy male spice, perhaps sandalwood and vanilla. It's disgusting.

I crane my neck to look up at him. "Stealthy, aren't you. That's not a question, but a rhetorical statement. What are you doing?" The pitch of my voice escalates as he eases closer.

"I know you." His voice has deepened, soft and silky.

"I have one of those faces. I'm a chameleon."

"Hmm." His eyes stare into mine, and this close, I see the ring of silver around his irises, like lightning. He drops his gaze to look at my unimpressive chest.

I resist the urge to straighten my shoulders.

"You follow the band?"

Oh. I glance down at the faded Four Dragons shirt, a Vane castoff, one I haven't been able to let go of. In the early days, I slept in it, wishing away the heartache, but now I wear it because it's roomy and clean and in my drawer. I can proudly say I put it on without even thinking of him.

I shrug nonchalantly. "Pretty sure I heard them a time or two." What I don't say is, *Well, I was with the lead singer for years then the world caught fire.* A tight feeling grows in my throat and I push those thoughts down, trap them in a box, wrap a thick chain around them, and toss them into a dark closet.

He takes his hat off, rakes a hand through his messy hair, and readjusts the cap so the bill is facing forward. "Crazy that those local guys now have songs on the Billboard charts. Makes me feel like I knew them. What was the lead singer's name? Vince? No..."

"Vane," I mutter. His band is alternative rock mixed with Delta blues, eccentric in sound and heavy on angsty lyrics. He even wrote a song about me after our breakup: "Sweet Serena". I picture him now, his midnight hair, his tattooed body—probably curled up next to a groupie.

"Right." He's studying me. I'm not sure he's stopped staring, as if I'm a puzzle he can't figure out. "What's *your* name?" He takes another step toward me, and I press back against the cookie shelf. He has no personal space bubble!

My heart skips and I get a strange prickle along my neck, an awareness of something rich and complicated threatening to suck me down. He's managed to get under my skin, though I'm impervious.

I inhale sharply as our eyes cling. Something about him jogs my memory—

"Excuse me." I maneuver my cart around his and disappear down the next aisle.

God. No video is worth putting up with some pigskin-toting Casanova.

A few minutes later, I head toward the checkout aisle and get in line. Mr. Hot Pants and his entourage come up behind me. Inside the narrow space, bracketed by candy on one side and magazines on the other, I inch forward, putting distance between us. I jerk up a copy of the *World Enquirer* and flip through it. UFOs spotted in Canada, a sea serpent spotted off the coast of Cornwall, Katy Perry pregnant with a bat baby… I huff. I can write better sensationalized fiction with my eyes closed.

He towers behind me, his body sending off enough heat to power an entire city. The woman ahead of me finishes with her purchase, and I move forward and set the four six-packs of Fat Tire on the belt.

Yeah. I grabbed them all.

The moment he sees what I have, the air charges with tension.

"Come on, now you're just being spiteful. You took all the beer," he says.

"What's wrong?" says the blonde.

"Is someone asking for your autograph again?" asks Mila/Bambi.

"She took your beer? Who is she?" Ashley asks suspiciously, sharp green eyes raking me up and down.

I huff. "No one you know."

He lowers his eyes to half-mast. "Fine. I'm open for a trade. A package of Oreos for a six-pack. What do you say, sweetheart?"

Feigning nonchalance, I shrug and repeat his words from earlier. "Fat Tire—so good, right? It's my favorite. The first beer, I drink in a frosted mug. The second one, well, I take my time, sit back in a chair on the deck, and take small sips so I can *lick* every malty drop." Okay, that doesn't make sense. Wouldn't I *savor* every malty drop? I mean, I wouldn't actually *lick* the beer or the mug. Yeah. That's a miss. But I had to get lick in there!

The cashier rings up the pricey beer and I blanch at the cost, my hands clenching. I may have to eat Ramen with my fruit and Nutter Butters this week.

"Random factoid: at any given time, 0.7% of the world is drunk. Fifty million people are trashed right now." I pat the beer. "I can't wait to suck one down." I hold my finger up before he can interrupt me, because he definitely wants to. "Hmm, maybe this one's more intriguing: beer and vaginas have almost the same acidity levels, with an average pH of 4.5. Makes you think, right? I wonder if it's the same if a guy puts his penis in a mug of brew…no? I guess not judging by your expression."

"Did she just say vagina?" the redhead yelps.

"She said penis—even better. Go, girl," says the blonde, and I decide I adore her.

"Son of a nutcracker," he murmurs as he shakes his head.

I swear under my breath. I missed it, having tucked my phone away to juggle the groceries and my debit card.

"Thanks for shopping at the Piggly Wiggly. Please take your receipt and come again," the slightly dazed young cashier says as she looks past me to the leather-clad hottie hovering behind me. "Are you Dillon McQueen? You're so amazing. And gorgeous. I don't care what they say, you're gonna be the starter this year, and if you aren't, you can always try the movies," she gushes, already digging around for a pen and paper.

He gives her that lazy smile. "Thanks." Then he focuses on me, his expression hardening, but he tries… "Let me have the beer, baby."

I've been upgraded to *baby*. How cute.

I put a little extra southern in my voice when I speak. "Bless your heart, if you'd only known who I was or batted your lashes at me. Check Walmart, sweetie..." I tip my hat at him and flip around, hips swaying as I leave the checkout area, smiling as I go out the door.

For the first time in eighteen months, I feel like myself again. Girl on fire indeed.

3
Dillon

We leave the Pig and walk through the dark parking lot to my black Escalade. The girls are chattering about the party, and I tune them out as I carry the bags. Between these ball-squeezing pants, the guys texting me snack preferences, and my worry about the season, my head spins. I should be excited about a house party, but I'm not.

Women elbowing each other to hold my hand is pissing me off.

All for the sake of a tradition I managed to get entangled in.

Dillon's never been to the Theta Fall Ball. He's not dating anyone. We will offer him as tribute, Sawyer told the team this past May before school ended. He riled them up, got them excited, and convinced them to vote for me.

Normally, I'd be willing to go along with the contest, if just to keep things fun, but this year is my last chance for the NFL. On the other hand, every year that we've participated in the Theta tradition, we've had stellar seasons. We won a national championship last year when Zane was the prize player. Now it's a superstition that we have to do it. I'm talking serious. We don't want to screw up the upcoming year, and that means repeating the rituals we did last year. We touch the tiger mural when we enter the stadium, we chant the fight song before we leave the locker room, Sawyer eats the grass, I kiss my hands before I leave the tunnel—and we do the Theta thing.

That means I have to deal with the girls' attention, trying to balance it with the inadequacy that keeps pricking at me. Even the cashier had to bring up my shortcomings.

I roll my neck.

For the past three years, I was Ryker's backup, but now that he's gone, I'm in charge. He was the number-one pick in the draft—how do I live up to that?

Does McQueen have what it takes to lead the Tigers? was this morning's trending topic on Twitter.

The worst part is my new backup is in the wings, just waiting to take the ball out of my hands. This team has been my family for three years, and it stings that Coach is pitting me against some untried freshman.

Owen Sinclair took his school to state. Won MVP. Runs like a gazelle. Rated a 5 by ESPN, he told me in a one-on-one meeting this week.

A muscle pops in my jaw. My father replaced me with a new family, and now my team is close to doing the same thing.

My gut swirls.

This season is mine, I tell myself. This is my shot and I can't blow—

What the hell?

I jerk to a halt at the girl I see. *Her*. Again? She's like a curse!

Four Dragons has jumped out of her vehicle, slammed the door, and is currently glaring at the hood of her car as if she expects it to tell her what's going on.

She kicks the tire with her boot then lets out a yelp of pain and hops around on one foot. "Just one more year. That's all I'm asking!"

She doesn't see me and I narrow my gaze, taking her in. She's downright frumpy in those pants and old shirt. Honestly, she looks like she just rolled out of bed, threw on a hat, and came to the store. I recall her heart-shaped face under the fluorescent lights, the smarty-pants curl to her lips, the sly barbs she directed at me. I couldn't even see the color of her eyes behind those nerdy glasses.

One of the girls asks me to unlock the car, and I click the fob.

I walk around to where the Four Dragons girl is. "Car

trouble?" I ask, and she jumps and whips around, a slow flush rising on her cheeks.

She fidgets and stares at the ground. "I think it's the alternator or the battery. Honestly, I have no idea, but I'm sure it's expensive."

"Ah, I see."

"Yeah." She glances back at her car, a frown worrying her forehead.

I grew up in a world where if a vehicle didn't work or was involved in a fender bender, another one took its place. When I was sixteen, my parents gave me a white tricked-out Hummer, and when I wrecked it six months later, they replaced it with a black one. A long sigh comes from me. I had material things, not denying that, but I would have traded it in for parents who cared about me.

She blows out a breath, full of defeat. "Son of a nutcracker."

"Hey, that's mine."

"No, it's Will Ferrell's. It would have been nice if you'd said it when I needed it. You cost me."

"Son of a nutcracker," I snap. "That work?"

"I don't have my phone handy, so no. It has to be spontaneous. I can't cheat. It has to be fair and square."

No clue what she's jabbering about.

We stare at each other, and a prickling sensation flutters over my neck—just like it did in the store. The vulnerable arch of her nape, the curve of her face, *those lips...*

She reminds me of—

Behind me, the girls break my train of thought as they argue and hash out a quick game of rock paper scissors to see who gets to sit up front with me. Exasperated with their antics, I glance back at them and sigh, then turn to Four Dragons. Courtesy demands I offer help. It didn't demand I give her a package of cookies, though. Maybe part of me wanted to annoy her. I saw her staring at us when we walked in, felt the way she dissected us. I know what she thinks—that I'm a guy with women all over me. This is true, but these girls are not by choice.

"You need a ride?" I ask gruffly.

"I'd call an Uber, but I don't..." She stops and shadows flit over her face, worry tightening her eyes.

She doesn't have the money for an Uber. Her Toyota is old, and there's a dent in the bumper. She winced when she paid for her groceries.

"Hey, Babycakes," Ashley calls from behind me. "You coming? I won and get to ride up front with you, wahoo! Can we listen to my songs? I have a playlist—"

"Sure, sweetheart, whatever," I call back, cutting her off, barely listening because Four Dragons has swiped up her bags from the car and is marching across the parking lot. I hear the clinking of the beer bottles as they bounce against each other.

"Hey!" I shout at her back. "Where are you going?"

"Walking home, duh," she says as I jog up next to her.

"Can't you call someone? A friend?"

"I know how to take care of myself." She throws her chin in the air—so proud—and picks up her pace, but she's no match for my long legs.

"You're running from me like you're scared. Are you?"

"No, Damon, I'm not. You annoy me. You refused to hand over just one package of Oreos because I wasn't attractive enough for you."

"I never said you weren't attractive!"

"It was on your face."

"No, it wasn't. Look, let me call you an Uber."

"I don't want an Uber, thank you."

"I just want to help." I'm worried about her. She's barely holding on to all those bags.

We've reached the edge of the parking lot and she's about to step onto the sidewalk. A big truck roars past us on the road a few feet away, and my gut clamors for her to stop, protective instincts flaring. "Come on, let's put aside the fact that we don't like each other. Since you don't want the Uber, let me give you a ride."

"I don't know who you are."

"I'm Dillon McQueen, the quarterback for the Tigers. I promise, you know me."

Her brows arch. "Um, never heard of you."

I take my cap off and rub at my disheveled hair as I laugh. *Sure, sure. Keep saying that...*

"You'll have to skirt around a few bars and dark alleys, and you're on your own with all those bags."

She inhales the humid night air, making her chest rise. She's maybe a B cup, but it's hard to tell in that loose shirt. My eyes linger there, watching as she breathes.

I can see the wheels in her mind turning, debating as she flicks her eyes down the darkened busy street, taking in the multiple red lights, and then back to me, her top teeth worrying her bottom lip.

"You think I'm a jerk," I say as I shrug, trying to be nonchalant and non-threatening. "I'm not, you know. I help old ladies cross the street, volunteer at the local schools. Cats like me, and they're finicky. Not gonna kidnap you. Plus, my posse is with me. You're fine."

"Posse...ugh." She scrunches her nose up. "And?"

"You want more?"

"Please. I want to hear all about how awesome you are."

I squint my eyes. She *is* infuriating. Why am I still talking to her?

Several moments pass as she searches my face, and then she looks back at her car, uncertainty on her face. "Alright, you convinced me. I live off Highland on Burgundy Street, if it's not too much trouble? Thank you."

"Cool. Driving past there anyway." Not on the way at all.

"You love it that you have the upper hand now, don't you?"

I huff under my breath. She thinks *I* have the upper hand? Holy... She ran circles around me in the Piggly Wiggly, and now I'm chasing her across a parking lot?

"Right." I tuck my hands in the pockets of my pants—and her gaze follows, as if she can't help it, lingering on my crotch. I smirk.

The streetlight illuminates one half of her face, devoid of makeup, a smattering of freckles dotting her dainty nose. Our eyes cling, and I'm aware of the moon coming out from behind the clouds above us, illuminating the hue of her eyes.

"Champagne," I murmur.

A frown puckers her brow. "What?"

I'm silent, just taking in the long lashes behind those glasses. My fingers itch to rip that ugly hat off her head. I want a good look at her.

Her shoulders rise and fall. "Stop staring."

"You're staring at me."

Her lips twitch, barely. "We sound like toddlers."

"It's your fault."

"No, it's yours." She dips her head, as if hiding a smile, then glances back up at me and I'm snared. I can't see much of her, one high cheekbone, a pointy chin, the pulse at her throat…

Cars whiz past and moments tick by, me looking at her, her looking back. A buzzing sensation runs over my body—

One of the girls, probably Ashley, blows the horn on the Escalade.

I let out a groan of frustration. "Dammit!"

"Your posse is waiting." She whips around and heads to my car.

4

Dillon

"You girls want a beer?" she says from the back seat a few minutes later as I pull out of the parking lot. I watch Four Dragons in the mirror as she looks over at her seatmates, Chantal and Bambi. They got chummy before I even got to the car. They probably got her name and I didn't. Fine. I'm not asking her again.

The girls decline while she opens one, takes a swig, and chokes.

"Love it, huh?" I say, my eyes holding hers in the mirror.

She takes another drink—just to spite me. "Wonderful balance, a little toasty with a hint of biscuit. Might pair well with a cookie." She bends down and I hear packaging tearing as she rustles around then pops back up with three Oreos clenched in her teeth.

"You're opening my stuff?" I snarl, my voice incredulous.

"Obviously," she says.

The girls pause and dart their eyes between us.

"You two know each other?" Chantal asks.

"No," I say as Four Dragons snips, "As if."

"Seems like you do. Could cut the tension in here with a knife," Chantal chirps as she takes a cookie from the sleeve. The girls tilt their heads together, talking, most of which I can't hear, so I turn down the music.

Ashley pouts and pokes me in the arm. "Hey, that's my playlist I made for you."

"I'll listen to it later, 'kay?" I tell her, my tone distracted. Did I just have a moment with Four Dragons in the parking lot? Nah. It was a fluke. She doesn't like me; I don't like her.

Ashley huffs then turns around to the girls in the back and says, "I've never seen you on campus, Serena. What's your major? Are you in a sorority?"

Serena! I rack my brain for a girl with that name but come up empty.

"I'm a grad student in journalism. I pledged Theta freshman year, then went inactive," she says.

"Oh no. What happened?" Bambi asks.

Serena pauses, her brow wrinkling. "Um, my parents

passed away my sophomore year. I tried to be part of the sorority, but I had to get a job and didn't have time to do the activities." A long sigh comes from her. "Plus, the dues were pricey." She says it matter-of-factly, but there's heaviness in her words.

"Oh, wow, sorry about your parents. That must have been tough," Chantal says quietly. "But, hey, small world. We're Thetas. You still know the secret handshake?"

Serena laughs as they do something weird with their hands.

"I'm thrilled to meet an alum," Bambi says. "We all pledged three years ago. We're seniors now."

Ashley frowns at Serena. "You don't look like a Theta."

"We don't all look the same, Ashley. Chill out," Bambi says. "She's one of us."

"I was a junior when y'all were freshmen, so I was already gone." She grins wryly. "My picture is up in the house if you want to check. I was president of my pledge class. My last name is Jensen."

"I'm the current president," is Ashley's curt reply.

The girls, being nosy and maybe a bit intrigued by the way she defied me in the checkout line then me chasing her through the parking lot, slam her with questions: how old is she (*twenty-four*), where's she from (*Magnolia*), who does she know (*a few people they do*), does she like football (*no*), what does she do in her free time (*yoga and sewing*). Sounds boring.

They continue to bombard her with questions, but she skillfully turns the conversation to them, asking about their majors, where they're from, and the party we're headed to. She compliments them on their leather attire, even asking Ashley where she got her dress. She talks to Bambi and Chantal about where they're applying to graduate school next year, offering tips and advice about the process. I'm listening to every word, analyzing her. She's much nicer to them than she was to me.

"So, you three and Drake," Serena says later as she licks at a piece of chocolate wafer at the corner of her mouth, "I can't help but notice you're all *together*. It feels like an episode of *The Bachelor*, campus style. How do you manage? Set up a schedule? Rock paper scissors for a night in his, um, bed?"

Ashley glares at her. "His name is Dillon."

"Oh," she replies innocently. "I don't follow lacrosse."

I roll my eyes. Her smartass remarks don't bug me like it did in the store. She's doing it on purpose, obviously, which means she *wants* to get under my skin.

They give her a confused look, and then Bambi, who's one of the kindest, most genuine girls at Waylon, offers, "He plays football, honey. You were inactive when the Thetas started the tradition to partner with the team. We pick three girls, usually officers, and we all get to spend time with the selected player. Then he'll take one of us to the Fall Ball. It's a lot of fun and we get to hang out with the team during the contest. It's considered bad luck not to do it. Athletes are very superstitious."

I make a turn onto Highland, keeping my eyes peeled for her street. "I'm sure Serena doesn't want to know the details of our contest."

Oh, but I do, her eyes tell me in the mirror.

And why is that, my eyes say back.

Serena nibbles on her cookie. "Tell me, how did you girls meet him?"

"He sat next to me in art class freshman year, and as soon as I realized he played football, I was a fan," comes from Bambi. "My dad's an NFL player so I grew up in the culture."

The guys on the team consider Bambi our little mascot.

"I met him at Cadillac's, he's hot, plus I'm not seeing anyone right now," Chantal explains with a dismissive shrug.

I hide my smile. Out of the three, she's the one most likely to ditch me.

"I've known him since freshman year, and he danced with me at our Theta party last spring. Three times, and you know what they say about three: it's the magic number..." Ashley gushes as she reaches over to stroke my arm.

"You're all half in love with him, I suppose?" Serena inquires.

"You ask a lot of questions," Ashley retorts.

"I'm a writer," Serena says with a shrug. "Actually, I'm interning for the *Magnolia Gazette*. I answer letters in the 'Asking For A Friend' advice column."

"Huh. Is that why you know how many ridges an Oreo has?" I ask.

"I collect random facts, yes. It's a quirk."

"Oh my God! I've read that," declares Chantal, turning in the seat to give Serena her full attention. "You're hilarious. I loved the one from the girl who said her boyfriend had to dress up like a superhero to have sexy times."

"Oh? What did you tell her?" Bambi asks.

Serena laughs, the sound husky. "I told her role-playing is fun as long as it's consensual. I might have said Spiderman could bite me any time. And Thor—hello, bring out the hammer. Then there's Benedict Cumberbatch as Doctor Strange, and Chris Pratt as Star-Lord, and who can forget Henry Cavill as Superman? Those lips are to die for, and of course Ironman—"

"We get it," I snap. "You have a fetish for capes." Irrational jealousy fires over me.

"It's Black Panther for me," Bambi whispers to Serena.

"Winter Soldier," Chantal throws in. "His long hair, mmmm…"

Ashley traces her red nails down my arm. "I don't fantasize about superheroes. I'd pick you any day, Dillon."

I give her a look. Maybe I'll cozy up to her tonight. I've

yet to mess around with any of them, and she's been giving me the *fuck me, please* eyes all week…

"Everyone wants Dillon," Bambi says. "He's perfect."

"He is *so* perfect," Serena says sweetly as our eyes hold in the mirror.

"What is love anyway? At this point, I just want some great sex," Chantal tells the car.

Serena holds her beer up in salute. "Vibrator. All day long."

"You just ran that stop sign, Dillon!" Chantal calls out as she and Bambi giggle.

Dammit. I ease up on the accelerator. Must stop looking at her in the mirror! I shift around in the seat to ease my erection. That's what I get for imagining Serena's orgasm face.

"Honestly, we're doing the contest because Dillon is a great guy. Plus, there's the competition," says Chantal. "I love to win. I'm the current vice president."

"Speaking of love, I miss my Pekingese. Her name was Taffy," Bambi says randomly. "The feeling isn't romantic, of course, but I never had any siblings and she kept me company. People say you can't really care for dogs like people, but you can. She died of old age my freshman year. I never got to say goodbye." She whips out her phone and shows Serena a picture, presumably Taffy. Serena coos at the image, murmuring her condolences. Chantal leans over and commiserates with them.

Chapter 4 | 55

I realize they've lowered their voices in the back.

"...boyfriend?" Bambi asks.

My eyes cling to Serena's face, watching expressions flit over her features. She takes a swig of beer, winces, then says something I don't catch. I turn the music completely off, ignoring Ashley's protests.

"Oh, goody, tell us," Bambi begs, clapping her hands together. "Maybe we know him."

"Oh, I'm sure you do," is Serena's reply.

Hang on... Her answer was vague. Does she have a guy or not? She mentioned a vibrator, but girls do that with or without a guy. I give myself a mental shake. Why do I care if she has a guy?

"Amen." Chantal nods. "Hey, do you want to come to the party with us? Trust me, there's nothing like athletes. I know some guys you should meet."

Okay, so no boyfriend.

Who does Chantal want her to meet?

"Sawyer is hot," Bambi says. "Dark hair, tight muscles, loves to sing."

"And Troy," Chantal muses. "Huh. I wonder if he'd wear a Winter Soldier outfit..."

"Please come!" Bambi gushes. "I'd love to get to know you. And if you like the guys and want to come to a game, I'll find you a jersey, crop it, bedazzle it."

"She has to go see her nana at the nursing home. Isn't

that right?" I say. "Which is interesting—you'd think all the old people would be in bed by now."

"Trust me, my nana is up, and she'd resent being called an *old person*. Meh, I may have lied about the nursing home. My nana is on a date with her man. I'll take you up on the invitation next time, Chantal." I hear Serena rattling off her digits.

"Here's my place," she says a few seconds later, tapping the back of my seat. "On the right. Just park on the street."

I pull over to the curb of an older two-story house with white siding and a detached, two-story garage. My headlights drape over the rundown residence, a faded red shutter askew on the front, weeds in the flower beds, an overgrown yard. Her streetlight is burned out, shrouding the area in darkness.

I'm out of the car in a heartbeat and open the door for her. She gives me a surprised glance as I grab the bags at her feet at the same time she does. We tussle over who's going to carry them. She gives up with a puzzled expression and steps down to the street. She stumbles over the curb and my hand reaches for her elbow, catching her before she falls. The brush of her skin against mine makes goose-bumps rise on my arm.

We disentangle, both of us giving each other wary looks.

The girls call out goodbyes to her as I walk toward the house and she follows.

"What are you doing?" she asks.

"I'm walking you to your door. I want to make sure you get inside."

She gives me an uncertain look, hesitating as she points away from the house and toward the detached garage. "I'm at the top, up there, but you don't have to."

I should just hand over the bags, but part of me doesn't want to let her disappear. What if I never see her again? It's an odd thought, but there it is. "I'd like to escort you to your door. If you don't mind?"

She pauses. "Fine, but my steps are narrow."

"I can handle it," I say as I head up the driveway, eyeing the myriad of rickety wooden stairs that lead to a blue door on the second floor of the garage. The steps are narrow, some missing, and I hear the telltale groan of the wood as I climb. Her footsteps pad behind me.

I reach the top landing, and the tall trees next to the garage hide the moon, making the night almost pitch black. I notice a blown bulb inside a rusted porch light that hangs off the wall. She needs to get that fixed. What if she trips and falls off this deck one night?

The area in front of her door is small, the landing barely wide enough for us to stand without touching, but somehow Serena manages, muttering about forgetting her car keys as she eases around me and leans down to pick up a little gnome, grab a key, and put it in the lock. She cracks her door, keeping it closed so I can't see inside.

"You need a porch light, Serena," I say, worried for her safety, even though I sense she's the kind of girl who knows how to take care of herself. "You shouldn't leave your key out for anybody to find."

"Thanks for the tip, Douglas."

I lean down until our faces are close and our breaths mingle in the night air. She smells like cherries. "You're gonna run out of D names soon."

"I'll buy a baby name book, lacrosse player." Her lips purse.

And my dick is a steel pipe.

I. Am. Insane.

"Open the door so I can set this beer down. Please."

She frowns. "You're sweating. What's wrong with you?"

I am sweating. The ride here was a little surreal, me hanging on to every word she said, watching her face in the mirror. My shirt feels sticky, and my heartbeat is faster than normal. A clawing feeling is growing in my gut, the sense that I'm about to get my world rocked. I feel light-headed. I eye the distance to the concrete below. If I fall...

I lick my lips, about to tell her *she's* what's wrong with me—

"Babycakes, you coming? Don't forget we're playing

darts tonight to see who gets a kiss, and my aim is feeling lucky—"

Frustration rushes at me. Can't I have any alone time?! "Give me a minute!" I call back at Ashley, who's obviously gotten out of the car.

Serena crosses her arms. "Ashley the redhead, Bambi the brunette, and Chantal the blonde. You're toying with them. They're nice women—well, the jury is still out on Ashley. She kept giving me the evil eye, but still, you are ridiculous!"

I'm part of a contest I wanted nothing to do with, but I refuse to defend myself.

She knocks open her door with her boot, making a loud clattering sound. "You want to come in? Help yourself, Casanova."

I shoulder past her and she clicks a light on behind me, illuminating the small apartment. I take a steadying breath of the cool air inside and look around, willing my chest to slow down. It's apparent she's put work into the interior, the walls a pale blue color featuring graphic artwork from the Beatles and Pink Floyd. A retro orange velour sofa sits against the window with pops of bright pink pillows. A green puffy chair sits in the corner, a basket of knitting supplies beside it, and a sewing machine sits on a desk beneath a window that overlooks the backyard. The place has a funky vibe and is fastidiously clean, yet cluttered with books and papers and magazines stacked on the coffee table. I see a collection of old albums. A laptop gleams from an end table. Two closed doors head to the right; I imagine it's her bedroom and a bathroom. Her kitchen is tiny, only a table with two modern looking chairs, a little stove, and a pink fridge that looks like it came from the fifties. Marching in, I set her groceries on the kitchen table and pivot around to face her, but she's already brushing past me to grab two of the bags.

She thrusts them at me, the clink of glass echoing in the quiet. "Here, take your beer, please. I doubt I'll drink it." She pauses and says grudgingly, "It was petty of me to buy them all."

I can't move. I'm rooted to the black and white linoleum tile on her floor as I stare at her. My chest rises, inhaling gulps of air. She took off her hat at the door, or somewhere, and pulled her hair out of her ponytail. Gleaming brown, copper, and blonde strands spill around her shoulders. Three colors in anyone's hair should be over the top, but on her it's...

My eyes scan over her face, clearly lit by the fluorescent lights in the apartment.

Adrenaline hits my bloodstream. Swaying on my feet, I right myself with effort.

She's—*holy shit*—the girl from the bonfire.

Same face, petite body, and fierceness.

I had the hints at the Pig, then the parking lot...

That night from three years ago rushes at me, playing back in my head: the movement of her hips, the dandelion on her nape...

"When can I see you again?" I blurt.

"What?" Confusion mars her features, her nose scrunching. "Are you crazy? I'm not one of your kittens!"

I'm barely registering what she says.

Maybe I am crazy.

She's...here.

Right here.

I try to speak and fail.

She nibbles on her bottom lip. It's lush and a pale pink color. I remember the fullness of her mouth, how she melted against me...

"We can't stand each other. I don't know you," she adds.

I swallow.

Oh...

Oh, she doesn't... I exhale gustily.

"You don't remember me," I murmur incredulously, more to myself than her.

She pauses for a second, frowns, looks away, then shrugs.

I huff out a breath. I'm used to girls knowing me by the way I walk from clear across campus, or at least that's what they say.

How could she *forget*?

I read the uncertainty on her face as she darts her gaze back to me.

She's... God, she has no clue.

I tore that party up looking for her, staked out the freshman girl dorms for a month, asking about her, describing her. I even checked out the dance studio on campus, all while enduring the trash talking the team tossed my way, the kissy noises they made.

She doesn't know that I've compared every girl I met to her, and they always came up short! All over a kiss!

The craziest part is, I was absurdly celibate for months, turning girls down left and right. Waiting. Holding out hope I'd find her. Am I the kind of guy who believes you can have a brief moment with a girl and fall hard? If anyone had asked me then, my answer would have been *hell yeah*, but now, after all this time? That's crazy talk.

Clarity sinks in, and I lean against the table.

You were just another guy who hit on her.

What sucks is that she wasn't even a freshman at the bonfire, so if the legend is true, would it apply to her? I don't know. I always assumed she was a freshman since most of the partiers were, but—

"Are you okay?" she asks.

No. I built up this idea of her, that one day we might see each other and, I don't know, be together?

*You don't even know **how** to be in a real relationship*, my head says.

Whatever. This is fine. It's going to be fine, dammit! I don't need feelings in my life. Not with the pressure of this season, and hello, she doesn't even like me as a person. That much was obvious from the Pig.

"Forget it." And then I'm stalking away to her door.

"Wait!" She catches up with me and tugs on my arm.

Her eyes meet mine, and they're a pale golden color, like topaz.

Our gazes cling and hope, unbidden, fires off like a rocket inside my chest.

"Yeah?" I say gruffly, shifting closer to her. Her skin is like porcelain, soft and creamy, the tilt of her eyes giving her an otherworldly, exotic look…

She toes her boots, fidgeting, her shoulders shrugging. "Thank you for the ride."

"I see. Thank you for the ride…that's all you got?"

A slow blush rides up her neck to her face, hinting at vulnerability. That makes twice. Does it mean anything? Is she even attracted to me at all?

"We rub each other the wrong way, but I am appreciative that you brought me home."

She's appreciative? I whip my cap off and scrub my face. "I can't believe this… Karma really is a bitch…"

"Believe what?"

I shake my head. "Just do one thing for me. Say my name."

"Dillon, thank you for the lift. Happy?"

No, I'm not. Not by any stretch. Frustration gnaws at me that there's a girl in front of me, one who has been in my head for three years, and she can't wait to see the back of me. It's a blow to my chest.

"I hope I never see you again," I mutter under my breath.

"Same!" she calls as I slam her door.

5

Dillon

I'm awake by six for a run, my goal to get some cardio in before our morning practice. After slipping on my running clothes and shoes, I enter the den. A disaster meets my gaze: red Solo cups on the floor, the TV still playing, empty beer cans on the end tables and on the kitchen counter. Chris, our tight end, doesn't live here, but he's sleeping on the couch, his mouth open as snores reverberate through the house. He's gonna be useless at practice today, and an angry rumble comes from me as I head out the door, shutting it hard to wake him up.

My usual route takes me through a quiet campus, the sky dusky, just a hint of the sunrise peeking over the horizon. It's my time to think, to assess, to focus, to work out this elephant that sits on my chest.

When I get back, Sawyer's in the kitchen, scrambling a skillet of eggs. Wearing his practice gear, he's got a frilly, pale pink apron tied around his frame. *Grandmas Never Run Out Of Cookies Or Hugs* is stitched on the bodice. It's faded with yellowed lace trimming the bottom. His granny passed last year, and it belonged to her.

"Got breakfast for us." His skin is dark brown, his voice a slow Southern drawl, a testament to his small-town Georgia roots.

"Where's Troy?"

"Still recovering from the party. I knocked on his door."

"He better get up if he doesn't want to be late." I grab a Gatorade from the fridge, my heart coming down from the adrenaline as I suck it down. He grabs us plates and divides the eggs while I get the oatmeal ready in the microwave, mixing in protein powder for both of us. We move around each other in a coordinated synchrony, our routine the same since we moved into the house at the beginning of summer camp. He pours the orange juice and grabs napkins. I get us forks and spoons. He unties his apron and drapes it over the oven handle, his fingers lingering on the worn fabric for a few beats before he takes his place across from me.

"You disappeared last night," he comments a little later as he sticks a spoonful of oatmeal in his mouth. "Dude, what a mood you were in—at your own party.

Those poor girls..." He chuckles. "Ashley kept knocking on your door."

"I slept with ear plugs."

"You'll be glad to know I drove Bambi home after she had too much to drink."

"Nice of you," I grunt and shovel eggs into my mouth. "Would be nicer if you were the prize in the contest and not me. Thank you again for nominating me. Asshole."

He smirks. "Cry me a river."

When we got back from dropping Serena off, my mood had soured, and I roamed the party for an hour before claiming a headache and going to my room. Before I escaped, Chantal was talking to Troy, Bambi was on her laptop, probably researching stats, and Ashley shadowed my every step, pouting.

"I saw *her* last night at the Pig." My words are flat, and he pauses mid sip of orange juice.

"Her?"

I jerk up from the table, rinse my plate and bowl, and stick them in the dishwasher. "Freshman year, bonfire party, the girl I never found. Remember?"

There's silence from him as he figures it out. He gives me a wide-eyed look. "Wait... Nah, you don't still believe in that legend, do you?"

I shrug. "Maverick mentioned witches. He straight-up told me about Delaney, and now he's wrapped around her finger. Take Blaze—he met Charisma the night of their freshman bonfire and now they're living together in New York."

He sings "Witchy Woman" by the Eagles.

I flip him off, and he stutters to a stop.

"Dude." A gasping laugh comes from him. "You're serious."

I throw my hands up. "I know! She doesn't remember me, and *I* dreamed about her last night. Again. She wore a white dress and was standing on the football field, right at the fifty-yard line, and I was…" I exhale and grip the top of the chair. "On my knees in front of her asking her to…"

"Yeah?"

"Marry me…" I stop.

"Shit."

"You were a zombie, by the way."

"Hope I was badass."

"I killed you with a sword."

"Zombies and swords at a wedding—pencil me in."

I lean against the fridge. "I know the legend is just a bunch of frat boy mumbo jumbo…"

"But?"

"She got in my head and then she ran away—from me."

"The nerve."

"It's not like that." I'm not being cocky. It just bugs me that she didn't feel the same for me that night. And Sawyer? He doesn't know everything. It's embarrassing to admit the torch I carried. "It feels like everything Maverick warned me about came true... That she'd haunt me."

He belts out the chorus to "Haunted" by Taylor Swift and I throw a dishtowel at him. He stops, a maniacal grin on his face. "So what if you saw her? She's just a girl. There are five thousand more on campus."

"I didn't know who she was at first, but as soon as we got close and I smelled her scent—"

"Smelled? What are you, a wolf?"

"—something niggled at me, like a ghost ran its hand down my back. It's like that whole destiny thing at work." I throw him an impatient glare. "Don't discount scent. Pheromones are no joke. They're behavior-altering chemicals you emit, and once you smell the right one, it triggers your instincts, and you'll want to mark your territory—"

"So you *are* half wolf. Always suspected."

"Go on, laugh all you want. Everyone emits pheromones. Why do you think cologne is so popular?"

His lips twitch. "What scent should I buy?"

"Keep on joking. The right kinds of pheromones elicit a sexual arousal response. Dude, I can't walk past cherries or any kind of fruit without thinking about her. For three years!" I shake my head. "Therapy—I need aversion therapy for this girl so I'll stop thinking about her. Maybe a hypnotist."

"I'm stuck on the fruit thing. Cherries give you a hard-on?"

"If you sing 'She's My Cherry Pie', I'll kick your ass."

Glee dances over his features and he laughs for several moments, wiping at his eyes. "Honestly? I'm blown away. You, the guy who's always in a good mood, are actually in a snit over some girl who doesn't recall a kiss. Who *are* you?"

I arch a brow. Oh, he wants to trash talk... "I know you still keep that stuffed tiger Bambi gave you freshman year. Under your *pillow*."

"I have no idea what you're talking about."

"Liar." I crack my knuckles. "I need another run this afternoon."

"Is the worst part that she doesn't remember you? Or is it that you've found her and don't know what to do with it?"

A long exhalation comes from me. "Both. I don't know."

He shrugs. "She was probably drunk at the bonfire. Most people were. I was. Woke up in my dorm on the floor with Troy curled around me like a girl. Slapped him silly and kneed him in the nuts. Good times."

"I didn't smell or taste alcohol on her, and my tongue was in her mouth long enough to know." Every detail from that kiss is etched in my mind as if I have a photographic memory. I don't.

He pops a cookie left over from last night in his mouth. "She was probably there with a boyfriend, kissed you, and freaked out."

Anger rushes at me. "She was dancing by herself."

"Okay, okay, obviously you've built this up in your head over all this time, created a shrine to her sweet cherry pie memory—"

"Smartass."

"Uh-huh. Let's break this down: wasn't one of your theories that she wasn't a student or was from out of town? What did you find out?"

"Nothing really except that she hates me. She's a grad student. Two years older." I'm almost twenty-two. I wonder when her birthday is...

"Ah, a girl you have to work for. This is new for you."

I sigh. Freshman year, I had a list of theories about the unicorn. Perhaps I was drunk with beer goggles and wouldn't recognize her. Perhaps she cut her hair. Perhaps she transferred. But those full lips... I just knew I'd know them anywhere. If it hadn't been for the hat and glasses last night, I would have spotted her right off the bat.

"I think you should have nailed her and didn't and that's why you're still wondering about her. She's the one who got away. Everybody's got one. Mine is some chick from middle school. She was my first kiss, and I thought she'd be my first everything, but she dumped me for a high school kid. Good thing—she got busted for money laundering for the mob a few years ago, but I still wonder..." He snaps his fingers in my face. "You know what this is, right? It's a challenge."

"Dude..."

"Nah, listen. This girl—she could be your lucky charm. Remember last year when Zane challenged me to knock him out in a boxing match?"

Zane is a defensive player and weighs close to three hundred pounds. Sawyer is muscular but wiry, his body perfect for playing wide receiver. Not boxing.

I nod. "Yeah, you practiced for six weeks, worked out your arms like crazy. You lost ten pounds, but your shoulders filled out—"

"Right! And I had the best season of my career—because I knocked him out and beat the challenge. Along the way, I overcame my fear of getting punched. I'm a lover, not a fighter."

I scrub my face.

His brown eyes narrow. "I'm serious. You need to work your magic and check her off. Mystery solved. No more wondering about the what-ifs. Flush her pheromones from your system. You have the game to focus on, but if your head is daydreaming about some girl..." He pops an eyebrow. "Do it for the team."

Screwing Serena for a challenge? Nah. I don't have a shot with her. Besides, the idea of using her to make my game better is inherently wrong—and the idea of *wooing* her makes me jittery. "That's a no-go. She couldn't wait for me to leave her place."

"So? You're Dillon McQueen. Has any girl ever turned you down when you turned on your smile? Come on."

She did three years ago.

Troy slinks out of his bedroom, his shoulder-length brown hair everywhere. A talented running back from Texas, he rounds out our roommate situation. I'm not as tight with him as I am with Sawyer, but he's cool. A stiff expression grows on his face as he approaches me, his eyes wary as he enters the kitchen.

"Uh, Dillon..." he says, his eyes shifting from me back to his bedroom.

"What's up?" I ask.

He exhales. "Don't be upset. It just happened. Well, I mean..." He chews on his bottom lip. "She looked so hot, man, and a little lonely. You weren't around." His look turns defensive.

I stalk toward him, towering over his six-one frame. For some reason, my mind goes to Serena. "What are you talking about?"

His fists curl. "Don't get pushy, man."

I rear back. I'm the charmer, Sawyer's the wise-cracking manipulator, and Troy's the quiet one—only right now, he looks pissed.

"Oh for the love of... He's talking about me," Chantal mutters as she stumbles out of his room, hopping around as she puts on one of her heels. Her blonde hair is mussed, mascara smudged, lips swollen. She darts her eyes at Troy then back to me. "Troy and I..." She blushes furiously and gives me an unsure look. "A girl has needs, Dillon. Are you terribly upset we hooked up?"

Hell no. She and I have never been a thing. "Winter Soldier, huh?"

She sighs heavily. "And tequila."

Troy stiffens, his body turned to Chantal. "We didn't *just* hook up."

Chantal frowns. "Hang on, it was fun, but—"

He juts out his chin. "You followed me outside last night. You sat next to me. You played with my hair."

She shrugs. "You're pretty and I was drunk. It was nice. Thanks for the orgasm."

I wince. *Burn.*

He gapes. "You used me?"

"Like that Chi-O last week meant something to you?" She tosses the strap of her purse over her shoulder. "You guys mess around with girls all the time. What's good for you is good for me. Men don't own the hook-up scenario. I can be with anyone I want, a different one each week if that's what I decide. I do adore football players—"

He sputters. "If you want a football player in your life, you come to me, jersey chaser."

"—but," she says, crossing her arms, "the next person who refers to me as a 'jersey chaser' is getting a fist in their face. I'm pre-law, for God's sake. I'm going to find a guy as smart as I am, maybe check out the Phi Beta Kappa honor society!"

"Hey now, ease up," I say. "I'm a psych major with a French minor." And decent grades. Not a 4.0, but considering how much time I spend on football, it's freaking exemplary. During my freshman and sophomore years, when I first realized Ryker was always going to be the starter, I even considered getting serious with it, but I wanted to play football. A job behind a desk would never suit me.

She smirks at me. "You like numbers so much, maybe you should be a *statistics* major."

Ahhh. "Good one."

"Are you saying I'm a Neanderthal?" Troy asks.

"Your words," she chirps. "All you alphas, sniffing around females like a, a—"

"Strange you should bring that up—Dillon is a wolf," comes from an amused Sawyer.

She ignores him. "You think we're just waiting to do your bidding, and I did. Last night, I followed Dillon around the grocery store like some love-starved kitten, and I'm done!"

I know when to keep my mouth shut.

Troy's lips tighten, his eyes holding Chantal's, a silent communication seeming to simmer between them. "Baby. Come on. This thing between us has been brewing since the contest started—"

"In your dreams," she smarts back.

"Damn. Where's the popcorn?" Sawyer says under his breath. "How did we miss this last night?"

I missed it because I ditched the party. I jump in to defuse the situation. "Hang on, Chantal. Obviously, you've changed your mind about the contest. I'm what you girls call high maintenance, and you made the right choice. You shouldn't ever feel like you have to do anyone's bidding. Be you. Be fierce, I say." I toss an arm around her and give her a quick hug.

Chantal gives me a thoughtful look. "Honestly? Seeing how Serena didn't fall under your spell like everyone else got to me. Being part of the contest is exciting, and I do love to win, especially beating Ashley"—her lips tighten—"but I don't relish the idea of spending the next few weeks researching team stats just for the chance of a date with you." She shrugs. "Besides, if I didn't know better, I'd think you were trying to get rid of us."

"What?" Sawyer says, eyes swiveling to me. "Is that true? Are you making the contest difficult? You know this is an important tradition."

"If it's so important, why didn't you do it? You're not dating anyone," I mutter.

"Yet."

Okay, not sure what that means... "I've done nothing but let the girls hang around, as asked!"

"Uh-huh," Chantal replies.

The sorority never set any rules for the contest, so there is some gray area. Perhaps I took some liberties by asking the girls to come up with the statistical analysis, but I'm desperate. Since classes started, the three of them have been following me around, offering to pick up my books, cleaning my room, rubbing my shoulders. Yeah, normally that's cool and girls have done this for me in the past with no expectation, but now, it's like a gnat in my ear. They're more vicious than a defensive player when it comes to competing, even sweet Bambi.

I heave out a breath. Of course, I could just be a dick to the girls to run them off. I'm just a trophy for them, a popular guy on their arm, but I don't want to let my team down. They're counting on this. Could I sit down with Sawyer and explain how this contest, coupled with my anxiety, is aggravating? Sure, but we're dudes, and I don't talk to him about deep things. I give off a carefree vibe, but on the inside, I keep my feelings locked down. I'm the team captain. I have to be strong and suck it up. Plus, it's too late. They voted in May and the deal is done. I have to follow through or risk the season. If it's a bad year and I don't do the rituals, the team might blame me.

"She isn't part of your posse anymore," Troy mutters as he elbows me out of the way, shuffling between Chantal and me as he attempts to take her arm.

"Stop assuming you know what I want, Troy," she snips, shaking him off.

As soon as they step out on the front porch, I punch into the air. "One girl down, baby."

Sawyer sighs. "I like having girls around though. It's our senior year. We need to soak it up. I'm going to arrange a pool tournament for Ashley and Bambi to compete in. We need to find another Theta to fill in for Chantal's spot. Their treasurer is a hot little strawberry blonde—"

"Nope. Don't you dare," I call out as I stalk back to my room to grab my duffle for practice.

His laughter follows me, a reminder that he can afford to be relaxed about this year. His stats are incredible. Not as good as Blaze's last season, but he'll be drafted. He's a starter and cool under pressure. Me—I'm freaking out.

I just hope *I'm* the one throwing him the ball this year.

6
Dillon

After a team meeting, we grab our helmets and head out to the field. "Alvarez is supposed to announce the quarterback today. You ready?" Sawyer asks as he slides his gloves on.

"It has to be me." I've put in the years, the work—

"Don't be so sure," Owen Sinclair says, interrupting as he jogs up with a football in his hand. About six one, he's lean and fast, his face smug as he rakes his pine green eyes over me. His hair is cobalt blue, a fauxhawk with lightning bolts shaved on the sides of his head.

I tense, waiting for his usual dig. Three, two, one...

"Coach loves how I throw, McQueen. Told me so himself every time he watched me play. Did I tell you he came to see me three times in Florida?"

"Almost every day."

He bounces a football in the air, one he's always holding, on the sidelines, in the locker room—hell, word is he even carries one to class. He also shows up for practice half an hour early every day. I know because I do too. He's a competitive little shit.

I snatch his ball in midair. "Timing in college is different than high school." I toss the ball back to him. "You'll get there by the end of the year, rookie."

His lips tighten as he palms the ball and spots Kendrick Rose, another super freshman. Sawyer's gaze is on that one. Yeah, welcome to my world, where the young guns have us in their sights. It's cool, I get it, but Sinclair takes it a step further, and I get the sense he's in it for the glory. I'm in it because it's *all* I have. I live and breathe this game. I have since I was ten years old and moved from Malibu to Alabama. While my parents' marriage was falling apart, I clung to the one thing I was good at.

"Keep talking, Grandpa," Sinclair says. "You think you're owed something 'cause you been here, but this team doesn't owe anyone anything. The starting quarterback has to earn it by working, not by partying."

I smile. "Ah, someone's pissed they weren't invited last night. Man, best party ever. Hot girls, every sorority on campus representing, all the cool frat guys…"

His face reddens. "While you were getting hammered and screwing your fan club, I was studying the playbook."

I was not hammered. Yeah, I can throw down at a party—been there, done that—but this year *is* different.

"I've got that playbook down." Ryker and I worked together to memorize every page.

Sinclair throws the ball to Rose, a perfect spiral, but his eyes are on me. "The difference between you and me is I won't stop working till I'm the best, not just *good enough*. You fill that role, backup."

My hands clench. What a dick...

"Line up!" calls out the offensive coordinator, adjusting his visor as he sweeps his gaze over us, lingering on Sinclair. There's appreciation there.

We head to the field, thoughts tumbling through my head. After we won the national championship, the entire team was on cloud nine, but that talk faded as the fans and media started talking about 'next year'.

At first everything online was positive about me becoming the next quarterback at Waylon, but the mood changed on national signing day in February when the number-one recruit in the country, Sinclair, picked Waylon over Oklahoma, Tennessee, and Alabama.

"Drill stations. Let's see what you boys have today." He announces a full situational scrimmage, first team offense versus first team defense with Owen and me switching out after each play.

"McQueen, you're first up," Alvarez calls. "Opening drive, first and ten."

After looking over the defense, I identify they're in zone coverage with a straight four-man pass rush. "Hike!" I rumble.

The team goes into motion, the defense dropping into a three-deep zone exactly like I expected. My line picks up the pass rush, and I throw to the tight end for an easy eight-yard gain on first down.

"Nice read. Sinclair, your turn," calls Alvarez while I jog to the sideline, victory thrumming through my veins.

"Hut!" Sinclair yells. The tight end runs a slant and is wide open in front for an easy ten yards—and Sinclair hits him in stride. He breaks the tackle and turns up the field for another fifteen yards before the safety can make it over to bring him down. A muscle pops in my jaw.

I'm up.

"Two minutes to go in the quarter. Down by five. First and ten from the twenty," Alvarez calls out from the sideline.

"Hike!" I growl.

Palming the ball, I study the blitz coming from both sides. I throw a perfect pass down the sideline to Sawyer. He catches it and heads to the endzone. Score.

I pass Sinclair on my way off the field. "Beat that, rookie."

He huffs and gets into the huddle at the twenty yard-line. Right away, I see the blitz coming as an overload on his right side. He'll need to keep the tight end in play to block and dump the ball off to his running back. It won't pick up a lot of yards, but it might move the ball downfield.

"Hut!"

The play starts and the blitz surprises him. Sinclair falters but spins at the last second and runs toward the sideline, looking for an open player. He waves his hand at Sawyer, who breaks off his slant route just as Sinclair throws the ball, a wobbly spiral that hits Sawyer around sixty yards. He walks into the end zone for a touchdown. The freshman players run out and smack Sinclair on the helmet.

My teeth grit. Yeah, it was pretty, but...

"What the hell was that?" snaps Alvarez as he stomps out to the field and gets in Sinclair's face. "That little spin worked this time, but it'll get you sacked and probably a fumble. That shit might have flown in high school, but you aren't the best athlete on the field anymore." Coach turns to the defense. "And you just let some fresh-as-a-daisy kid beat you deep on what would have been a game-winning play. You have to contain..."

He continues to yell at the defense as I swagger over to Sinclair. "You know what he's looking for? Experience. This is real football, not a one-man show."

He bumps me with his shoulder and stalks to the sideline.

Walking into the locker room after practice, Alvarez

motions for me to come to his office. Sinclair is already there, hovering in the background.

Coach scans his eyes over us, and I think I see a glimmer of uncertainty there. He crosses his arms, determination on his face.

My heart pounds in my chest, but I keep my face cool.

Sinclair sends me dark looks, his fists clenching and unclenching.

"You both did fine today."

And...

"I'll be announcing Dillon as the starter this afternoon at a press conference."

Yes! Elation rushes over me as the weight of summer camp eases.

Sinclair exhales a breath and looks at the floor.

Coach's eyes narrow as he takes us in. "It's no secret you two are at odds, and I get it. You both have different styles. McQueen, you're steady and balanced. Sinclair, you're talented but have a lot to learn. McQueen, I want you to spend some personal time with Sinclair—"

"Sir?" I interrupt. "What do you mean?"

Coach's lips flatten. "You claim you want to lead this team, so do it. You're the captain, and that means welcoming the new talent and teaching him what you know. I'm assigning you two to run together every day—on your own time. It would be good if you spent more time together as well. Eat together, hang out, whatever you boys do."

My personal time? I shoot a glance at Sinclair, and he curls his lips at me.

Coach looks down at the mess of papers on his desk. "Sinclair, you may go."

He bumps his shoulder against me as he heads out the door, and I shake my head. Was I ever that much of a pill? No. I was an eager learner and deferred to Ryker, letting him mentor me. Hell, I welcomed his friendship with open arms. I might even have been a little needy. That first year was a hard time in my life, adjusting to college and the ghost of my brother.

Coach leans back in his chair. "Congrats on the position. Take a seat."

My stomach jumps. Why do I feel like I still haven't won? "Thank you, sir. I promise I'll put the team ahead of everything. This means the world to me."

He nods. "You've been patiently waiting for your turn, and I have a lot of respect for your dedication. This is it for you, son. If you're tight this year, the scouts are going to notice."

But? Is he just letting me start because he feels like he owes it to me and not because I'm the best? Insecurities rise up, and I tap my fingers on my knee.

His gaze goes back to the door Sinclair left through.

"He is good, you know, but he's impulsive and makes it up as he goes along."

I'm impulsive too, but never on the field. Everything I do with football is calculated and sure.

"Just because I'm naming you starter today doesn't mean I can't change my mind. Don't flake out under the pressure, because trust me, you've never seen the kind of intensity you're about to face. If you aren't the best on the team at the end of each week, you won't be playing." He assesses me. "I need Sinclair to fall in line. Teach him what you know."

Oh, I see. Teach him my tricks... "So he can step up and take my place?"

Coach frowns. "This isn't a pissing contest between two players. Ryker taught you. You teach Sinclair. Regardless of who starts our games, it's all about winning."

Right. This is cut-throat college football, and we have a championship to live up to. I'll have to prove myself every day. Tension builds in my head. Definitely gonna need another run today, maybe another lifting session...

A long sigh comes from me. "I understand."

7

Serena

Dear Asking for a Friend,

Does it make me a slut if I swipe right on every hot guy I see on Tinder?

A year ago, my ex cheated on me with my best friend, and they just got married in Hawaii. It feels impossible to move past the rage and betrayal—hence the Tinder addiction. These sexual encounters work for a little while, but I'm worried it's a spiral of behavior. I want to stop screwing my dates and meet someone nice, but how?

Sincerely,
Dating App Addicted

Dear DAA,

First, let's take the word "slut" and put it where it belongs:

in the trash. That word is degrading to yourself and other women, which is ironic considering it first appeared in the early 1300s when Chaucer used it to describe a male character as untidy. You are simply a person in charge of your own sexuality.

Your ex and ex-bestie are not worthy of you. (Alexa, play "thank u, next" by Ariana Grande.) It would have been better if they'd approached their relationship in a thoughtful, honest manner, and I'm sorry you went through this turmoil. You're right, seeking happiness in the arms of a hot guy might fill certain holes (heh), but it won't nourish your soul.

Instead of sex with your booty call, suggest coffee or a walk. If you still can't resist getting tangled in the sheets, find a new hobby, adopt a pet, join a club, or take up knitting. Personally, I enjoy cookies. People say not to eat your emotions, but seriously, have you ever had a deep-fried Oreo? Orgasmic.

~Asking for a Friend

"Serena! Need you now! Get in here!"

Warren's booming voice reverberates through the office just as I hit send to the editor for next week's column. Jumping up from my cubicle, I grab a notepad and a pen and dash down the hall.

He's talking on the phone while pacing behind his desk, and he waves me in. I plop down in the brown chair and immediately smell Irish Spring and leather. The owner of the *Gazette*, he's fiftyish and stout with a head full of graying dirty blond hair that brushes his blue button-up.

There's a glint of excitement in his eyes as he clicks off his call, comes around his desk, and sits on the edge. I straighten my gray pencil skirt and cross my legs. I didn't have a lot of professional clothing when I got the internship, but I did buy a few pieces from a secondhand store downtown. My one rebellion is my black Doc Martens with red roses embroidered on the sides. They're a little loud, true, but a girl needs personal flair.

"How's your day?" His voice rumbles.

"Column is sent. Marriage announcements and obituaries are done."

He grins. "Bored out of your head, aren't you?"

True. I love to write fiction stories, the more fantastical the better, but that isn't what the *Gazette* wants. My undergrad degree is in creative writing. Journalism for grad school was the option to ensure I have a paycheck, and I do enjoy talking to people. "Got a call this morning about a lady who turned a hundred and five. It's rather mundane, but she's seen a lot of history in Magnolia—"

"Gotta wait on that. I need you on special assignment for the next few weeks. You can hang on to the column, but I'm going to put Traci on anything local. Pass the birthday story to her. What do you know about football at Waylon?"

Oh. Crap. "There's a kicker and a band at halftime?"

He grimaces. "I see. In case you've been living under a rock, the Tigers won a national championship this past January and put our town on the map. Some of the guys on the team are pretty interesting, different backgrounds, and you might find an angle there. The starting quarterback is Dillon McQueen, a rich kid who attended Menton Academy, one of the best football prep schools in the South..." He keeps listing players, but my brain has stopped on Dillon's name.

I hope I never see you again.

Yet, before that, he asked to see me again.

He already has Charlie's Angels—so why me?

My hands tap the chair. After he left, I looked him up online, scrolling through his Insta. I saw pics of him with girls, and more girls, wearing that dazzling smile, his muscles bulked up like he works out twenty-four seven. The man has half a million followers and countless *I <3 Dillon 4EVR* comments. Verdict? He's as shallow as a rain puddle. A jock with rocks for brains.

I interrupt Warren. "Wouldn't George want this assignment? He's the sports guy."

"George and his partner just adopted a baby. He's got no interest in hanging around a bunch of rowdy football players." He raises an eyebrow.

In other words, I'm the intern who does whatever...

I wince, recalling Bambi reciting football stats. "I'm the least athletic person I know. Maybe Traci—"

"I asked her and she said no."

So. I'm the *third* choice. He must be desperate.

"I spend a lot of time with my sister. She's young and needs guidance."

"And the *Gazette* needs you to say yes."

I exhale, reminding myself that I'll need his recommendation when I graduate in May. "Right."

He leans in. "ESPN is predicting the Tigers won't be able to live up to last season, and it's created some heat with the athletic director. You know him, right?"

No.

"We're good friends, so don't screw up, be a professional, and write solid."

I always do.

"I'd like you to go to the home games, give them a homespun, authentic appeal. Get people excited."

"I'm so excited," I deadpan.

It isn't lost on him. He smirks. "Buy some football books. You're smart, Serena. You'll figure it out. These are our boys, and we need to light a fire under the fans." He pauses. "Do an article about McQueen, maybe midseason."

Anyone but him!

He stares at me, as if reading my expression. His

bushy brows lower like he's daring me to utter another excuse.

"When do I start?"

He smiles. "The first game is this weekend at home. After that, another home game, and then LSU, away. I want you at that one. LSU is ranked high in the polls and we've lost at their stadium several times. Should be a tight game. You like Louisiana?"

"Never been," I say faintly. Who has time or money for vacations with bills I can't pay...

He hands me an address on a sticky note. "Here's the location of the stadium."

I grimace. "I've been to a game—although the last time was probably a few years ago."

He pauses, concern appearing on his face. "Are you doing okay, you know, after everything that happened..."

I know what he's asking. Not a lot of people know about my short marriage to Vane. We kept it low-key, but Warren knows Nana, and Nana has a big mouth. There's no doubt he got the sordid details.

My hands pleat the material of my skirt. "I'm great."

"Good. How's *he* doing? Nancy mentioned he..."

I sigh. "Last I heard Four Dragons was opening for One Republic, so I assume he's awesome." I push up a smile.

"You're giving me your fake smile and it's creepy."

"Actually, forcing yourself to smile can boost your

mood. It tricks your body into releasing chemicals to your brain."

He nods, waving his hands at me, already done with the personal questions. "Good. There's someone better out there for you. You're young." He hands me a business card. "Here's the contact for the media person for the Tigers. He can get you situated with a press card and give you an itinerary. Of course, you need to see the team—they have an afternoon practice today if you want to pop in." He pauses. "Are you excited? Really?" He gives me a hopeful smile.

Just thrilled to bits. I give him the creepy smile.

I'm about to approach a man who clearly said he never wanted to see me again. An image of him spins around in my head, those tight leather pants, the steel six-pack under his shirt. Unbidden, another memory stirs inside me, of a long ago forbidden kiss. I shut it down hard.

"You bet."

~

It's two miles from the *Gazette* to the stadium, not that far considering how much I walk, although when I exercise, I usually wear sneakers. I send up a silent prayer for my car, which is still stuck at the Piggly Wiggly. I know no one will steal it; it's too ugly. I called the manager of the

Pig the morning after it wouldn't start, and she assured me I could let it sit in the parking lot until I can pay for a tow or get my brother out there to take a look at it.

By the time I've made my way through the winding hills of campus to the stadium, my white silk shell clings to my skin and my face is damp from sweat.

Waylon University Tigers is painted in bright orange at the south end entrance. I brush my fingers over the paw print mural. Superstition says you can't enter without touching it, and if you don't, it brings bad luck to the team. I may not have attended many games, but I'm willing. I touch the paw. If this is my new assignment, I'm going to tackle it with my usual excellent work ethic.

After getting lost for several minutes, bemused by the number of stairwells and halls, I find a directory and take the elevator to the offices upstairs. I meet the media director, get my press pass, the itinerary, a list of players' and coaches' names, and a bundle of promotional materials, as well as a map of the stadium. An hour later, I take the elevator down and wince at my reflection in the mirrored walls. At least I've worn my contacts today. I whip out my sunglasses and push them on my face, hoping it makes me a little incognito in case I run into *him*.

I step out of one of the upper-level tunnels. The heat may have diminished slightly, but the humidity feels thick inside a facility that seats over a hundred thousand fans. Considering the student enrollment of Waylon is smaller compared to other SEC schools, the stadium is a testament to how important football is here. Brightly colored championship banners dance in the wind, and sky rooms with tinted windows sit high in the air, arching out over the lower decks.

"You know nothing about football," I mutter to myself. I'll need to find a way to relate, and to do that, I'll need to get closer. I head down the stairs to the seats near the sidelines on the fifty-yard line. The field already has players on it, most of them running drills and working in small groups.

A tall guy in a dress shirt and slacks is already in a seat with his laptop out as I approach. I figure he might be press and head that way. He's handsome with sandy-colored hair and fashionable square-cut black glasses. His eyes flare when he looks up and sees me. "Serena?"

I rack my brain then smile broadly. "Neil? Hey!" I'm used to seeing him in casual attire, mostly jeans and Waylon basketball shirts.

He laughs. "You didn't know who I was! How long since we had that horrible class together?"

"Dr. Cartwright," I say when he reaches over to sweep me up in a hug. "Sophomore year. I loved that class! Having to write down our secret thoughts was awesome."

He laughs. "Until he calls on you and your comment is *This professor needs to get laid* and you have to read it aloud."

I sit next to him. "He didn't like you much after that. He called on me once and my comment was *Cereal is soup*. We debated for ten minutes."

"It isn't," he says with a smirk.

"I have a valid point. You eat both with a spoon. You crush crackers in soup, and cereal is made from grains. Maybe soup is just warm cereal. It's a fine line. Admit it."

He laughs, his gaze warm. "Sure."

I pull out my ponytail and redo it, arranging it in a messy knot. My hair develops a life of its own in the humidity, but Nana says it's my best attribute. The length is mid-back and it's thick, the color a rich brown with natural copper glints. I add the blonde highlights on my own. Once upon a time, I used to get it done at the salon, but that was one of the first things to go after my parents died.

"So you're going to be traveling with the team?" he asks.

"Just LSU. You?"

"I go to them all. I started following the Tigers last year at the sports desk for WBBJ Memphis. I'm aiming for the head sports position in a few years. You ever think about a career in front of the camera?"

"I'm just a writer." My dream is to write for a magazine or maybe publish my own collection of short stories and essays.

He leans back, his torso trim, his chest taut inside his

button-up shirt. The sleeves are rolled up, showing toned, roped forearms. He smiles and straightens his glasses, a small dimple popping out on his cheek. He's a studious hottie.

He played basketball for Waylon, and we saw each other frequently at parties, even had coffee a few times. But, then came Vane, my grades went to hell, and I lost touch with most people.

His brow arches. "You're more fun than George, that's for sure. We'll be spending a lot of weekends together," he muses as a wry grin flashes across his face. "I contemplated asking you out, you know, but it never was quite right. Either I was seeing someone or you were."

"Timing is everything," I say.

He gives me a crooked smile.

A tingle dances over me, as if someone has stroked the curve of my face, and I turn away from Neil to glance out at the field, sucking in my breath when I see a player on the sidelines.

Facing me, he's looking up into the stands, his shielded gaze pinning me like a butterfly. His helmet is on, shoulders impossibly broad, muscled legs in white football pants. The rest of the team moves around him, but he doesn't flinch. Even though I can't see his eyes, I feel them, digging into my skin.

"Who's number ten, Neil?" I ask softly.

"Can't be a decent sports reporter if you don't know

who the players are."

"Haven't had the time," I murmur, feeling frozen, my attention locked on the man on the field.

"Dillon McQueen," he replies, leaning over to brace his arms on the seats in front of us. "Quarterback—for now. A good, solid player, but his backup has a prettier pass. There's talk of him losing his starting position to the freshman. You know him? He's staring."

"We've met."

Dillon whips off his helmet, his honey brown hair cascading around those chiseled cheekbones, accentuating the black smudges under his eyes. Yards between us, but I feel his scrutiny, his intensity—his dislike?

He flicks his gaze to Neil then back to me. His lips curl up in a smirk as he tucks his helmet under his arm.

I stare back, refusing to be the one who breaks eye contact first.

I recall him slamming my door as he left. I peeked out my window and watched him walk down my steps, his shoulders stiff and tense. He stopped at the bottom of my driveway and turned around to look back up at my place. I quickly ducked out of his view. I went to bed thinking about him, about the turbulent look in his gaze as we stared at each other.

A wiry player a few inches shorter than Dillon runs over and calls his name, and finally Dillon turns his back and takes off down the field.

8

Serena

Later, I've wrapped up some research about Dillon on my laptop and look up to see that practice has ended. All I gleaned about him was a breakdown of his early career, when he not only played backup quarterback but was also a solid running back. He sustained a wrist injury last year but recovered, and he scored a touchdown in the national championship game in January.

Neil has ventured down to the field to talk to the offensive coach, and the sun has started a slow descent in the sky. I grab my laptop, stuff it in my leather bag, and hoist it over my shoulder, already dreading the walk home. Standing, I cry out at the sting of pain where the leather has rubbed the side of my foot. It hurts like the devil. I plop back down in a seat, unlace my boots, and frown at the raw skin. "Dammit," I mutter. I remembered to pack my sneakers earlier in the week but was running late today.

"Problems?" a deep voice says, and I whip my head around.

And there he is, standing at the end of the row, freshly showered with damp hair, wearing a white Tigers shirt, low-slung designer jeans, and orange Converse. He looks good enough to lick from head to toe—

Nope.

I stick my feet back in my boots quickly, "Nothing serious."

He steps up to the section and walks toward me as his hand pushes his messy hair to the side. "Blisters?"

I dip my head. "Meh, they rarely need medical attention. Fact: the feet are particularly prone to them."

"You're just a regular walking, talking Wikipedia." He's reached me and hovers there, hands on his hips. Why does he have to be so dang tall? And his hands…they are huge! I mean, not weirdly so, but proportionally. My body is drawn to other things as well, the way the sun highlights the gold in his hair, the fullness of his lips. They're luscious, puffy clouds! It's just wrong.

I stand up. "It's worse when I'm nervous."

"I'll file that away."

"Do that. Now, if you'll move and let me pass, I need to be going." No way am I going to ask him if he'd be open to talking to me, not when I look like something the cat dragged in off the street.

He checks out my press pass. "You're covering the team?"

"It appears so," I say dryly.

"That's just great," he replies just as dryly. "I'll have to see your face."

"My sentiments exactly."

"Oh, the fun we'll have, Serena..."

"Bring it. I'm so excited I can't stand it."

"I can tell. You're frowning. Lighten up." He smiles, a perfect flash of white, and I feel the effect of it like a slap in the face. Why does he have to be hot AF?

"Does it hurt?" he asks.

"When I fell from heaven?"

"You don't think much of me, do you? I meant your blisters."

I clear my throat, my face warming. "No, I'm fine." Screw this. If he won't move, I'll just go the long way around. I pivot and stalk off in the opposite direction, sucking in a breath at the extra steps I'll need to take to get to the exit. Bolts of pain dance through my feet and I steel myself, yet a hiss comes out. I ease down in a seat and take a fortifying breath. I'd walk home barefooted if I could, but... Obviously, I need to call Nana. Frustration bubbles. Twenty-four and I need to call my grandmother...

"Really hurts, huh?"

I exhale. "Yeah."

Leaning down, he takes my elbow. "Come on. I'll get you some bandages." He pauses, inhaling a deep breath. "Mmmm, cherries. Is that your shampoo?"

"Like it?"

"Hate it."

"Not surprised." I move to pull away—

"You're the most stubborn person I've ever met," he declares as he jumps up to the row behind and then hops back down in front of me. It happens so fast I can barely track him. "You asked for it." He bends down and picks me straight up until my body is pressed against him, my legs dangling. He smells like vanilla, again, and I barely keep myself from pressing my nose to his chest. It smells divine. Ridiculous!

My arms flail. "Dillon, this is crazy. Put me down!"

A huff comes from him as he hitches me up and swings me around until I'm lying in his arms like a bride, my cheek pressed against his stupid broad chest.

"If you wiggle, I might drop you. You're heavier than I thought."

Ah! The nerve... "You can't just throw me around like a sack of potatoes!" I swing my hand and my bag gains more momentum than I anticipated, smacking him in the shoulder.

"You can't walk! I'm trying to help you." He stomps

down the aisle and into the darkness of the hallways that lead to the tunnels.

"If I wanted your help, I would have said so."

"You're in pain," he growls, and I shiver at the tingles that go down my spine.

"Why do you care?"

"I'd help anyone," he mutters. "I gave *you* a ride, didn't I?"

"Jersey chaser giving you trouble, Grandpa?" comes from another player who's coming down the tunnel. Tall and lean with blue hair, he watches us, amusement on his face.

"Don't be dissing jersey chasers," I snap. I liked Chantal and Bambi. Yeah, I called them kittens, but come on, they *are* adorable.

"You heard her, Sinclair. Women rule," Dillon rumbles, hoisting me up higher. "Get out of the way. She needs first aid."

"Feisty one. When you're done, pass her along." He runs a hand through his spiky hair and marches out of sight.

"Friend of yours, I presume," I mutter.

"Owen Sinclair. Big chip on his shoulder. My nemesis."

"Your rival?"

"I prefer archenemy. Sounds more dramatic."

"So you're Superman to his Lex Luther? Batman to his Joker, Spiderman to his Green Goblin—"

"You really do have a thing for superheroes."

"I have a whole list in my head if you want me to continue."

He grunts as he takes the stairs, jostling me around, and I squeal when it feels like I might fall. "Please don't drop me." I peek up through my lashes and study his face then look away quickly. He's too much this close, too heady, too perfect.

He carries me into the locker room and sets me on top of a table. The space is vacant, yet I hear the distant sound of showers running, the rumble of male voices just around the corner.

He walks to the cabinet, pulls out a first aid kit, and stalks back to where I am, the fabric of his jeans brushing against my thighs as he moves between my legs. He kneels on his haunches in front of me, slowly unlacing both of my boots and easing them off, hissing under his breath at the torn red skin on both ankles. A drop of blood slides down my leg. Gross.

"*Merde.* This looks bad."

I start. "Did you just curse in French?"

He shrugs. "My minor. The curse words are the easiest. New shoes?" He frowns as he glances at my footwear. "You walk a lot, Serena? You need sneakers."

Tell me about it.

"A person walks 65,000 miles in their lifetime. That's enough to go around the earth three times."

"I make you nervous. This explains a lot about how you acted at the Pig."

"No. It. Doesn't." I give the words a little extra clip.

"Maybe wear socks next time you go around the world." His hair falls in his face, obscuring his features as he hovers over my feet, holding them in his hands. His fingers are long and nimble, his nails blunt as he tears open an antiseptic pad, pulls it out, and brushes it over my ankle. My skin sizzles.

I flinch and gasp. "Oh my God, it feels like a blowtorch!"

His lips quirk. "You gonna pass out?"

My face feels clammy, the air in the room sparse. I lick my lips. "I hate to admit this, but I banged my toe on the coffee table last month. Blood everywhere. Total carnage. I woke up five minutes after the murder scene. So, maybe I have a tendency—" My hands clench as he touches another blister, ramping up the sting.

"Hmmm, you're pale. Talk to me, it will help." He blows on my skin, soothing the burn.

I suck in a breath. "Well, back to nemeses, there's my favorite, Harry Potter and Voldemort—" I pause, my heart skipping as another bead of blood trickles down my foot. "Oh, no..." I sway on the table, my throat moving convulsively.

He looks up at me, searching my face. "Just breathe. Big inhale, long exhale."

The room spins, and I lean forward, resting my forehead on his chest.

He pulls my face up. "Serena? Hey, baby, focus on me."

"Don't call me baby," I whisper. That was Vane's nickname for me.

I stare into his ocean gaze, trying to focus, but the sting isn't going away, and the crimson color that's dripping down my foot... "This is incredibly embarrassing, because I'd like to believe I'm tough, and I apologize in advance, but I think I might..." The room darkens, dots flashing in my field of vision. "Pass out."

He presses my face down between my legs, maneuvering me until my back is bent. "That's it, breathe for me."

I suck in air and blow it out, trying to ignore his hands in my hair, the way his fingers knead my nape. It's not a sexual touch, but careful and deep. My muscles unlock as I let out a long breath.

"I like your dandelion tattoo," he says quietly. "What does it mean?"

The image on my nape is about four inches long, a blue dandelion with the seeds flying away on one side. "Thanks," I say, my head still bent. "Second chances. It's a weed, but has deep roots, like a close family, and comes back again and again. Got it when I was seventeen with a fake ID. There might have been vodka involved. My parents grounded me for a month." I pause, feeling better already. Talking does help. "These days, it symbolizes hope for happiness and love. I'm a bit of a dreamer, I guess."

A gruff laugh comes from him. "Seventeen? You're a rebel."

"Not so much lately."

He pauses, as his fingers drift over my tattoo. "To me, a dandelion means wishing for something. I happen to know a lot about that."

"Oh. What do you wish for?"

There's a silence, then, "Besides being a good quarterback, I wish I could go back in time, knowing what I know now, so I don't screw it up. Do you have any more tattoos?"

"No. I was a little wild when I got it, I guess, but in my defense, my dad was covered in tattoos. He was upset about the drinking. He was a cop. He is—*was*—the best man I ever met. Yours are nice. I like the roses."

"You noticed them," he purrs.

I rise up and look at him. I imagine my face is flushed from being bent, and I can feel the color deepening.

"I saw your"—magnificent chest—"tattoos at the Pig."

"You might feel better if you let this down." He pulls my hair out of the messy bun and spreads it out with his hands.

"Yeah?" he asks.

"Yeah." My eyes land on his lips then dart away. Oh, man. Is he flirting?

That question is answered when his hands fall away from me as he gets back to work, kneeling down and inspecting my ankles. He wipes the rest of the blood away with another alcohol pad. "What about Seinfeld and Newman?"

What? Oh...

"Oldie but a goodie."

"Ever watch *Alien*? Ripley and the alien were arch-enemies."

"Kept my eyes closed through most of it, especially the nightmare scene where she delivers a baby alien..." I wince. "Let's talk about something else. That movie isn't helping."

"You know... One could say I have the upper hand with you right now."

"You're the one on your knees."

"Ah, there you are, ornery as usual. I best get used to being on my knees around you."

I start. "Why?"

"No reason." He dips his face so I can't read him as he pulls out a square bandage from the kit, rips the package with his teeth, and removes the backing. Carefully, he holds my foot and applies the beige bandage, his fingers dancing over my foot. Goosebumps rise on my body and I glare at them. *Dear Body, ignore the fine example of male hotness in front of you. He is a womanizer as was evidenced in the Pig! Yes, he speaks French, the language of love, but you must ignore it!*

Moments of silence pass as he takes my other ankle and performs his ministrations.

I clear my throat. "Are you what everyone thinks? Party boy who's just passing time before he goes to the NFL?" I recall the countless girls on his social media, hugging him, kissing his cheek, smiling up at him...

"People see what they want to. What do you think?"

I think he's got layers underneath that carefree demeanor. Or, at least, I hope he does.

He looks up, and I realize I haven't answered his question. Instead, something weird comes out of my mouth. "When I look at you, I see storms in your eyes." Maybe a glimmer of sadness. "It makes me wonder who you really are."

He gives me a searching look then drops his gaze. "You're not what I expected."

"What did you expect?"

There are ten beats of silence. I know because I count them.

"I figured a girl like you, you'd be hard to hold onto." His eyes hold mine, intensely, as if willing me to understand the meaning of his words. When I don't take the bait, he exhales, a frustrated look on his face. "Anyway.

Back to your earlier question. Most think I have everything, but no one ever does. I lost my brother."

I hear the hint of barely suppressed grief in his voice.

He stands, too close for comfort yet not touching me. I have to hold myself back from leaning in and inhaling him. The air between us crackles, and part of me—the insane crazy girl part—wants him to kiss me. Maybe it's because he's being honest with me. This isn't the guy in leather pants at the Pig.

"When was that?" I ask softly.

He studies my face. "Four years ago."

Compassion fills me. "My parents passed four years ago as well. I'm sorry you lost him. There's not much else people can say to make it better, is there?"

"No," he says. "Most don't get it. Your parents...what happened?" He pauses. "Sorry. Is that rude? I never quite know. I don't talk about my brother much so..."

"No. It reminds me that they were real." I dip my head, thinking of another loss I dealt with, a baby's fragile heartbeat that faded away before it even had a chance. "They went for a ride on their motorcycle, and just never came back." A long exhalation comes from my chest, emotion clawing at me. "It was a Saturday in September, and my mom made breakfast for all of us that morning. She spilled coffee on her shirt and Dad called her a klutz and kissed her on the nose. I remember how hot it still was when they rode off..." I swallow thickly. "Then, a state trooper showed up at the door, and the solemn expression on his face... I just knew. My life was never the same again."

His throat bobs and he looks away, then back. "My brother died in June at a party with my friends at the lake. It was a beautiful day, sunshine and low humidity, not a cloud in sight. He wore these bright yellow swimming trunks with pink flamingos on them. Some of us were diving off a cliff, and he wanted to try." He blinks rapidly. "He jumped before I could stop him."

My heart clenches. "That wish. You'd want to go back in time to save him?"

"I never would have gone to that party with him."

"Same. I'd save my parents."

"There's another thing I'd wish for..." His voice trails off, a guarded look flashing on his chiseled face.

"What?"

He shakes his head. "Nah, never mind."

"Tell me." I cross my heart. "I promise I won't tell anyone."

He chews on his lush bottom lip and shrugs as he stares at the floor. "Alright. I'd wish for someone in my life who's real, you know, not just some hanger-on, but someone who gets me."

His head rises and our gazes lock as butterflies take off in my stomach.

Is this the real Dillon McQueen?

My heart pounds as the intimacy between us deepens, a sense of connection growing in the air. I decide that eye contact with him is a rollercoaster ride. One moment you're at the top, about to lose your breath, and the next you're soaring down a hill and clenching the railing.

"What else?" I ask softly.

He inhales a deep breath and glances away from me. I picture walls going up around him. "What does it matter? Wishes aren't real."

I study him as he avoids my eyes, taking in the sharp jawline, the straight nose, the proud stance of his shoulders.

I keep coming back to the fact that we lost loved ones the same year.

Is that why I feel this attraction to him? This kinship?

No, girl, you'd like to kiss him, admit it. It's been eighteen months!

"I'd like to write a story about you. Everyone already knows your stats and how good you are, but I want to focus on who you really are, what makes you tick. Would you want to talk about your brother?"

He lets out a heavy breath. "No. It's too..." He shakes his head and lifts his hands in an expression of *I don't know*.

"Painful?"

"Yeah." He scrubs his face as he takes a step back from

me. Several moments tick by as we stare at each other. I can feel him retreating from the topic of his brother.

He smirks. "I've got something interesting. You believe in legends?"

"People find them fascinating. 'Bigfoot Marries Coed in Mississippi'—I wrote that short story for the *World Enquirer*, freelance, and it paid for last year's tuition." It also helped with a small portion of my sister's private school. I danced around my apartment with that check in my hands for an hour. It was my first real success.

"Jesus, and now you're doing sports?"

"Scary, right? In 2014, a study showed that more people believe in Bigfoot than the Big Bang theory."

"Bigfoot is a myth, Serena."

"Maybe he's just a really tall, hairy guy who's forsaken society for the forest. It could happen."

"Weird." He huffs out a laugh and walks away, tucking the first aid kit inside the cabinet as I slip my boots back on. Returning to me, he takes my hand and helps me off the table. "Give me your number."

My breath hitches. "For?"

He gives me that lazy grin from the Pig, the one he gave his posse and the checkout girl. "You'll need to talk to me if you want a story. Do you want to stop by the house? Practice is done and the night is mine, sweetheart." His voice has deepened, his gaze lowering as he rakes it over me, lingering on my chest before coming back to my face.

I sigh. I prefer the other Dillon, the melancholy one who wishes for his brother.

"Real subtle. Phone is fine." Which sucks. Normally, I *would* like to sit across from him, get a feel for him, but he's more than I can handle.

I recite my digits and he adds them to his phone.

"When will you call?" I say. "I'm usually free after seven at night."

"Looking forward to it, sweetheart?"

And here we go...

"Egotistical jock. You aren't used to girls not being into you, are you?"

"Ah, if you only remembered... You *are* into me." His eyes glitter like jewels.

"You don't even like me," I say, putting my hands on my hips. "Wouldn't I be just another notch on your bedpost?"

"I notch my belt."

"Classy. I won't be on it."

"You sure?"

"Positive."

"Too bad."

"Yeah, too bad, Dominick." I really suck at comebacks.

He smiles and a tingle dances over my skin.

Ugh. What is it with him and my body? Must resist! (Alexa, play "Womanizer" by Britney Spears.)

He holds my eyes for several moments, until I can feel the blush on my face.

"I'm not interested in you like that," I say. Liar, liar pants on fire.

He blinks, a resigned expression settling on his face. "I seem to never say the right thing in front of you." He dips his head, then looks back up at me. "Honest? You make me a little nervous."

I don't believe him. "Right."

"It's true."

"Why?"

Someone out in the hall calls out, breaking into our silence. He tucks his hands in his jeans and fidgets. "Your ankle should be good with the bandages. You need anything else?"

A ride home, but I'd never ask him.

"No."

He hesitates, watching me, looking like he might say something else, then… "See you at the games, Serena."

Before I can respond, he's gone without another glance at me.

9

Dillon

"You're a real bastard, Grandpa," Sinclair pants noisily as he runs next to me, his feet slapping the road. "And why the hell are we running in the burbs? Wouldn't campus be better? Or a treadmill with air conditioning?"

"Ah, Mississippi, I love you." I inhale humid air.

"It's a hundred degrees," he snarls.

"Hold up..." I stop and stretch, easing some of the tension out of my shoulders, although it feels impossible. Day by day, the closer we get to our first game, the stress continues to build and escalate.

He jogs back to me, sweaty and tired, and I smirk at the memory of the first day I dragged him out of his dorm room and made him run. He bitched and moaned the entire way then vomited in the bushes at mile five.

His chest rises up and down as he puts his hands on his hips and nods his head at the driveway. "You know who lives here? We've stopped here a few times."

"Nah."

My eyes dart up to the garage where Serena lives. Where is her car at six thirty in the morning? She said she doesn't have a boyfriend, but is she fucking someone?

Thoughts of her in the locker room tumble around in my head, the softness of her skin under my hands, the way she leaned on my shoulder, her story about her parents—and my impulse to kiss her.

Then, I had to go and open my mouth... *I'd wish for someone who's real, you know, not just some hanger-on, but someone who gets me.* What possessed me to say that? Jesus! I totally freaked during our conversation, surprised by the level of intimacy between us, how easy she was to talk to. I got anxious and reverted to being a jackass. I acted like a douche, telling her I notch my belt. Not true. Please. Sure, I date girls, never staying with one too long, but I never leave them with hurt feelings. I treat them well and never fool around. My brief relationships come and go and that's been cool for the past three years. I never formed a real connection. I never found the *right* one. Well, I thought I did three years ago, but...

I couldn't wait to get away from Serena, afraid I was going to blurt out everything from freshman year right in front of her. *Hello, we kissed once. I may have imagined us as a couple. I looked for you for months. Yes, I'm a lunatic.* Yeah, not cool.

A sigh comes from me. Sawyer has thrown down the challenge, and I've accepted just to shut him up, but I have no intention of wooing her.

I'm not interested in you like that. Boom. Message received.

Maybe we can be friends?

But... I'm not unaware that her eyes linger on me. I see the pulse in her throat that beats faster than normal. There *is* something there. The question is, what do I want to do about it?

Her number has been in my phone for two days, and last night I almost called her, the urge eating at me like crazy as Sawyer and I played video games. Instead, I took a cold shower and went to bed. Frustration swirls, part of me wanting to knock on her door and see if she's home, the other part ready to rip my hair out to get her off my mind. And last night's dream? Her naked in my bed, hips rolling on top of me, her hair tumbling down her back—

I huff out a long breath.

Sinclair mimics me, doing his own stretches, eyeing me as he touches his toes. "My hamstrings are killing me," he moans. "Let's call it a day."

Tearing my eyes away from Serena's place, I look over at him. "When you figure out that football isn't just about you, we can run on a treadmill."

He snorts—as much as he can while trying to regulate his breathing. "You think being older makes you wiser? I went to school with rich pricks like you who think the world owes them."

I click my tongue. The world hasn't been kind to me. Sure, it may look like that from the outside, but... "You got siblings, Sinclair? Family?"

"Two younger sisters and my mom. My dad split."

At least we have that in common, yet he has family who needs him. No one *needs* me. Once my brother did, but he died. My dad did, but he left. My mom never needed me, period.

I never talk about Myles, but with Serena I had.

I can dive from here, Dillon, just like you...

My head spins with images of my brother, his small body a direct contrast to my bigger size. Four years younger than me, we looked nothing alike, me the athlete, him the intellectual who'd rather hold a book than a football. Barely thirteen, and all he wanted was to hang out with me. I should have watched him better, should have stopped him from jumping off that cliff into the water below.

"You?"

It's the first time he's asked me about myself, and I start, coming back to the present. "My cousin Mary attends Waylon, but we're not close. My mom travels a lot. My dad moved back to Malibu and got remarried. My bio dad died in a private plane crash with my grandparents when I was a month old." It's as if my real dad never existed. All I have are photos of him, a tall dark-haired man with my eyes. He was an only child so there's no connection to that side of my family. Wes McQueen adopted me when he married my mom two years later, and he's the only father I've ever known.

He blinks. "That sucks. My mom is tuned in to every game. She can't afford to fly in from Florida, but I'm getting her tickets when we play the Gators. She'll be there wearing my jersey. You should see her twerk when I score. She's badass."

My chest pangs. My dad didn't come to any games last year because of his new family. Mom didn't either.

"Plan on going out early for the draft?" I ask, needing to change the topic.

"I have to look out for myself."

"Yeah? I'm here for my team. Those guys have been my rock, my *family* for three years. Ryker could have been drafted early but chose to stay and grow stronger."

"Really tired of hearing about your friendship with Ryker and how great the team was before I came."

I scoff. "Do you know what the difference is between a thermostat and a thermometer?"

He rolls his eyes. "Lessons with Dillon. You are so fucking boring."

I ignore that. "A thermostat sets the temperature,

decides the tone for the room, for the team. A thermometer simply records the temperature of a space, nothing more. It takes more than skill to be a quarterback. A thermostat is a confident voice, a leader who isn't only thinking about how good he looks. Also, you can't read a blitz for shit."

"Then why aren't we looking at game tape to figure it out?"

"I like seeing you puke, rookie." I take off in a run and he jogs up next to me, edging ahead. I push myself, my chest burning as I pump my arms and pass him. "Try to keep up."

He calls out a juicy curse and attempts to run ahead. Sure, he manages it for about twenty seconds—until my longer legs and better conditioning leave him in the dust.

∼

BY THE TIME the game rolls around the next day, I'm wound up as I take the field against Auburn with my offense. Unlike us, most of their older guys have returned, and it's a seasoned team we'll be facing.

It's a balmy September afternoon when I snap the first play then throw to Sawyer, and he dodges the defensive lineman to get our first down. Inch by inch, we move the ball against a beefy team, and everything flows like silk, every pass tight and sure. By the end of the first quarter, we're fourteen points ahead, and by halftime, when they still haven't scored, we celebrate as we walk back to the locker room.

"Badass game, McQueen," one of the coaches calls to me, patting me on my pads.

"Way to read the defense," Alvarez says with a rare smile.

When we come out of the tunnel for the second half, my eyes go up to the press section near the fifty-yard line. Serena is there, sitting next to the guy from WBBJ. She's laughing at something he's saying, her full lips curved up in a smile. My throat tightens. Why can't I say the right things in front of her? All the way back to the bonfire, I acted like an ass, assuming she'd be interested in me.

As if she feels my gaze, her head turns and our eyes cling, that familiar humming starting up in my chest.

"Yo! Let's kick Auburn out of our stadium," Sawyer calls as he runs up and slaps my ass.

Yeah, let's. I pull my eyes off Serena and imagine Myles in the stands cheering me on, giving me his wide grin as he waves a foam hand. I gaze up at the blue sky. "This one's for you, bro." I kiss the tops of my hands.

This *is* going to be my year to shine. It has to be. Football is all I have left.

10

Serena

I send a wave to Neil from my balcony at the top of the stairs before I head inside my apartment. We had dinner after the game with a few other reporters and then he gave me a ride home. Just as I shut the door, my phone pings with a text from an unknown number.

Hey. I saw Bigfoot earlier. He was wearing an Auburn football shirt and tried to mow me down. Had more hair than a grizzly.

Dillon. Has to be.

Hey yourself, I reply as I smile. **Congrats on the first win of your senior year.**

Thx. I saw you there. Want to text me questions for your story?

Text? Not really. Using my phone, I FaceTime him two times before he picks up.

He's in a bar, probably Cadillac's, the loud murmur of voices echoing through the phone. He looks freshly showered, his diamond-cut jawline filling up my screen. He's walking through a throng of people, several of them slapping him on the back. "Serena, hey," he says.

I plop down on my bed, scooting my pillows up and leaning back as I hold the phone up. "You're celebrating your win."

He glances away again as someone squeals his name —a girl I can't see. "Yeah. Sorry, I can't really talk in here. I just thought, you know, if you text me the questions, I'll reply to them later."

Mortification washes over me, and I try to keep my face from showing it. *Be cool, be cool.* God, why *did* I FaceTime him when he specifically asked for me to text him? Of course he's out with his buddies, no doubt about to pick some lucky girl to take home.

Ashley pops up on the screen, her red hair piled in an elaborate chignon, her lips a hot pink. "Come on, let's do some shots."

"Give me a minute." He eases away and steps into a less crowded hallway. "Are you in bed?"

"Obviously." I grab a couple of Oreos from my nightstand and munch on one. Nana picked them up at Walmart earlier this week.

"It's Saturday—don't you ever go out?"

"I'm not really a party girl." I used to hang out in bars with Vane and his crew all the time, most of them out of town. I haven't been to Caddy's in years.

His eyes gleam as I pick up another cookie. "You need to lick the cream now. I promise, it's the way to eat it."

"Like this?" I manage to ease the wafers apart with one hand and run my tongue over the white center, closing my eyes as I lick my lips. "Mmmm, you're right. So good."

"You almost make me forget I don't like you."

An unexpected laugh comes from me. "Will any girl do, Dillon?"

"Not lately."

"Is the big bad football player having a dry spell?"

"You have no idea. It's been months—"

A girl comes around the corner from behind him, cutting him off as she screams his name and jumps on his back, wrapping her legs around his waist. The phone falls and the camera lens spins then goes black as it slaps the floor. I hear Dillon's muffled voice, the laughter in it. After a few moments, his face appears again and he smirks at me ruefully. "It's crazy in here."

I can see that.

She saunters off, but she's behind him in the camera, looking over her shoulder and running her eyes over him.

"Looks like you have plenty to pick from tonight." I toss my cookie on the bed, too annoyed to eat it.

"Maybe I want this particular one, but she's giving me trouble."

"Who is she, Dimitri?"

A slow smile curls his lips. It's real and genuine—and I melt. "You love to play games, don't you?"

"Dillon, come on!" comes Ashley's sugary voice.

"Carry on without me. This call is important," he tells her in a muffled voice off-screen before looking back at me. "Sorry. How are your feet?"

"Better."

"You have"—his lips quirk—"nice feet. I liked your chipped pink polish."

"I dig capes, you like podiatry."

He turns up a beer and takes a sip.

"Fat Tire, I see."

"Every time I drink one, I see you at the Pig. Fierce."

"I made an impression."

He stares at me, a deep look, and it feels as if he's in the room with me. "Oh, yeah. *First* impressions." He shakes his head. "Ever hear of the 7-11 rule?"

"No."

"People make seven decisions about a person in the first eleven seconds of seeing them."

I gasp. "Are you spouting random facts?"

"Hush. Within seconds, we make decisions about

sexual orientation, economic status, cultural beliefs, religion, desirability, kinks, level of intelligence—what are you doing?"

Propping my phone on my knees, I wave my notebook and pen at him. "Writing this down. Go on, tell me what you assumed from your first meeting with me."

He huffs out a husky laugh. "You're different. You don't care who I am. You give it back as good as I give, and most girls don't. What was your impression of me?"

"A pigskin-toting Casanova."

And the *very* first time I ever saw him? Well, I thought the same...

"You hate me." He smiles.

"Who can hate the best lacrosse player at Waylon? You're so good-looking you should be in movies—the cashier's words, not mine." He chuckles and I smile at how easy it is to talk to him, at the way he can find humor in himself.

"I need someone like you to keep me in line. Reminds me I'm just a regular guy," he murmurs, staring at me, his gaze warm. "Want to get out of your place and join me?" he says. "I'll wait for you outside in the parking lot."

My mind goes back to watching him perform on the field. He's a warrior, a big majestic fighter. I sat in my seat and watched him far more than was professional. Temptation unfurls inside me, yearning to see those broad shoulders in person... "I shouldn't."

"You know what I'm thinking right now?" His voice deepens.

I resist the urge to fan myself. "What?"

"About that rapid pulse I see in your throat. Hmmm?"

I place my hand over my throat as he holds my gaze. He walks through the crowd and steps outside the back door of Cadillac's. The background noise is quieter, but I still hear the strum of music from the speakers in the bar.

I stifle a groan. The truth is, Dillon is the hottest freaking man alive, and when he gets close, I'm a firework waiting to be lit. I denied it at the Pig, but it's always been there, just waiting to blow up.

"Know what I'm thinking?" I ask.

"That I'm irresistible—"

"Ha. I'm thinking you'd have a hard time keeping up with me." Yeah. I just said that.

"I'm hard, alright." He lowers his gaze, his top teeth tugging at his bottom lip.

I burst out laughing. "And people say romance is dead!"

He levels me with his searching turquoise gaze. "You said you weren't interested. Is that true?" An anxious expression flits over his face as he frowns. "I don't want to bother you or say suggestive things if, uh, if you think I'm terrible. I'll, um, rein it in…" His words peter out as his eyes shut briefly. "I suck at this. Sometimes, I have no filter. Pretend we're in middle school. For real, all jokes aside. Do you like me, you know, as a person? Check yes or no." He squints at me, as if dreading the answer.

He *is* irresistible.

"I check *yes*." I feel like a twelve-year-old talking to the popular guy.

He exhales. "Thank you, Jesus. Hop in your car and come have a drink with me."

I swallow. Why not take him up on that offer—only I don't have a car.

He looks away briefly. "Hey, they're playing your song inside."

"What?"

"Listen. 'Sweet Serena'…it's a sign."

I hear the slow beat of the Four Dragons hit, the guitar strumming the angsty ballad.

Teardrops on my hands,
   Red lips and an angelic face,
   Come on and give me a twirl,
   How do I get the girl?
   Sweet, sweet Serena…

Teardrops on my guitar,
   It's worth fighting for,
   Sand turned to pearls,

How do I keep the girl?
Sweet, sweet Serena...

T*EARDROPS ON MY BED,*
Whiskey bottles and broken stilettos,
Long lashes that curl,
How did I lose the girl?
Sweet, sweet Serena...

T*EARDROPS ON MY HEART,*
Stumbling through goodbye,
Making me crack, baby,
How do I get you back?
Sweet, sweet Serena...

"H*EY, WHAT'S WRONG?*" he asks, holding the phone closer, the blue-green of his gaze searching mine.

Everything. Bad memories. Old heartaches. Loneliness wraps around me like a vise, and a long exhalation comes from my chest.

It is a sign—a bad one.

"Nothing." I clear my throat and rush my words before I change my mind. "I need to go. If I didn't say thank you for the first aid this week, thank you so much.

Have fun tonight. You had a great game. I'll text you questions soon. Bye."

"Serena. Wait a minute—"

I click my cell off and throw it on the bed, lying back on my pillows and staring up at the ceiling fan. My chest feels heavy as my mind flips to Dillon and then Vane, comparing how similar they are, both hot, talented guys with women begging to be with them. I'd be a fool to get sucked into Dillon's world. I refuse to repeat past mistakes.

But... What's wrong with a little tango in the sheets? Or, as Nana says, *making the bam-bam in the ham?*

Without getting my heart involved?

There's no doubt he's open to that. I get the sense that's the way he operates, easy come, easy go.

Dillon's emotional eyes appear into my head, the pain and sadness in him from the loss of his brother, and I groan and throw my hand over my face. There's no way I can tango with him. He's exactly my type: sexy as hell with issues.

Must. Stop. Thinking. About. Him.

11

Serena

The next morning when I walk over to the house where Nana and my sister Romy live, there's a lanky teenage boy crawling out of the top-story window. His bleached hair sticks straight up, there are piercings in both of his eyebrows, and his chest is bare. Probably left his shirt behind. Here we go again.

He tiptoes over the roof and jumps to the big oak tree in the front yard. There's a *crack* as he lands, the limb swaying under his weight. Would serve him right if it broke.

I stand under the tree and wait, tapping my foot as he jumps to another branch and slithers down the tree, landing with a thump at the bottom. There are red scratches on his chest from the twigs and limbs.

"Good morning," I drawl. "Don't you think it would be

easier to use the front door? Oh, wait—you can't, because you spent the night with my baby sister!" My voice rises at the end, my hands planted on my hips.

He was about to dash down the street but flips around to face me, eyes flaring. "Uhhhhhh..."

"Leave him alone, Serena! I'm seventeen, for fuck's sake!" I hear my hellcat of a sister call from the window, probably watching to see if he made a clean getaway.

"Language! I told you about letting boys in your room! Do you want me to nail your window shut?" I yell back, not taking my eyes off Tree Boy. "You," I say in a low voice. "Don't you dare move. We're gonna talk."

His mouth flaps open then he looks up at Romy, who sends him a shrug. Her wavy auburn hair is mussed, and my eyes narrow at the hickey on her neck.

The roar of a motorcycle reverberates as it turns down our street, and I smile. "You hear that? That's my brother Julian on his way for Sunday brunch." I let out a long whistle. "Twenty-six years old, muscles, prison tattoos, and a pretty little Glock. He's in a motorcycle club. Lots of mean friends. You know what he's going to do to you when he finds out about you?"

"Don't believe her, Liam!" Romy shrieks. "He's a cop! His motorcycle club is just a bunch of old farts!"

"Heh. Old farts with guns. That any better?" I smart back.

He gasps. "No."

I edge closer to Liam as my fingers imitate a gun and I aim for his heart. "Last boy who came out of that window disappeared in the Mississippi River—"

"He moved! Serena, quit scaring him!" comes from my sister. "That was months ago! I haven't done it since then! I swear!"

"Or I haven't caught you!"

The Harley roars into the driveway and parks behind Nana's faded brown Avalon. Julian's six-three frame eases off the bike, all muscled thighs and carefully leashed power as he whips off his helmet and stretches. He's wearing faded jeans, a black wife beater, and dirty motorcycle boots. Roses and gold daggers decorate his upper left shoulder. A gold python starts at his right bicep and wraps all the way down to his wrist. I laugh under my breath.

Liam sputters and darts his gaze back at me. "Look, uh, we were just studying and it got late—"

My arms cross. "On a Saturday night? How conscientious of you…"

Red flushes up his face.

I poke him in the chest. "Now, here's how it's going to go. You're on my blacklist, which means the next time you want to see Romy, you have to trudge over to my place above the garage…" I tilt my head back toward my apartment. "You knock on my door and ask real polite if you can knock on Nana's and see Romy. Then, if I say it's okay, *if you have a shirt on,* you come over here and be polite to my grandmother, maybe take out her trash, help her cook dinner, and for sure you help her wash dishes, and then you can sit in the den and watch TV or study with Romy. You leave *through the front door* at her curfew, which is midnight. Under no circumstances do you go to her room. It's disrespectful to Nana and to Romy. I'd prefer you abstain from sex, but if you are having sex, well, I can't stop you, *but don't do it in the house.* Also, please use a condom. Venereal disease, simply put, will rot your penis, and teen pregnancy—"

"Serena, for the love of... Don't make me cuss!" Romy calls.

"—is no joke," I continue. "Seven hundred and fifty thousand teen girls get pregnant every year. Do you want to be a dad right now?"

"No," he whispers.

"Don't let the sex muddle your brain, and don't think her being on the pill is enough. Even condoms are not completely safe." Been there, done that.

He pales. "You can get pregnant with condoms?"

"Yes, Liam, I see you're catching on. Nothing is impossible, and sex is a big responsibility. Think you're ready for it?"

He sways on his feet.

"Should we discuss venereal disease?"

"No," he whispers. "Please."

"I'm going to jump out of this window if you give him the sex talk!" Romy yells.

"No, you won't!" I call back to her, eyes still on Liam. I clear my throat. "First, and most people don't realize this, there are more than twenty-five different venereal diseases, and some of those you can get even with a condom. Look it up—it's true. Some, such as chlamydia and gonorrhea, have no symptoms but can be deadly if left untreated. I won't go into what happens to the female, but for the male, well, it begins as a disgusting penile discharge and mild pain when urinating that becomes more severe. Then it progresses to epididymitis, an inflammation of the tube-like structure that stores and transports sperm..." I pause. "You look a bit green, Liam. Should I tell you about the rectal issues?"

"No."

"Problem, sis?" Julian murmurs as he steps up next to me.

"Is there a problem?" I ask Liam.

He sucks in a breath and looks up at Romy, back at me, and then lands on Julian as he licks his lips. He comes back to me, a pleading look in his eyes. "I understand completely, ma'am. I'm so sorry."

Ma'am. I laugh. "Good. Now, I'd love for you to meet my big brother. He bench-presses two hundred and fifty pounds. How much do you weigh, Liam?"

"One forty."

"Julian's a decorated state trooper and a former Navy SEAL. Wanna know what he did in the Navy? Sniper. My brother can kill a man from a thousand yards. He's very protective of his baby sister. How do you think it makes him feel when a guy climbs out of her window?"

"Pissed off," Julian mutters.

Liam flinches. "Won't happen again, I swear. I'll come see you first, before I see Romy."

His body is pointed to the street, and I sigh. "You may go," I say, and he pauses for half a second then takes off in a run down the street toward a bright yellow Chevelle. He cranks it and drives past us very, very slowly.

"Call me!" Romy yells at him.

"Navy SEAL? Damn, I sound good." Julian chuckles.

"I improvised. I'm pissed at Romy, but catching him coming down the tree—now that was just fortuitous fun."

"You're crazy! I hate both of you!" Romy yells before slamming her window shut.

Oh, the bliss of mentoring a teenager. Technically, Nana has guardianship of her, but I'm the one she gravitates to. There's only seven years between us, so it makes sense. Did I do crazy stuff when I was a teenager? Um, yeah, hello, tattoo and vodka. I used to sneak out of my bedroom on the weekends. I gave my virginity to a bad boy in high school who dropped me afterward. I just want Romy to make better decisions than I did.

Julian throws an arm around me as we walk to the front door. "You mentioned the gun?"

"Told him you took the last guy out."

He shakes his head. "What are we gonna do with her?"

A long sigh comes from me. "Heaven help me, I've tried. You should talk to her…"

He winces. "Serena, nah, don't make me. I wouldn't know what to say."

"Maybe if you sat down with her and told her a guy's point of view on sex, how they may not feel the same emotional attachments—"

He sucks his teeth. "Look, you're a girl, she's a girl… you got it."

Then why is she always in some kind of trouble? Frustration builds in my stomach. In March of her junior year, while I was in the middle of dealing with the fallout from Vane, she hooked up with a bad crowd at the public school. The administrators caught her and two other girls smoking pot under the football bleachers. Drugs on school grounds are an automatic 180-day expulsion and admittance to an alternative school. I scrambled to find the money and managed to get her accepted at the local private school. Lucky for us, one of the board members is a policeman and worked with my dad, otherwise they wouldn't have taken her.

An hour later, I'm slicing strawberries while Romy

takes the chicken breasts out of the oven. A plate of warm waffles sits on the counter next to a bowl of eggs ready to be scrambled, just waiting for Julian to come in from mowing the yard.

My gaze drifts over the soft blue curtains in the breakfast area, the faded filigree wallpaper, the ancient oak table with a centerpiece of grapes and apples. The house is old and ramshackle, but tidy. Selling our family home was never an option after my parents died.

"How's school? It's your senior year, so that has to be exciting," I ask Romy, offering an olive branch after I talked to her in her room. While she glowered, I sat on her bed and went through my checklist with her about teen sex, how she's experiencing raging hormones, that sex doesn't mean love…

Now in the kitchen, she shrugs, a wary expression on her face. Deep purple lipstick colors her mouth and her eyes are heavy with eyeliner. Magenta streaks pop in her hair. That's new.

"Two weeks in and calculus sucks. I flunked the first test." Her shoulders dip, and a panicked look flashes over her face before she turns back to the stove. "The uniforms drive me batty, and the girls are snotty. Headmaster Roberts glares at me like he expects me to fire up a joint at any moment. Same as last year."

"Would you prefer I homeschool you?" I could, I guess, in between catering jobs and writing.

Her face reddens and her eyes grow shiny. "I miss my old school is all."

"How's the hip hop?"

"Tryouts are soon." She turns away, giving me her rigid back.

"I can help you, if you want." I took dance classes for years, ranging from ballet to modern. Once I thought I might do it professionally, maybe own a studio and teach, but the uncertainty of that career choice made me wary—especially after my parents died. I had to grow up quick.

"You're busy." She shrugs.

I sigh. "I'm sorry I'm not always here. Nana is."

"At least I see you more now that Vane is gone. Asshole."

"Language," I murmur.

"Like you don't say worse."

I am trying.

"I'm sorry about letting Liam stay. We honestly just fell asleep." Her lips twist. "Do you believe me?" Her eyes find mine and hold them.

I nod. "Just…don't rush into anything, okay?"

"Like you did with Vane?"

A long exhalation comes from my chest. "Yeah." The first night I met him, I slept with him. She knows about the pregnancy, the rushed marriage, the quickie divorce when he cheated.

My almost-seventy-year-old nana flounces in, her

two Yorkies, Buster and Betty, behind her, their nails clicking on the hardwood. An unlit cigarette dangles from her pink lips, sponge rollers still in her graying brown hair.

"Nana, those are bad for you," I warn. She claims she quit smoking ten years ago after her COPD diagnosis, but she sneaks them when she takes the dogs for a walk.

"Just one of those days when I like to have one in my mouth." She stops at the butcher block island in the middle of the kitchen. "Girls, would you be willing to eat a bowl of live crickets for twenty thousand dollars?"

"Gross! No!" Romy takes a chicken breast and sets it on a stack of paper towels.

"How many crickets are in the bowl?" I ask.

Nana scoops up Betty, the sweeter of the dogs, and scratches behind her jeweled pink collar. "Twenty."

"Maybe." Money is always tight. My parents had insurance, but a lot of that was used to pay off the house, Julian's college loans, mine, Nana's medical bills, and now Romy's private school. I'm also socking money away for Romy's freshman year at college. Julian contributes to her college fund, but he doesn't live here with us, and sometimes it feels like an uphill battle just to stay afloat with the day-to-day.

She pats me on the cheek. "I asked Turo, and he said he'd eat anything. His eyes got all sexy like and he waggled his eyebrows. That's a come-on if I ever heard it."

She sucks on the end of her unlit cig. "I'm gonna bang him. Have I mentioned he's Italian?"

"Yes!" Romy and I say at the same time.

Romy smirks. "Your senior citizen center is a hotbed. Geriatrics are the most likely to contract venereal diseases. Just ask Serena." Her tone is sharp as she darts her eyes at me and then away.

"Serena!" Julian sticks his head in the front door. "Someone's pulling up with your car."

"My car?" My voice rises.

What in the world?

How are they driving it? It's at the Pig...

I wipe my hands on a dishtowel and head to the front door, then stop. Oh, oh, right! I was distracted when the quarterback showed up in the parking lot. I've been meaning to get a ride to grab my keys, but it's slipped my mind.

My eyes flare wide as I stop on the porch and watch as Sawyer gets out of my car. I have the team profiles and photos memorized. Dillon's Escalade pulls up behind my car at the curb. Owen Sinclair is in his passenger seat.

My eyes are on Dillon as he exits his vehicle.

He sweeps his gaze over the house, briefly glancing to my apartment over the garage. He's wearing workout clothes, gym shorts, and a Tigers vented tank. The ends of his hair curl around a ball cap.

His eyes flash over to me, lingering.

I gaze down at my gauzy teal harem pants and orange-striped bandeau top that cups my breasts and loops around my neck. I'm showing a liberal amount of midriff. It's a far cry from my Piggly Wiggly outfit or my stadium clothes.

This is the real me, football player. A little wild. A little scared of you.

"Serena," he murmurs as he stalks toward me.

"This is..."—*shocking*—"a surprise." My gaze flits to my Toyota. "What's going on?"

"Your car—don't you need it?"

"Yeah, but how..." My words stop as Owen comes around the Escalade.

His gaze darts between us. "Hey, Serena. Dillon said I owe you an apology."

"He did?" I ask, bemused.

"Apparently I was a dick at the stadium."

"And..." Dillon prompts.

Owen grunts. "And I shouldn't have said, '*Pass her along when you're done.*'"

"Ah, okay. You fixed my car?" I glance at my sad excuse for a Highlander, wincing at the rust around the edges of the wheels, the dent Romy put in the bumper.

"Not me. *Dillon*," Owen says. "I've got no clue what you see in him. He's the biggest asshole—"

Dillon pops him on the arm, shutting him up. "What Owen meant is, we ran past the Pig this morning and saw your car. We checked it out, spied the keys in the console, so I popped the hood. Turns out, you needed a battery. You should have told me you didn't have a car. I would have driven you home from the stadium that day."

"So you decided to drive to AutoZone and get a new battery?" My tone is incredulous. He fixed my car!

Sawyer raises his hand and says, "He called me and I brought them one." He flashes me a wide grin. He's handsome, his wavy black hair chin-length, his skin a dark bronze. Small silver hoops hang in his earlobes. "Dillon wanted to repair it and deliver it to you. So, we did. Now that I see you, well, all is clear. Crystal. Nice to meet you."

I murmur the same back to him.

"How much do I owe you?" I ask Dillon.

Before he can answer, Julian juts in and gives me a prod in my ribs. "Why didn't you tell me your car was stuck at the Pig? How long?"

I sigh. "A week. You were working late shifts and I was going to get around to it today at some point. I didn't have any catering gigs this week, just class and the *Gazette*. I was fine." I explain how I called the manager and she told me it was cool to leave the Highlander.

He gives me a disgruntled look.

My chin tilts. "I like to walk." Magnolia doesn't have a bussing system, and Nana needs her car for her visits to the senior center and to drive Romy to and from school. If we had more money, I'd buy my sister a car, but we don't.

Julian exhales. "It wouldn't have taken much for me to run over there."

The truth is, he's got a new, demanding girlfriend and spends most of his extra time with her. I've heard him on the phone with her trying to explain why he's over here repairing this or that. Two weeks ago, it was the garbage disposal. The week before that it was a gutter that came down in a storm.

"Well, well, who do we have here?" Nana's voice comes from the porch. She approaches us wearing leopard-print leggings and a black Guns 'N Roses shirt. Her unlit cig still dangles from her lips, but thankfully she's taken out the rollers and teased her hair up in the back, the ends flipped up à la 1950s. Betty is in her arms.

Buster paces the porch and yips, sending indignant looks at the crowd until he gets the nerve to jump down the steps and trot after her.

I start with introductions—

"Oh my God! Dillon McQueen!" is shrieked from the front door as Romy throws it open.

Dillon laughs as he looks at my face. I laugh with him and he stops, pausing, something on my face making him blink. Butterflies take off in my stomach. *Stop*, I yell at them.

"Why didn't you tell me you invited friends over!" Romy grouses as she makes her way over to us. She fluffs her hair, an excited look on her face. "Eek! I need an autograph!"

"Sure," Owen and Dillon say at the same time then glare at each other.

Romy runs off to get a piece of notebook paper and a pen, comes back, and all three guys sign it as if it's something they do all the time.

Dillon rakes his eyes over Julian. "You with Serena?"

I start. When Julian and I go out, people do sometimes think we're together. We grew up as an affectionate family and often hug and tease each other, and we don't look alike. He's got the bulk of Dad, the dark hair and blue eyes, while I'm petite with light brown eyes. "Brother. A protective one," Julian says, eyes glowering at Dillon.

Yeah, that was subtle. He's (understandably) wary since Vane.

"Hmm." Dillon's gaze comes back to me.

"It's not every day I get to meet Serena's friends. Why, I didn't even know she knew any football players," Nana says, thrusting Betty into an unprepared Sawyer's arms. He blinks and cradles the dog as she licks his face.

Nana smiles at them, lasering in on Dillon. "So, what I want to know is… Would you eat a bowl of live crickets for twenty thousand dollars?"

Romy chokes, and I groan inwardly.

Dillon looks at me. "I see where you get it."

I shrug. "We're Southern—you should see the relative we have locked up in the attic."

"Uncle Charles is dead and you know it," Nana quips.

"He wasn't locked in the attic. He passed away in Miami," I retort.

Dillon laughs. "How many crickets are in the bowl?"

"Twenty. A thousand dollars for each cricket," she declares.

Dillon tucks his hands into his shorts and speaks in his lazy tone. "Well, ma'am, the NCAA doesn't allow us to accept gifts from anyone, but if we're speaking hypothetically, I suppose I would. I like a good challenge." His eyes drift over me.

"Are you a Southern boy? You talk like it, but there's no accent," she asks, eyes narrowed.

"Nana doesn't trust Yankees," I warn him.

"I was born in California but moved to Alabama when I was a kid. My mama's from Montgomery so I have Southern roots."

She walks a circle around him. "My parents were from Montgomery. What's her family name?"

"St. Claire."

Nana's lips purse. "Is she the one who married that man who owns all the hotels? McQueen! That's your family, isn't it?"

"Yes, ma'am."

She puffs on her unlit cig. "Holy cow. Butter my butt and call me a biscuit. Good job, Serena."

I wince. "Nana, it's not like that."

"Does your mama know how to hunt and fish? Or is she one of those highfalutin' debutante types?" she asks him.

"Nana..." I start.

"Shopping is hunting for my mom. She's in Paris right now."

His lips have compressed, a tightness in his eyes. She didn't come to his first game? I frown. That sucks. It's his senior year.

Nana mulls that over. "I can turn you into a country boy in no time, show you how to put a worm on a hook or shoot a squirrel. Serena hid my shotgun, but I'm gonna find it one of these days... You interested?"

"I swear we aren't hillbillies," I tell him.

He chuckles, his face softening. "I'm game."

Buster trots over, sniffs around Dillon's sneakers, and then inexplicably puts his paw on his shoe and looks up at him.

"Buster hates everyone." Nana studies Dillon, and I can already see the wheels turning in her head. One night after dinner, I overheard her on the phone asking Turo if his son's divorce was final "because Serena needs a good seeing to".

She goes on. "So you're the one who brought her

home from the Pig? She should have called me, but I was deep in my bingo game and, well, Turo was there, and I've got my sights set on him. She assumed I wouldn't want to leave, and she was right. He's Italian." She takes a breath, gearing up for more. "Serena's a good girl. She's been through a lot, putting others first, trying to raise her sister. She was my little angel—until she fell in with that musician. He was a sexy devil, sings with a forked tongue probably, but bless, he was a pile of dog poo, as useless as a screen door on a submarine. I reckon if you want to see her, we need rules. First rule is, when she starts spouting off random stuff, just listen. Her looks make up for it, and it does grow on you. Second rule is, she needs to get hers first, if you know what I mean—"

"Nana," I interrupt, my face growing hot. "He doesn't need my life story. He's dating *three* other women." I can't resist throwing it in.

"Just two," chimes in Sawyer with dancing eyes. "Chantal jumped ship. Something about the Winter Soldier, tequila, and Neanderthals. I couldn't keep up."

"Good for her," I murmur.

"I'm *not* dating other women. I'm in a contest," Dillon says to Nana. "But Serena keeps turning me down."

She bats her eyes. "Call me Nancy, boys. I'm a football fan, you know. Now, since you've been sweet to my Serena, do y'all want to stay and have some chicken and waffles?"

"Nana!" I interject as unease spikes. I'm not ready for Dillon to sit across the table with my family and me. Yes, we shared some confidences in the locker room, but... "I'm sure they have places to go—"

"Heck yeah," Owen says. "I'm starving!"

"I'd love a home-cooked meal," Sawyer murmurs.

Dillon studies my face, frowns, then says, "Thank you for the offer. Some other time, Nancy. The rookie and I have a meeting with the quarterback coach anyway. Sawyer, you need to watch game tape." He pauses. "I'll see you at the next game?"

I nod. "Yeah."

He hesitates, as if he might say more, then moves past me, his hand briefly brushing against mine, and my traitorous eyes track the slope of his broad shoulders, his trim hips, the flex of his long muscular legs—

"Are you really going to let that hot piece leave?" Nana hisses as soon as he's out of earshot.

"Yeah," Romy says under her breath, adding her two cents as she slides in next to me. "You haven't had a man in eighteen months, and I, for one, am tired of you harassing my love interests because you're jealous—"

"Of *Tree Boy*?" I hiss. "Please. He gave you a hickey!"

"His name is Liam, and I prefer love bite. You should see the one I gave him."

"He has braces! Doesn't that hurt? Never mind, don't

answer that," I mutter. "If I was Daddy, I'd snap a switch off the tree he climbed down and tan your hide—"

"You'd never," she snips. "You don't approve of corporal punishment, and you hate to see me cry."

True.

"'Spare the rod, spoil the child,'" I quote. "Starting to see the value in that."

"Be quiet, both of you. The football players are leaving, and I think you need to be polite and give a proper thank you to that handsome young man," Nana says.

She isn't wrong.

"Wait!" I call out and dash over to Dillon, and he pauses before opening his door. He turns to look at me, and my breath feels rushed as I speak. "Thank you for the battery. That was kind and it's been, um, a while since someone did something that sweet for me. You never said how much it was..."

"Nah, I don't want money."

"What do you want?"

An uncertain look flits over his face. He stares at me long enough that my face grows warm. "A kiss. Promise me a kiss." He dips his head, hiding his eyes. "Um, is that okay?"

"One?"

"Maybe two." His gaze rises to find mine.

I trace the sensuous curves of his mouth and my breath hitches. What's the harm? "Okay. Now?"

"Later." He gives me a lingering look then gets in his car and cranks it.

Owen crawls in the back and rolls his window down, his gaze sliding to Romy, and of course, she's checking him out, lashes batting. I lean in. "She's jailbait, Sinclair, and has a boyfriend." Tree Boy is on my shit list, but a college boy is the last thing I need.

Owen flashes a sly smirk. "Looking doesn't hurt."

"With her, it does," I say as I reach into the car and thump him on the forehead.

"Dude!" Owen calls, rearing back from me. "Your women are crazy, Dillon."

"I'm not one of his women!"

"Hard to believe, but true," Dillon muses.

"Then why are we running past her house every morning?" Owen says.

My eyes flare. Aha!

Dillon gets a wide look in his eyes—*caught*—and flushes red. He rolls his window up, our eyes holding through the glass.

Sawyer walks to the Escalade and meets me in the yard. His gaze flicks to the car. "You know, I think he can be kind of shy when it comes to you. Odd."

He chuckles and murmurs goodbye and gets in the car. Dillon throws up a wave, and they drive away.

"Blue hair is hot," Romy murmurs as we watch them disappear down the road.

I glower at her. "Remember Liam?"

She chortles. "Oh my God, his face when you said rectal issues...."

I throw an arm around her and press my lips against her temple. "You're a minx. You know I'm grounding you, right? No phone, video games, or Liam for two weeks. Then, we'll talk and reassess."

She shuts her eyes briefly. "Please, Serena. I invited him to the tryouts. You know how anxious I am about it." She's mentioned some of the other girls are catty.

"Fine, he can come, but that's it for two weeks."

She releases a long sigh. "I won't let him stay again, Serena. I promise."

We walk back inside, and my mind is on Dillon and the kiss I promised him.

12

Serena

Wearing my gray tie-dyed leggings and a cropped pink workout top, I head into the student center. As I'm taking the steps to the upper level, my phone rings and I snatch it up without looking to see who the caller is.

If I'd known, I never would have answered.

"*Serena.*" Vane's voice dances down my spine, and I inhale a sharp breath, ready to hang up, but he jumps in, "Baby, baby—wait. Come on, now, don't hang up, not like last time. Just for a few minutes, let me talk to you. *Please.*"

My hand clenches around the phone. It's been two months since he called, the longest he's gone, and I thought he was finally done. Holding the phone to my ear, I sit down in a chair in one of the lounging spaces. "Okay."

Background noise fills up the silence between us, muted rock music playing, glasses clinking together—female giggling.

"Hang on, let me go out on the balcony. Too loud in here, and I can't hear you." His words are husky with a slight slur.

I picture him in a hotel room, probably the penthouse suite somewhere, his riotous black hair swishing around his shoulders as he cradles the phone to his ear, moving past his bandmates, the alcohol bottles littering the tables.

We met at a bar in Magnolia my sophomore year after my parents died. I was in a weird place, still grieving, and he provided the perfect distraction. When he sang that night, I was mesmerized by the tender way his hands clutched the mic, his ripped-up jeans that hung on his lean hips. His songs called to the music lover in me. He was charismatic, the kind of sexy that tells you he's going to be a star someday. He kept his gaze on me the entire night, and after he finished his set, he jumped off the stage and took me in his arms. *Be mine tonight*, he whispered in my ear.

I was his—for several nights that morphed into months, then years.

I dip my head, keeping my voice low. "You have to stop calling me. I need to go. Take care of yourself, okay? Lay off the booze."

"Baby, baby, the sound of your voice…it's like the sun after a storm, like a candle in a dark tunnel—"

"Pretty words you don't mean," I say faintly, memories of him tugging on my heart.

He exhales gustily. "Tour is over, baby. You should have been here. Sold-out crowd in Chicago last night, fifty thousand screaming fans. I'm leaving soon, coming home to Memphis."

"That's good. I'm sure you need the rest and your family misses you."

"It's been over a year since…" he murmurs thickly.

Our divorce was final. My lungs squeeze.

"Do you need anything? Money?"

"You don't owe me anything, Vane."

"I wish you'd let me see you. We have unfinished business, you and me, things I need to say, and if you give me a chance, I'll make it right, I promise."

So many promises… "You can't fix what you did."

"I'm gonna work on the new album, and you can come to my house on the river. It'll be just like old times."

Old times? My jaw tightens. Like the times I skipped class to see him? Or the entire weekends I spent at his house, leaving Romy with Nana? Other memories batter me, a darkened tour bus after a show in Nashville, the drummer of his band trying and failing to hold me back from going inside. The sounds of moans, the naked girl kneeling at Vane's feet, his hands cupping her scalp as she—

He knows exactly where my head is... "Serena. Please. Let me explain about that night—"

"I saw what I needed to."

"*Just listen.* I should have loved you better, *I should have*, and now look at us, look at what we are...just let me see you..." His voice breaks and I hear him gasping for air. "We lost each other, and the baby, and you were it for me. Please, baby. I fucked up, *I fucked up*..."

My eyes shut, willing my voice to be calm and firm. Should I have let him explain himself after what I saw? No. He cheated, probably more than I'm aware of. He broke all his promises to me. End of. I divorced him, and lucky for me, he didn't even have to be there.

"I'm happy, Vane. Don't call me anymore."

There's a long pause from him. Then, "Who is he, Serena? Who are you dating?"

Leave it to a man to assume I need *another* man to be happy...

I swear under my breath and throw a glance around the student center, my chest hitching when my eyes catch on Dillon's. Through the glass wall of the pizza place, I see him sitting at a table. Bambi is next to Sawyer, and Ashley is next to him. Guess she won rock paper scissors today.

"I have to go." I click my phone off and tuck it in the pocket of my leggings.

Dillon...

This past Saturday, the Tigers defeated Virginia Tech on our home field. I watched him with rapt attention as he kissed his hands and ran out to his teammates. At halftime, he stopped in front of the fifty-yard line and sent me a long look, seeming to soak me in. Then, he shook his head as if to clear it and ran to the locker room. As far as the game, he led his team like a maestro, orchestrating passes that always hit their target. I loved that quote from my last article, although it was a bitch to write, dry as toast. Warren was happy at least.

Over this past week, I've seen him around, once at a red light a few blocks from campus while I was on my way to the *Gazette*; another time I glimpsed him leaving the library as I peered over the third-floor railing. The third time was yesterday morning when I looked out my window and saw him and Owen jogging past my house.

And now, tonight. The universe is tossing him into my path at every turn.

As if he knows I've spotted him, he looks up and freezes. He watches me, deep and penetrating. My eyes shut briefly, trying to break this weird *thing* between us, and when I open them, he's weaving his way through the crowd to the exit.

I dash for the right hallway. I tell myself I'm running

because I'm late, but the truth is, I can't get Dillon out of my head.

The yoga room is darkened and quiet except for the rainforest music our instructor Zena likes. I grab a spare mat and lay it out in the back.

The door opens and I turn to see who else is late.

"Dillon," I sputter. "What are you doing?"

"No clue," he murmurs as he takes a moment to check out the room then walks to the back, picks up a mat, and sets it too close to mine.

"We're going to bump into each other."

"I'll live." Wearing gym shorts and a practice shirt, he takes in my stance, legs spread with one bent, and my arms extended straight out to each side. "Cute."

"Warrior pose. You try it and see how long you can hold it."

He mimics me, and I'm annoyed when he accomplishes it perfectly, moderating his breathing, not one quiver in his muscles. "How long have you been coming to this class?"

I think. "Three years, twice a week. It's free for students."

A look of incredulity flashes over his face. "You've been coming to the student center all this time and I've never once seen you!"

"We weren't meant to meet, I guess."

"Timing," he mutters.

Zena, a willowy attractive lady in her late forties, leaves her mat and walks around. She works for the university in the catering department, and since I pick up the odd job with them, we've known each other a while.

She stops at Dillon's mat. "Hello, handsome. You sure brighten the place up." She cocks her hip, a smirk on her face as she takes him in, appreciation in her glance.

He grins broadly. "Came with Serena. She insisted. How's my form?"

"Excellent," she replies.

I snort. "He's my stalker."

Dillon rolls his eyes. "Pot, kettle. You were waiting for me at the Oreos and don't deny it."

"Well, he's in for a treat," Zena murmurs to me and pops a questioning eyebrow. *Do you want to tell him?* her face says, and I shake my head. Nope.

A laugh tinkles from her as she moves on. "Carry on, then. Welcome to class, Dillon. Invite your football friends."

He smiles. "*She* knows me, Serena, and it's dark in here." There's triumph in his voice as he whips off his shirt and tosses it to the side. His skin is golden, his pecs firm...

"Cat pose, class," Zena calls.

I ignore him—dang, so hard—and maneuver into the pose on my hands and knees, arching my back to the ceiling. He watches, lips pursed as he attempts to mimic me, only his bulk doesn't allow for much arch and his hands are in the wrong place.

"Hey, Kitty, try again," I murmur. "Round your spine toward the ceiling."

"Meow," is his response.

I bite my lip.

"Make sure your knees are set below your hips, everyone, and center your head in a neutral position with eyes on the floor," Zena says.

"How do you get your back up that high?"

"Practice." I stifle a laugh as he tries again and fails.

"Ladies, this pose will gently warm up your pelvic floor and open your hips—which is crucial for a top-shelf orgasm, the kind that reverberates through your body for several seconds. Flexibility and relaxation are key, especially if he goes in for round two. That's the best, isn't it?"

A round of *yeses* comes from the ladies.

Dillon starts. "Hang on. I thought this was a *yoga* class?"

"For ladies," I chirp. "Zena is all about using yoga for, um, the bedroom. Usually it's only women in here, and the men who show up tend to never come back. You don't do exercises like this at lacrosse practice?"

"No, and don't think I'm not keeping tabs on every time you call me a lacrosse player. So far your debt is so big I don't think you'll ever pay it off."

"Hmm, how will I repay you?"

His eyes glitter. "A kiss for every infraction—"

"I owe you one and you haven't collected." Maybe I'm a little miffed about that.

Zena says, "On the exhale, round your spine up toward the ceiling. Yes, that's it...engage those abs and warm up your core...open your body, feel the heat..."

"Why are you smirking?" Dillon asks a few reps later.

"Because you make a very large cat." I scoot over and touch his spine with light fingers. "Now let your stomach drop to the floor...right, now back up...you got it."

"Can you do the splits? 'Cause that's cool—"

"Shhh," comes from the older lady on the other side of Dillon.

"Well? Can you?" he whispers.

"Oh, Dillon, my body can do anything."

His eyes heat; I stick my tongue out at him.

"Alright, let's move to downward facing dog, my favorite for spicing up the bedroom. In fact, as an inversion pose, it clears your head and gives your face a glow that's irresistible to your partner. When you're feeling frisky, I suggest ditching your bed and trying this on the floor," Zena says in a saucy tone.

I move into the stance, adjusting my body into an A shape, my hips in the air.

My eyes dart to him as he aligns his body and sinks his heels to the mat. He looks magnificent, his leg muscles taut, his forearms bunched and tight.

He pops an eyebrow. "You're supposed to be looking at your navel."

"Yeah? Then why are you staring at me?"

"You're staring at *me*."

"You wish."

He laughs as his eyes glow at me. "Champagne. Is it crazy that I love how you spar with me?"

I shrug. "What is up with you and champagne?"

"It's your eye color, like sunshine." He bites his lip, his face flushing. "I kind of, um, well..."

"What?" I cock my head.

His face grows redder, embarrassment growing. "I may have thought about popping a cork and pouring it on you, you know, um, when we, um, make out some time in the future. Maybe." He blows out a breath. "I can't believe I just said that. I can't get anything right with you. Kill me now."

Oh. He's getting it right. He's part smooth charmer, part uncertain college boy, and it ticks all my boxes. Help.

"Move to the happy baby position, class," Zena says. "We all know what a baby looks like when they lie down and hold their feet."

"These are the weirdest exercises I've ever done," Dillon says as he rolls to his back and puts his legs in the air.

"Lie on your back and bring those knees to your belly, good. Now, open your knees slightly wider than your torso. Show the ceiling your feet and wrap two fingers around your big toe..." Zena calls, her voice low and soothing. "This is a deep hip relaxer, related to the Kama Sutra. It opens your sacral chakra, your pleasure center... that's right, you got it...breathe deeply...think about your orgasm..."

He attempts it but loses his balance and rolls over on his side.

I shake, biting my lip.

"I know I'm making a fool of myself, but I had to see you."

"You could have called."

"I almost did, about a hundred times."

So why didn't he?

Zena darkens the room even more and lowers the music. "Alright, class, let's cool down with a friend for the back-to-back partner twist."

"Be my friend?" Dillon asks.

"Sure," I say, preparing myself for the torture of being near Dillon's body.

He edges over to my mat. His hair is messy from exertion, one side of it sticking out. "We get to touch each other," he whispers in my ear.

Yeah. My heart pounds at the thought. He hasn't really touched me since he tended to my feet.

I clear my throat. "See the people in front of us...do that. Sit cross-legged with your back to mine."

With an eager expression on his face, he flips around and does as instructed. I inhale a deep breath at the feel of his powerful body against me. Vane was fit, but lean and wiry. Dillon, though, his muscles are firm and hard, a work of art I'd like to—

"What's next?" he asks.

"We get as close as possible."

"Yeah, we're doing that." His voice is gruff. "You feel good."

"So do you."

"Knew it."

"Hush. Okay, now, as you exhale, put your right hand on the inside of my left knee."

"Like this..." His hand lands on my knee, fingers on my inner thigh. My breath hitches and I shiver as heat pools in my body. *It's just yoga*, I repeat in my head.

"Mmm, yeah. I'll do the same to you on your right knee." I move my hand to the muscles in his inner thigh.

"Finally," he breathes out.

Same.

I say, "Now, we twist our shoulders in opposite directions to feel the stretch. We're supposed to trust each other to hold us steady as we deepen the twist—"

"Deepen?"

"You are going to die when this is over," I say on a laugh as I clench my hand around his leg.

He groans and I freeze, moving my hand back to his

knee. "Sorry," I say softly, grimacing. I'm not the only one who's built up a little lust.

A long exhalation comes from him. "Not complaining."

My senses are on overload as I feel the ripple of his back, the tautness of his muscles. I picture his magnificent body on top of me, sliding inside me...

"Good class," Zena says a few minutes later, her voice low and subdued. "If you'd like meditation time, I'll leave the music on and you can leave when you're ready. Please disinfect your mats before you go. Refreshments are in the kitchen if you need water or tea. See you next week."

We disentangle ourselves and I lie back on my mat, willing my heart to slow down—and it isn't from the exercise. He seems to be doing the same.

"Who's the musician?" His question comes as a surprise, and I glance over at him as he reclines, his hands behind his head as he peers up at the ceiling. "I looked at your socials. You really don't post a lot, but I saw someone who'd commented on a picture of you with your sister." He turns and catches my gaze. "Vane Winchester was the profile it led me to, the lead singer of Four Dragons. Then, I recalled you wearing their shirt, and *then*, 'Sweet Serena'." He pauses. "Did you date a rock star?"

Oh, well, here we go. I exhale. "I married him, then divorced him."

His eyes flare.

I chew on my lips. "Yeah. Crazy. Did you know it only takes sixty days to get an uncontested divorce in Mississippi? You don't need a real lawyer or even have to see your spouse. Just go to the courthouse, file the papers, and wait for the judge to sign them."

He eases up and props his head on his hand. Dimly, I'm aware of the last person in class leaving the room, the door clicking shut, leaving us.

"What happened?"

My throat feels tight as I push out the words. "I was pregnant and we'd been together a long time. I was ready to raise my baby on my own, but he convinced me to..." I stop and let out a long breath. "Anyway, we got married at City Hall and he left for his tour a week later."

"You have a kid?" He toys with the end of the mat.

"I miscarried at twelve weeks." My breath hitches.

"I'm sorry, Serena." He pauses, seemingly at a loss for words. He studies my face. "I can't imagine...wow. That must have been tough."

It was the worst time of my life other than when my parents died. I remember the day I missed my period, the anxiousness that ran through me at the idea of having a baby. Vane and I were up and down at the time, him traveling further and further away from Magnolia for gigs, ones I couldn't go to. We argued over the phone when I saw pics of him online, cozying up to groupies. He promised me nothing was going on, that it was just part of being a musician. Right.

I wait for the stinging betrayal that comes with those memories, and it's there, just waiting, but I take a breath and set them aside. "I was terrified to be pregnant. We barely saw each other, I still hadn't finished school, and I had Romy at home with Nana. I didn't even realize how much I wanted the baby until…" I stop, tears forming in the corners of my eyes. I will them to not fall. "Forgive me. I've always wanted kids, and it felt too soon, it did, but I was excited. Romy was over the moon. Nana had doubts, but she was knitting booties. Julian, well, he was pissed. He never approved of Vane. Ugh, I shouldn't tell you this."

"Hey. It's okay. Some people are just easy to talk to. Catharsis is good. The verbal expression of past painful emotions helps smooth over bad memories. It's like the brain merges the original painful memory with the new less painful version of sharing the memory."

"You're full of facts." I give him a wan smile as I sit up on my mat. He does the same, and we face each other.

"Psych major. Tell me anything. I joke a lot, but I'm a good listener."

"Vane, well, I was beginning to suspect that we wouldn't last, and I figured he was cheating on the road, but when you're in the middle of something, it's hard to see what's ahead. I pretended like everything was fine. I wanted it to be fine, so I ignored the warning signs.

Maybe I compartmentalized? I don't know. He had a lot of fame thrown at him. We were young."

"You still care about him."

"He was the center of my world for a long time."

"Come here," he says softly.

I do, inching forward until our knees touch. He smells divine, vanilla mixed with virile male. Something electric zings between us as we look at each other.

"*Je promets d'être bon avec toi,*" he murmurs, holding my gaze.

My heart skips at his soft words. "I caught *I promise*, but what does the rest of it mean?"

"I promise I'll be good to you." He tilts my chin up and leans in and—

I pull away and maneuver up to standing.

"Serena, wait—"

No. I'm already walking into the small kitchen that's to the left of the yoga space. I don't believe in promises from guys anymore. F that. Dillon is trouble with a capital T. I should run out of this room and go straight home.

I hear him following me. Swallowing down my anxiousness, I open the fridge and reach for one of the waters Zena keeps for us. His hands land on my shoulders. He's right there, the heat from his bare chest against my back. Tension crackles in the air around us.

"Serena." He pauses, uncertainty in his voice. "Look, I'm sorry if I came on too strong. The truth is, I met you my freshman year at the bonfire party." A small huff comes from him. "I kissed you. Twice. I said some douchey stuff about who I was and you ran off." His hands stroke over the straps of my halter top, touching my skin with the barest touch. He drifts down to my hips, and I lean back against him.

"You don't remember, do you?"

Oh, Dillon.

"I remember."

The silence builds in the room as we stand there, my hand tightening on the handle of the fridge. He turns me around and looks down at me intently, his eyes searching mine. "When?"

I can feel my face warming. "I had an inkling at the Oreo encounter, but I knew for sure when you came in my apartment. I didn't admit to it because I thought it would inflate your ego." I dip my head. "You looked different then."

"I wore bleached out dreadlocks in my hair. I also grew two inches that year."

"And you've bulked up more."

A dawning hits his eyes. "It's more than that though. Did you feel guilty about the kiss? It was his band that night. Were you married then?"

"I wasn't married, but yeah, I felt guilty. I told him what happened after his set was finished." A scoff comes from me. "He just laughed. I guess he was just that confident that I loved him—which I did. I adored him. You kind of came out of nowhere and took me by surprise."

Dillon exhales. "I would have been livid." He pauses. "I've thought about that night..." He bites his bottom lip. "A lot."

"Yeah?"

"We need a new kiss to replace it. I'm going to call in that promise you owe me, Serena."

My eyes dart to his mouth as nerves fly at me. *Just do it, Serena!* "Then take it."

His head lowers and his lips land on mine, hesitant at first, our tongues tangling as he moves his hands to my face, cradling my cheeks. It's as if I've been waiting forever for this moment, his touch, and I sink into the pleasure, the pressure of our mouths increasing. His hand slides up to my hair, and he cups my nape, pulling me closer.

It's my first kiss in eighteen months, and passion roars. Our mouths fit together instinctively, knowing how to play and tease then delve in deeper. My hands skate up his chest, trailing over the defined muscles, mapping out the hills and valleys. Sparks pop and heat spears me. We part to breathe, and my hands tug on his hair, bringing his mouth back to mine. "Again."

"Serena..." He presses me against the fridge, his hips against my pelvis. His lips own me, sucking at my bottom lip, then going right back to slanting his mouth over mine. The tent in his shorts aims for my center, and my legs part, inviting him in. His hands find mine, his thumbs teasing over the rapid pulse in my wrists. The gesture is romantic, as if he's counting the beats of my pulse.

"So good with you…" he whispers as he moves across my cheek and down my neck, his teeth scraping down my throat, his tongue lapping at my skin.

My need grows, and I feel hot, like the small room is a furnace. "Yes…" I murmur as my hand drifts over his gym shorts to caress him, and he groans, his lashes fluttering.

"Serena…"

"Touch me." *Please*. It's been so long.

His lips take mine, and this time his hands are everywhere, cupping my breasts and palming me. My nipples push through the material, hard and erect. He eases the straps down, pushing at the shirt, and gazes down at me, a flush on his cheekbones.

His pupils are blown as his mouth latches onto a breast, his tongue darting around the dusky pink areola like I'm a feast. My head bangs against the fridge as he devours me, switching from one breast to the other. My leg hooks around his waist as I meet his cock through his shorts and roll my hips.

"Crazy…" He breathes against my skin. "You've got no idea how long…"

His fingers ease under the waistband of my leggings, sliding around to squeeze my ass.

This, this is the point where I should call a halt, but I

don't. I touch him, the strong column of his throat, the top of his broad shoulders, the tattoos on his chest. I want to inhale him, every single masculine piece.

His hands move as he slides aside my thong and puts a finger inside me, and I'm drenched. A primal sound erupts from his throat. His forehead presses against mine. "Too much?" is pulled from him.

"No," I gasp out. "More."

"Serena..." Another finger joins the first. He parts the top of my mound, his thumb finding my clit and rotating.

I'm awash in sensation, my breath coming in pants. I'm going to fly apart any moment. Electricity sizzles in my body as tingles build at the base of my spine.

He bites my earlobe, his breathing as erratic as mine. "I want to fuck you, Serena," he says in a guttural voice and just that one dirty word that sounds as if it came from the depths of his lungs, pushes me over the edge. My nails dig into his shoulders as I ride his hand and go over the edge, my world shattering, a rush of fireworks bursting into sparkling lights as I call out.

I press my face into his chest, shuddering against him, my body undulating. He pulls back, his chest heaving as he sticks his fingers in his mouth and licks them slowly, his eyes heavy on me. I whimper at the open eroticism on his face.

The sound of a door opening pierces the haze of my

muddled senses. Dillon stiffens, using his body to cover me as he looks over his shoulder. "Someone's here."

"What?" I will my heart to slow, trying to focus. I see a cleaning crew through the window to the yoga room. My hands tremble as I work to pull my clothes together.

"You okay?" I ask, nodding at his shorts.

He grimaces as he adjusts himself. "Yeah."

I put some distance between us, walking over to the sink and throwing water on my face. I pat my face with a paper towel, and when I turn around, he's behind me.

His eyes lower to half-mast. "Come back to my place—"

My eyes shut briefly. Part of me wants that, but common sense is sneaking back in. I lick my lips. "Not a good idea."

His brow furrows. "Things are hot between us. I want you; you want me. What am I missing?"

I swallow thickly. "This was fun, but..." *You are dangerous to my heart.*

He scrubs his face, then stares at the floor for a few moments as if searching for words. He's about to speak when a clang of metal comes from the yoga room.

"Come on. Let's get out of here." He takes my elbow and steers me out the door, past the two women who are sweeping. We walk down the hall, making our way to the center meeting area. "I'll walk you to your car and we can talk," he says.

"You're messing around with two other girls, Dillon. I won't be the third. I've been down that road."

He pulls me to a stop, staring down at me with turbulent eyes as frustration flashes on his face. "Let's get this straight. I'm not having sex with them. I've never been with them, ever. You...*this*...has nothing to do with them. I tend to rush, I do, but we can go slow, Serena. Based on what you've told me, it feels like you need that. Just tell me how—"

"Dillon!" comes a high, shrill voice, interrupting us. "Where have you been? We've been looking everywhere!"

My hands clench as I turn to look at her.

It's Ashley, hands on her hips as she stands at the fountain in front of the pizzeria, flanked by Bambi and Sawyer. She's wearing a cream linen sheath dress that complements her pale coloring and red hair. Bambi looks more casual with skinny jeans and a cropped Tigers jersey.

Ashley's lips curl as she makes a beeline for Dillon. I keep my face expressionless as I step away from him.

"You ditched us," she says to him. "Where did you go?"

"Yoga."

She looks at me. "With her?" She says it like I'm a serial killer.

He frowns. "Yeah. Get over it."

"Oh, good grief, Ashley! The man has a life. Look who

he found," Bambi says as she rushes forward and wraps me up in a hug. *She's a touchy kind of girl*, I think as she leans in and straightens my hair, a twinkle in her eye. "It must have been an invigorating class—why look how flushed you both are! Was it that sex one? I saw you at the game on Saturday, but the crowd was so thick I couldn't get to you. Chantal says she called you and you guys are planning a girls' night." A wistful expression crosses her face. "If you want a third..."

Chantal did call, and we are going out. I'm looking forward to it because I never go anywhere. Plus, she's helping me with football jargon, and I owe her some drinks. "You're welcome to come," I offer, wondering how anyone can tell a girl like her no. I've been a fan of Mila Kunis since *Bad Moms*.

She squeals and gives me another hug, this one tighter as she whispers in my ear. "He's deliciously sweet underneath that cockiness, isn't he?" She winks as we pull apart.

I start. Something is up with her reasons for being in this competition, because it can't be for Dillon, can it?

"I have an idea," Bambi says as she crooks her arm in mine. "Chantal said your girls' night is at Cadillac's tomorrow, right?"

"Yeah." I get a sinking feeling.

"Why don't we all meet you there? It will be fun. All of us together." Her gaze sweeps over the group. "We'll play pool for a prize," Bambi adds, a gleam in her eyes. "And Serena will compete—"

"She's not in the contest," Ashley interrupts. "She doesn't even go to the formal. She's not an active Theta, didn't hold a real office—"

"Oh, please," Bambi says. "She's a Theta and I want to get to know her."

"I second all of that," Sawyer adds.

Ashley fumes, her face flushing. "Dillon, this isn't fair."

"It's fair," he replies to Ashley, still holding my eyes with an intensity that makes me quake. "But I don't think Serena likes the contest."

"Then she shouldn't play," Ashley declares.

"Scared I'll win?" I chirp, glancing at her.

She sniffs. "No."

I turn to Dillon and he's moved closer to me. *Let's ditch them and get out of here,* his eyes seem to say.

I fidget. Need to get out of here before I take him up on that offer.

"Please, Serena. You don't have to be part of the contest per se, but I insist you at least hang out with us. Are you any good at pool?" Bambi says, sending me a pleading look.

"There's a cue stick," I say vaguely.

"There, Ashley, does that make you happy? She won't win." Bambi smiles at her.

Ashley shrugs, her eyes hard, but she puts a smile on as she grudgingly says, "Whatever. If you want her to play, fine with me."

"Just this once, Serena?" Bambi implores. "Come on, say yes."

Sawyer cocks an eyebrow at me. "You in for some fun?"

My eyes are firmly not looking at Dillon. Do I want to hang out with Ashley while she competes for Dillon's attention? Hell no. But this was *my* night out, and nothing is keeping me from it. "I'll be at Cadillac's tomorrow."

I rush out a goodbye and flip around.

"Serena, let me walk you—" comes from Dillon as he attempts to follow me, but I cut him off with a hand over my back. As long as he has an entourage, I just can't go there. Yeah, I'll play pool with them, but...

"Later," I say, my feet moving fast until I'm at a jog and out the door.

13

Dillon

"*Closer*" by Nine Inch Nails plays from the speakers in the den, the song drifting into my room as I rifle through my closet for something to wear to Cadillac's. Nope, not the button-up shirt (dressy and screams *trying too hard*), and no, not anything loose (I need to show off my assets), and not the Henley (it's too damn hot). *Yeah!* I snag a faded navy Tigers shirt with the orange paw on the pocket. It's an oldie, all the way back to my sophomore days, and it's snug, but not too snug. Passed a killer psychology test and won a wet T-shirt contest with it last year.

"You gonna stare into your closet all night, bro?" It's Sawyer from the door. "Ah, the lucky shirt."

"Don't need luck," I lie as I slip the shirt on and tuck it loosely into my jeans. The orange Converse are next. The truth is, she brushed me off—after getting off. A long sigh comes from me. So, yeah, I want another chance. I did avoid her after I took her car to her. She cut her nana off while she was inviting us, and I get it, I do. We just showed up out of the blue, and Serena is what I call a "runner". Because of Vane, she's built a fortress around herself. Yeah, I asked for the kiss as payment for her car, but got nervous about it later and wondered if I put her in the uncomfortable position of agreeing.

When she's around, my usual charm is just *poof*, gone. I've never been this unsure over a girl. I don't need *more* anxiety. I mean, freshman year, I imagined the day I'd find her, but now that it's here... What if I fuck this up? What if I've built up this idea of her and she's just going to mess with my head?

Sure, she remembers me at the bonfire, but she was *in love* with another man.

I adored him. Those were her words. I frown.

"Just nail her. I'm sick of your moping."

My brow furrows as I give him a sharp look. "Don't talk about her like that."

His voice is surprised. "So it's like that. I apologize. You're gonna be cuddling up and watching Netflix in no time."

"This coming from the guy who teared up at *A Star is Born*, *The Big Sick*, and *Crazy Rich Asians*, which is a comedy." My words are grouchy. I'm thinking about Vane and

Serena together as a couple. My hands clench. I'm assuming she went home with Vane the night of the bonfire—was in *his* arms. I push those images out of my head.

"I had a cold. It was a sniffle, and you swore you'd never tell anyone that." He tucks his hands in the pockets of his jeans. "First of all, *A Star is Born* has been made four times. It's iconic, and if a person doesn't cry when watching it, they're a psychopath. Second, *The Big Sick* is original. She's in a coma, and they somehow manage to have a relationship. Third, *Crazy Rich Asians* portrays a rich heritage that I appreciate, and you have to admit, the scenery is amazing. Constance Wu is drop-dead gorgeous—"

"Ah, you do love brunettes."

He starts, his eyes narrowing. "I prefer blondes. This is law. I've proclaimed it many times."

"Uh-huh."

"You're insinuating something. Spit it out."

I've noticed this past week who he's been eyeing lately, and she isn't blonde.

He leans against the doorjamb. "Anyway. Tonight's like a date for you and Serena."

I fidget in front of the mirror. Damn, my hair needs a cut. "Technically, it's girls' night, and you and Bambi weaseled us an invite."

"You're nervous."

I am. "Never."

"You keep touching your hair. Sadly, you don't enjoy romantic movies, so you can't wow her with your sappy side. Let's prep what not to do. These rules are foolproof and came straight from my dearly departed granny. Ready?"

I adored that woman. I went home with Sawyer several times on the weekends during the off-season. She baked us cookies and enjoyed scary movies. She gave me hugs like I was her own. When she passed away last summer, I drove to Georgia, went to the funeral, and spent two weeks with Sawyer, helping him get her things packed up. Thinking of her makes me soften. "If Granny had rules, they must have been from God's own lips. Go for it."

He nods, hearing the respect in my voice and accepting it. "Obviously, don't talk about her ex, the famous Vane Winchester. You're already in the con column because you're three years younger—"

"Two! I'm almost twenty-two!"

"—and a college student. He's got a voice like honey and a megawatt smile women scream over."

Thoughts of Vane make my hands twitch. "Thanks for the vote of confidence."

"Don't forget your manners."

I spread my hands, exasperation rushing in as I recall

the night I took her home. "I try." Maybe I tried too hard? Yeah. I was overbearing. Damn.

"Don't stare at her tits."

She barely has any. And I don't care. I just want my hands on them. I recall her against the fridge, the silky feel of her nipples in my mouth—the way she came on my fingers.

"Don't bring up the L word."

My eyes jerk to him and my throat dries.

"Don't ask if she wants to go to a strip club."

"Dude... I am not that bad."

"Don't mention that you want ten kids. That should be introduced around date ten."

I gape. Kids? Maybe in the future—after I've found my groove in the NFL.

"Don't reply to any texts from other people."

"Jesus. What are you, Dear Abby?"

"Don't take the Lord's name in vain. You do it a lot. On that note, don't ask if she's found Jesus. Granny was pretty insistent about that one. She was a hardcore Bible thumper but wasn't in your face about it, and she respected other people's religion."

I know what he's doing. He's seen me in a weird funk for the past few weeks and wants to lighten me up.

"Make her laugh. Best way to bond. Women like funny guys."

"I'm funny?"

"And if her nana comes up, see if you can wrangle an invite to their chicken and waffles again."

I arch a brow at the wistful tone in his voice. He misses Granny. "Nana is a little different." Like Serena.

"The best ones are."

"Is that all, o wise one?"

"I'll come up with more later." He pivots to leave, singing "Witchy Woman".

After he's gone, I dash to the bathroom and try to fix my hair, running a hand through it. She likes my hair... right? I falter, my hand dropping. I brush my teeth, again, and study my reflection.

"You're pretty enough," Troy calls as he darts in and edges around me, grabs the cologne and lets loose a long spritz, spreads his arms and walks through it. "Ah, yeah, that's it. The smell of salt and sun, come to me."

I choke as some of it drifts over and hits me in the face. "Winter Soldier dabs on gasoline and gun oil before he goes out."

Troy freezes. "She won't even talk to me."

No need to ask who...

"Ah, sorry. Maybe dress all in black? Leave the cowboy hat at home. Tame your hair."

"Tame?"

"You know what I mean. You look like a wild man with that frizz. Bigfoot," I say with a laugh, thinking of Serena. "Use some product."

He scrunches up his face and looks at his hair, then digs around on the counter and holds up a tube of gel. "This?" He reads the text on the container. "Strong hold, brilliant shine, style versatility... Are you sure?"

"You're a cowboy, so let me educate you." I squirt out a dab and run it through the top of my hair in quick, expert movements, pushing the longer strands back, pulling on it a little to create volume at the top. "Just a little. You don't want that wet gigolo look—"

Bambi appears at the door, phone in hand as she snaps a pic. "Grooming with Dillon and Troy. Think I'll post this. Oh, and send it to Serena so she can see what *girls* y'all are."

Sawyer's voice comes from the den. "Tried to stop her from snooping!"

"Guys use gel," I say defensively.

She grins, her nose wrinkling delicately as she taps on her phone then shoves it in Troy's face. "Here's a pic of the Winter Soldier. Look how he scowls—do that. Got any black football cream for your face? He's got it around his eyes. Looks emo to me, but Chantal likes it. She talks about him a lot."

Troy's face flushes, his jaw working. "Nah, hell nah. Not wearing any makeup!" He takes her phone and stares at it. "He is dressed in black..." He stares down at his green shirt, blows out a breath, and stomps out of the bathroom.

"You're welcome! Any time you need style advice, I'm here all day," she calls out, gives me a smirk, and then heads back out to the den.

My phone rings and I make a dash for my bedroom as my stomach jumps, wondering if it's Serena.

The phone screen shows it's Mom, and my chest squeezes. "Mom! Hey! How are you?" It's been several weeks since I heard her voice. Sure, we text periodically, but it's on the surface stuff. *How are classes? Are you eating well?*

"Good! Happy! You?" I picture her at some fancy locale, her blonde hair cut in a sleek, modern bob that swings against her high cheekbones. She's a beautiful woman in her mid forties. We aren't close, like Sawyer was to his granny, like Serena is with her family. I recall snippets of her, mostly on her way out of town.

I'm headed to the beach with my friends, darling.

There's a gala I can't miss, sweetheart. Hope you win your game.

Give me a kiss and go ask your father, dear.

When I was a kid, I used to cling to the dream that my parents would magically fall back in love, but that dream died the day my dad packed his bags for Malibu after my brother's funeral. He asked me to come with him, but it was my senior year. I had college scouts coming to every game that fall and transferring to another school would have screwed up my choices. I didn't want him to *leave*, but he did. Their divorce came six months later. He wanted to erase Montgomery from his mind, to forget the pain of losing Myles—but he forgot about me too.

"I'm good. You missed my first game."

She sighs. "Yeah, sorry. I had to be in Paris for their Autumn Festival, but I'm back in the States." She pauses. "I know how important it is that you're getting to shine." Her voice lowers. "Look, I can't chat long. I'm at a spa in Little Rock with someone…" There's a rustling, and I hear her talking to a person in the room, *My son, yeah*. A male tone replies.

"We'll be at LSU soon," I say. "Little Rock isn't that far away." It's several hours, but still…

"I wish I could, darling."

I think about Sinclair's mom, wearing his jersey and dancing in the stands. I squash those feelings down. This is Mom's usual. Why am I even asking?

I exhale. "Maybe Thanksgiving? Might be easier if you came here since I'll have a game that weekend. We could hit a restaurant if you want, somewhere nice, maybe spend the night in Memphis—"

She speaks to the guy in the room, her words muffled, then comes back. "Wait. Dillon, I'm on the yacht to the Virgin Islands for Thanksgiving. Theo reminded me. I should have checked with you first, but, well, it came up and we invited some friends. Can you make it?"

No, Mom. I can't jump on a plane to get on a yacht. *I have a game.* "Theo?"

A long sigh comes from her, more rustling, as if she's walking. "I wanted to tell you in person, but there doesn't seem to be a good time. I'm engaged!"

What?

I sit down on my bed. She goes through men like shoes. Last Christmas, it was a Major League Baseball player. The year before that, it was a Greek millionaire.

"To this Theo?"

"You haven't met him."

"No shit."

"Don't be like that. Theo's wonderful. Age-appropriate." She laughs. "We're planning the wedding, no date yet, but soon. We'll come see you, um, let's see, Christmas? I like the hotel idea. I'll call the Peabody in Memphis today and reserve two suites."

The holidays with my mom and her new fiancé? I sigh. "I haven't even met this guy and we're gonna sing Christmas carols?"

She sighs heavily. "You'll like him. Don't be mad. I just...fell in love fast. You know how it is."

Yeah.

"How's your father?"

"He texted last week. He's going to New York with Brianna's family for Christmas. He asked me to come..." My voice trails off. Brianna is dad's new wife, ten years younger than him and his former personal assistant. I passed on his invite. I'd be a stranger to Brianna's family, and deep down, my dad doesn't want me around.

"Maybe next time, you can come on the yacht with us..." She details the particulars of her planned trip, the islands they'll be stopping at, and I respond in the right places, saying what she needs to hear. When we hang up, I lie back on my bed and stare up at the ceiling, wanting to erase the ache in my chest.

I'm an afterthought to my mom and my dad has a new family. Loneliness creeps in, snaking over me, and I exhale. Being alone is a feeling I'm accustomed to since Myles died. He was always my little buddy, needing me. I miss him. I scrub my face, my head tumbling. People think I have it all. What a joke.

Sawyer pops his head in and says they're ready to go. I get up and grab my keys. I may not have a real family, but I have Sawyer. I have my team.

~

SHE WALKS into Cadillac's at eight on the nose and my body buzzes, a long breath coming from me. I feel her pull, that little something about her that makes my skin hum. This, *this* is how I know she never came within my vicinity in the past three years, because if she had, I would have known.

She is so damn hot. Devastating.

Every male in the place looks at her.

Some of the girls, too, with sweeping gazes of envy.

I groan. She's wearing a pair of tiny black dressy shorts that hug her ass and a filmy red shirt with spaghetti straps. It has a split around the midriff, and her belly button piercing flashes. Red heels are on her feet, showcasing her tanned legs.

She tosses her head and her hair is sleek and straight tonight, the color of honey and mahogany as it tumbles around her shoulders. Her eyes are thickly lashed, her full lips a deep red, currently curved up in one of her cute smirks as she takes the place in.

My breathing increases as she glides through the crowd then stops at the bar to order a drink. The bartender stares at her with hungry eyes and rushes over.

"Whoa," Sawyer murmurs from his seat next to me. "Damn, she cleans up good. I can see her with a rock star..." He laughs. "She is *so* out of your league, man. Hot, feisty, doesn't care who you are—"

"I get it," I grunt as we sit at a table near the back next to a row of several pool tables. Yeah, how do I compete with a rock star? One she *married*.

Sawyer takes a swig of his beer. "Does she have any clue?"

I pause mid-sip of my water. "About?"

"How long you looked for her? Or the fact that you didn't screw anyone for months?"

"No." My eyes watch her at the bar. "Why isn't she coming over here?"

"She hates the contest, man. Maybe she's going to ignore us."

"This Theta thing is driving me crazy," I grind out. Ashley showed up this afternoon to "check on me" and bring us donuts. First, I don't eat a lot of sugar during the season, but I accepted them politely. Then, she plopped down at the kitchen table and rambled for an hour about her audition for a local musical. I was in the middle of studying and wanted her gone. Finally, Bambi texted her and they left for a sorority meeting.

He grimaces. "I've noticed, but we need to stick to our guns. We did the contest last year and won a *national championship*. The guys will freak out if we change anything—"

"I get it," I say sharply. "It's a big deal, but it shouldn't have been me. I've got enough on me with football. Sinclair can take my starting spot at any moment."

He grows quiet, studying me. "Dude. I know you're wound up this season, and I wish I hadn't suggested you. You're right. It should have been me or Troy or someone else. We've won our first two games. Just hang in there."

I sigh. "It's fine. I can manage it." I have to. "Once it's over, though, I don't want Ashley around. Feel me?"

He nods.

Chantal walks in and makes a beeline for Serena. I watch as they hug then do their secret handshake. Serena picks up one of the shots she ordered and puts it in Chantal's hands, and they throw them back. Serena leans over the bar, waving at the bartender, and two more appear—just as four Kappa guys circle around them. Serena smiles at them, and jealousy spears me in the gut.

Fuck that.

I stand and head her way, barreling through the crowd. I've decided. No more messing around. She might send me in a tailspin, but I'm willing to take a chance. I pat the gift in my pocket, checking to make sure it's there.

14

Serena

Dillon's leg is pressed against mine as we sit at the table, his hand around the back of my chair as he leans back. His fingers idly play with my hair, unseen by the others, but oh, I know it's there, the little circles he periodically brushes against the bare skin of my back. I'm strong though. My breathing is regulated, careful and slow, even though every nerve ending he touches is connected directly to my core. Have I thought about us in the kitchen about a billion times? Yeah. We've been waiting for a pool table to open, and the minutes next to him are driving me crazy.

"You want another drink?" he whispers in my ear.

Two tequilas in and I've got a warm buzz, so no. Must maintain control. I slant my eyes toward him. "I can get my own."

His gaze lowers, skating over the cleavage of my silk top. "I want to do things for you."

"Trying to get me drunk?"

A slow smile eases over his face. "I want you fully aware when we go at each other again."

"There won't be another *again*." I smile.

"So you say. Win this game tonight and you can have whatever you want."

"I'd rather knock myself in the face with a cue stick."

"Damn, I like your smart mouth."

I set down my iced water just as Ashley comes back from the bathroom.

Troy walks up from the bar with a drink and plops down next to Chantal. He edges closer to her, and she gives him a cool look but doesn't move away.

"Why are you wearing all black?" Chantal asks him. "Where's your cowboy hat? You *always* wear it out."

"I left it." He frowns and sits straighter, smoothing down his dark shirt. He touches his hair then drops his hand. "Um..." His throat bobs and he darts his eyes around the room. "Just... What's wrong with my shirt?"

She sniffs. "Nothing."

He picks up his beer and takes a long swig.

I smirk at the memory of Dillon showing up at the bar earlier, elbowing his way through the frat boys. He smiled at them tightly, nodding at their pats of congrats on the games, then threw his arm around me, pulled me close, and brushed his lips over mine—right there in front of everyone. Claiming me! He even let it drop that I was there *with* him. I glared at him, but he looked so damn pleased when the guys left abruptly that I could only shake my head. I've softened since we've been sitting here. It's clear he doesn't want Ashley. The man keeps looking at *me*.

I refocus on Sawyer as he explains how we're going to play pool with three players. "...pool game we made up one night, a version of Cutthroat, but easier. We call it Crazy Three. Since you're new, you'll go first, Serena, and break. If you hit a low ball, 1 through 5, those are yours and what you want to pocket. You don't have to call them unless you want to."

"It's been a while since I played," I say evasively.

Ashley, who's sitting across from us, smirks. "I can call them," she gloats. "We have a table at the sorority house."

Bambi says with a sigh, "Ashley's good."

Sawyer tugs on Bambi's hair. "I've seen you play—you're not bad."

She blushes, dipping her face.

He continues, "If you hit a ball from 6 to 10, you're medium, if you hit 11 to 15, you're high. Easy peasy. We'll play three games. Obviously, the first player to get her balls in wins that round."

"Alright," I say.

"Let's get this over with," Ashley says with a triumphant expression as she stands.

I'm muttering under my breath as we approach the pool tables. Dillon gets me a cue stick and rubs the chalk over it then puts it in my hands. "You need any last-minute tips?" he murmurs, his gaze searching mine.

"Yeah—how did I get myself involved in this?"

"I know it crawls all over you to play for me, but if we don't participate, it might screw with our season. Some of the guys get weird about traditions." A hesitant look settles on his face. "Sawyer, he loves it, and he's…" His words trail off.

"Important to you?"

He gives me a slow nod. "Blaze and Ryker graduated. Sawyer is my family now." He winces. "Plus, I can be a little superstitious myself."

Realization clicks. "Oh my…the bonfire…and you and I…" I gape at him. "No, you can't believe that Wiccan thing. You do! It's right there on your face! You think we're like, fated?"

"You have any Magnolia witches in your family tree?"

"Nana's mom."

"Shut up."

"Kidding."

"Can't you have a good time? Just for an hour or so?" His fingers brush over my cheek. "You're the one I want, Serena."

My eyes fly to his. Yeah? Until he gets me, then moves on?

And why is that bad? a voice in my head replies. *You don't want a relationship.*

"If you're done flirting, come break the balls," Ashley's acid tone says.

Dillon ignores her and whispers in my ear, "Since the moment you walked in, I've wanted to kiss you."

"You did. At the bar."

"That wasn't a real kiss. I just marked my territory."

"Like a wolf," Sawyer murmurs from behind Dillon.

I snort.

"Just you, Serena," he says for my ears only. "I promise."

I tense. "Promises, promises."

"Fine. You want to leave? We can make up some excuse, walk out that door, and drive to your place, and I'll show you what's been going through my mind since you walked in."

A shiver races over me. "No, Dillon, I'd show *you* what I want."

His chest rises. "Damn."

"Let the girl go," Sawyer murmurs. "The rest of us are waiting."

"Aw, they look so adorable together, don't they?" comes Bambi's voice as she addresses the group. "Serena and Dillon. They need one of those combo names. Dillrena?"

Chantal huffs. "Serdilla is better. Put the woman first."

"I put women first," Troy quips. "Isn't that right, Chantal?" There's a sly tone to his question and I can't hear her muttered response, but it sounded something like *Just a hook-up.*

I can't see any of their faces, but I smile, something easing in my chest. The truth is, despite Ashley's animosity, I've missed hanging with friends. I needed a night out without helping Romy with her homework or paying bills.

"Watch and learn, pretty boy." With a last look at Dillon, I duck under his arms and head their way.

Chantal gives me a fist bump. "Clean the floor with her, sister." She nods her head at Ashley, and I smile.

~

I BARELY WIN the first game, and Ashley destroys me on the second.

Bambi played poorly in both rounds, not one ball making it to a pocket. Declaring herself out, she sashays over to the others at the table and settles next to Sawyer. His arm goes around her shoulders and his eyes soften.

Well, well, well.

Dillon leans against the wall, not saying much. A few

girls have ambled over, soft laughter and teasing comments, but he's brushed them off, his eyes coming back to me.

Time to focus.

Sawyer tweaked the rules since Bambi is out, and it's now an 8-ball game.

Ashley breaks, leaning over in her red mini skirt, her shot sure and true, snapping the 9 into the top right pocket. "Stripes," she calls, giving me a little smile. She hits another one in, causing one of the solids to go in as well.

"Oh, too bad," I say, positioning myself for my shot. "Move over—you're in my way," I chirp. "In fact, take a seat and stop hovering."

She huffs and walks away.

Lining up with the cue, I've got a possible shot to the right pocket, and another one, maybe getting two into the left bottom, but...

Bending my back over on the long side of the table, I aim the cue—just like someone taught me—and make the harder shot. Both solids zip in. I move to the other side, line up the 3, and hit it in the right pocket.

"Whoa," Sawyer says, perking up.

I walk to the other side, eyeing the table. I want to avoid the 8 ball, and it's next to the solid by the bottom left. It's going to be tight. I lean in, stroke the cue, aim, and shoot. The solid clunks in.

"Shark. She played us," Dillon muses. "Why am I not surprised?"

"Not fair," Ashley says. "You aren't calling them."

I don't even look at her. I snap another solid in, an easier one. "They go where I want them to go."

"Who taught you?" Bambi asks, jumping up to linger by the table.

"I hung out in a lot of bars during my undergrad. Most of them out of town." I played pool while the band set up, sometimes while they sang, and always while they packed up. Vane showed me tricks when he had time, his arms wrapped around me as he explained how to play. The memory doesn't cut as deep as usual, just a soft slice, but I miss my next shot, knocking Ashley's ball in. I grimace.

"You insinuated you were terrible," Ashley says as she elbows me out of the way, calls her shot, and sinks one of hers.

"I've been known to play dirty," I murmur.

She scratches on the next one and stamps her foot.

"Finish her up," Chantal calls to me as she raises her glass, another tequila.

"Be sweet, ya'll," comes from Bambi. "Remember we're sisters."

Ashley tosses her hair and levels me with a narrow-eyed look as she leans over to whisper only for my ears. "Even if you win, you won't be part of our other games, and one way or another, he'll be mine." Green eyes scan over me. "Dillon gets tired of his toys fast, and you're not any different. I've been around him. I know exactly what he wants."

I smile at her, shaking my head. If that's the best she can do… Whatever. I have fond memories of my sorority sisters, supporting them and straightening their crowns, but some women don't get it. They prefer to tear others down. I harness my annoyance and stuff it down. Stooping to her level does no good.

"I'm teaching Romy to not be like you," I say instead.

"Who's Romy?"

No one you'll ever meet. I brush past her, aim my cue, stroke the wood, and slam in the next solid. Another goes in. Satisfaction settles in my gut. *Vane, you dick, you were good for something.*

"For the win, the 8 ball in the top right pocket," I say.

The air crackles and I glance over at a tense Dillon then look away. Moving to the other side, I aim, shoot, and the 8 ball flies down the table, spins in the pocket, comes out for a second, then drops in.

"Oh my God, that was awesome!" comes from a squealing Bambi. She rushes me and smothers me in a hug.

Chantal whoops and slaps me on the ass, and I shriek.

Sawyer ambles over. "So, what do you want?"

"A trophy and a million dollars," I declare.

"More tequila?" Chantal inquires. "Ohhh, ask for his shirt. It's his lucky one."

Dillon grimaces, the look on his face saying, *I'm sorry this is beneath you.*

I'm cool, I am, and I've had a blast. Beating Ashley trumps the particulars of the contest.

"What's it gonna be, Serena?" Troy says.

Bambi elbows me in the ribs. "When I won at Monopoly, I asked him to watch *The Notebook*. Sawyer managed to stay awake. Dillon didn't."

"I saw enough. Saddest movie ever," comes from Dillon.

"I made him watch *Pride and Prejudice*. He played Candy Crush on his phone," chirps Chantal.

"I love that movie!" I exclaim. "Not the Colin Firth one, but the Matthew Macfadyen version."

Dillon groans. "Boy meets girl, they butt heads, he falls for her, she misconstrues his motivations, they work it out, and live happily ever after. Bah."

"Nailed it. You sure you didn't watch it?" I ask.

"Call me Mr. Darcy if you want." He does a weird bow, then puts his hand over his heart. "'You have bewitched me, body and soul.'"

I burst out laughing. "Nice quote, but your curtsey needs work." I straighten my posture, fix my feet in the correct positions, and execute one, dipping my knees. I place my hand over my heart. "'It is a truth universally acknowledged, that a single man in possession of a fortune, must be in want of a wife.'"

"That opening line is actually ironic. Jane Austen had a great sense of humor," Dillon adds.

"You did watch it! Or read it?" I ask.

"I'll never tell," he says as our gazes cling. His face softens. "Okay, I might have read it in prep school."

I get warm all over. A stupid smile is on my face. My family loves *Pride and Prejudice*.

"Y'all are weird," Chantal says as she cocks her head, eyeing me and Dillon.

"Serena's fault," Dillon muses. "She brings out the cheesy in me."

Sawyer clears his throat. "Whatever you request, Serena, we'll do our best."

Hmmm, decisions, decisions. Dillon wants a kiss, and maybe I do as well.

But...

I plant my hands on my hips and look at Sawyer. "This Theta tradition... Normally the winner would ask for something from Dillon, but could I ask any football player?"

"Hey now—" Dillon mutters.

Sawyer gives me a wary look, cutting him off. "I guess that would be fair since you aren't officially part of the contest. You've got me and Troy here. Zane and Sinclair are at the bar. What do you want from us?"

Doing the unexpected is part of my personality, a side of me I've banked since Vane, and the minx within is roaring to be let off her leash. (Alexa, play "Girl on Fire" by Alicia Keys.)

I take a tiny sip of the tequila Chantal thrusts in my hands then press my fingers to my lips, pretending to think.

"Spit it out," Ashley snips. "We all know you're going to pick Dillon."

I ignore her, my eyes on the wide receiver. "Sawyer, I want you to kiss Bambi."

I'm greeted with silence.

Bambi sputters, Sawyer blinks, and Chantal grins. Troy looks confused.

I throw my head back and chuckle, catching Dillon's eyes, and we have a weird moment when he pauses, a slow smile of appreciation growing on his face as he stares. I feel tingles, as if he's brushed his fingers over my skin.

He lifts his glass in my direction. "Touché."

～

"You didn't have to walk me to my car," I tell Dillon as we maneuver through the crowded lot to my Highlander.

"Let me follow you home."

"No. I'm not buzzing, and I have work to do."

"'Bigfoot Is A Pool Shark?'"

"Nice. It's in the queue."

He threads his fingers with mine. "I'm good at several things."

We reach my car. "I have a feeling where this will go…"

His hand tightens. "Nah, get your head out of the gutter. First, I can cook. My chili is the best. Sawyer begs me to make it. My omelets are ugly but good—I use the good cheese. I'm a good friend, loyal. I'm tidy. My room is the cleanest at the house. I, uh, like the stars. There are so, so many stars in the sky at night." He exhales and closes his eyes briefly.

"So many," I can't help but deadpan.

He mutters, "I swear, I'm not this awkward."

I bite back a smile as he continues.

"And running, yeah, it helps me figure things out. I dig nature, like mountains and stuff. There aren't any mountains here, of course, just flat plains. Jesus, I suck!"

I'm entranced by his struggle.

"Anyway, um, long story short, I enjoy giving presents." He holds out a package and sets it in my hands slowly, as if it might explode.

"What…" I stop and look up at him. "You got me a gift? Why?"

He dips his face. "Um, no reason, uh, just saw it and

thought it suited you. It's not a big deal, I don't know…" He rakes a hand through his hair. "Just open it."

I tear at the delicate tissue paper, tugging on the pink bow around it, and out falls a small dandelion charm. It's sterling silver with a slightly bent stem, the seeds on one side fading away.

"It's, uh, like your tattoo."

"I know," I murmur. "Why?"

"Can't a guy just get a girl a gift?"

"Sure." No. It's personal.

He takes a deep breath, gearing up. "You said it symbolized hope and happiness for you, so I thought, um, you know, that I'd give you something you could see everyday…since your tattoo is on your nape. Does that make sense? I mean, I guess you could just pull your hair up and look in the mirror if you needed a reminder." He scrubs his face. "Anyway. The girl who sold it to me said you could wear it on a necklace or a bracelet, or you can just stick it in a drawer."

"It's so delicate. I don't have anything to put it on…"

"See… I fucked up." He exhales heavily.

"No, no, you didn't. It's beautiful and means a lot—especially because of our conversation. You remembered. Thank you."

We stare at each other, the moment stretching under the streetlights. He looks away. "Seeing Sawyer and Bambi kiss was spectacular."

"Watching them try to figure out where to put their arms..." I laugh. "Then we timed them."

"Sixty seconds is a long kiss." His eyes hold mine. "We can beat that record."

My heart skips a beat. "Yeah."

"They hooked up freshman year." He moves closer, the smell of him making me sigh. He tilts my chin up. "He's got a thing for her."

My head is not thinking about Sawyer and Bambi.

"Fact: lips have more nerve endings than most of the body. People remember kissing more vividly than sex."

"True?"

"I read it somewhere. Can't recall..." I stop as his nose runs up my neck.

"You nervous, Serena?"

"A little."

"Good. I am too. You make me feel..." His hand slides around my nape, drifting over my tattoo. "Like I don't know which way is up." He brushes his lips over mine. Long and soft and thorough, he kisses me, his tongue lazily teasing. It goes on for longer than sixty seconds as he presses me against my car. Desire rushes at me like a whip and I sigh as he pulls away. My chest rises rapidly.

His eyes search my face. "You're really going home?"

"I need to check Romy's calculus homework."

"Excuse?"

Maybe... Yes. I'm just not ready. This, *whatever it is*, is hurtling toward me like a whirlwind. I've done that before, and it blew up in my face.

"Let me follow you then."

"Dillon..."

He puts his fingers on my lips. "I just want to make sure you're okay."

"My neighborhood isn't that bad."

"No, it isn't that." He pauses. "I like knowing you're safe. Even the night at the Pig...just... I haven't always watched after people..." He frowns.

"Your brother?"

He sticks his hands in the pockets of his jeans. "Yeah. He died on my watch. I think he dove off that cliff because he wanted my approval, you know? He wanted to impress me and my friends."

Guilt about his brother plagues him. He's internalized that pain and therefore does acts of service. Maybe it's his way of saying he cares? Not that he *cares* for me. This heat between us is about sexual attraction. Right?

But this soft side of him... It gets to me. He isn't the nothing-bothers-me pretty boy people see.

I open my door. "Alright. Follow me home, and when I get inside, I'll blink the lights at you."

"Done."

A rush of anxiety hits me as I gaze down at the charm in my hand. What possesses a man to buy a meaningful gift for a girl he barely knows? I look back up at him. "Dillon?"

"Yeah?"

"Don't hurt me." I don't know why I say it. It's not appropriate considering we're not dating or even hooking up, yet there's a niggling feeling in my gut.

His eyes widen. "Never. I promise."

Later, I'd remember his lie.

15

Dillon

I'm coming to the LSU game, is the text from my dad the next day when I step out of the shower after practice. I sit down on my bed, trying to decipher how I feel about it. Is his new family coming? I rub my chest. Hope trickles in, a sliver of excitement.

I reply back, **Looking forward to it.** At least someone will be there.

A few minutes later, my phone pings with a text from Serena. **When's your birthday?**

I smile and lie back on the bed. October 23rd. You?

Same.

My eyes flare. STFU.

Ha, just messing with you. February 14.

An image comes through the text, a picture of her at a coffee shop. She's drinking a latte, and there's a smudge of cream on her lips. Wait—who's the other coffee on the table for?

Who are you with?

WBBJ guy. Neil. We had classes together back in the day. Discussing football.

My lips compress. I haven't missed the way he's been gazing at her during the games. **I can help you if you need it.**

Maybe. What do you love about football?

Ah, I get it. She isn't texting to talk. This is about her story. **I'll tell you in person. Come see me or let's meet.**

Those three dots dance on my screen, go away, then come back. **Can't. Sister has hip hop tryouts at six. Give me your email and I'll send some questions. Texting doesn't work.**

Email? Oh, Serena, no. Talking to you—in person— never gets old like it does with other girls, and the next time it happens, I want you alone...

I don't reply, set my phone down, and get dressed. I inhale a deep breath, remembering her face when I gave her the charm. If she knew the secret of that purchase, the exact *when* of the day I bought it... What would she think? That I'm crazy?

Even Sawyer doesn't know.

An hour later, after deciding I can't stay away from her today, I check my hair in the mirror, smoothing it back over my head, then get out of the Escalade.

Magnolia Prep looms in front of me, a two-story gray stone school with turrets bookending either side. I've been to the public school and here a few times to talk to the football players. High school coaches love it, and it's good press and shows a connection to the community.

Unease curls in my gut. I hope this is okay, just showing up here. I'm just...trying to figure out how to woo her. She needs slow and easy, but what if she doesn't like surprises?

"There you are."

I start and glance over at the lady quickstepping it to catch up with me. A small dog trots behind her with a pink bow in her hair.

"Nancy?" I say.

She pats my cheek. "You remembered." She scoops up the dog and puts her in my arms. "You carry him. They don't like to let me in with Betty, but you're semi-famous around here. She cries if I leave her at home. Buster, now, he hates everyone, so he stays home. I should say she's my emotional support, but I'm hers. What a conundrum."

I blink.

She hooks her arm in mine, and I hold the dog in one hand as we enter the cool interior of the school. "You came to support Serena and Romy—I like it. Shows initiative. Serena, bless her heart, she didn't invite you, that's for sure, or she would have mentioned it. She's about as useful as a steering wheel on a mule when it comes to men. I was going to set her up with Turo's son, but his divorce is still pending. And he's forty. I reckon that dog won't hunt."

"I see."

"He sent me an orchid today."

"Turo?"

"Mmm. We had sex for the first time last night. I do love a good orchid. Exotic. Classy. They need a lot of care though—like my Serena." A mischievous grin crosses her face. "Did I mention Turo's Italian?"

"Um, maybe?"

"Ah." She bobs her head, sliding on the glasses hanging from a chain around her neck. "Vane... Don't make his mistakes, honey. She walked in on him, you know. Saw the BJ."

Oh, shit. Serena didn't give me particulars.

"Are you better than him?"

I nod. I've had one-night stands before, even threesomes with girls, but I don't cheat in my brief relationships. Fidelity means something. Loyalty is essential. Maybe because I suspect both my parents found their love in other places before they divorced.

Vane must have been out of his mind.

She leads me into the basketball gymnasium. Loud music blares from one end of the court. I rove the stands, my eyes landing on Serena, her head bent, laptop in hand. Several adults sit around her, but she's got an area saved. Her glasses are on and her lips are pursed. She twirls a piece of hair.

Nana sighs. "She's pretty, huh?"

"Beautiful." My breath hitches.

"She's smart too. On the other hand, she's as confused as a fart in a fan factory when it comes to the stove. I fudge the truth and say the meatloaf's good, but she puts too much ketchup in it. I gag every time. If she offers to cook for you, ask for spaghetti. It's not the best, but edible."

"Okay." *Should I be taking notes?*

"She snores and likes to hog the TV. She gets crabby on her period. She loves music. She adored her parents, bless them. My son and Tamara were so in love, like kittens in a basket, a match made in heaven. She needs that, something real and solid." She darts her eyes at me.

I'm solid, I say in my head.

"Serena!" she calls, flapping her hands. "Look at the cute nugget I found! Sexy football player! For you! If I had a bow, I'd put it on him!"

A flush rises on my face as people stop talking and look over at us. *Geeze, Nancy.*

Serena's head rises, and I sigh, feeling that fist of pressure lighten since she told me she had coffee with Neil. She stands to walk toward us, a frown on her face.

"Well, I'm worn out. Hold on to Betty, honey. I'm

gonna go talk to Tree Boy about condoms." She sashays away to the bleachers.

"Dillon McQueen!" is the screech heard from the sidelines as Romy runs toward me. She's wearing bright green booty shorts and a tight shirt with the Hornets Dance Team logo on it. "You came to my tryouts?" Her mouth gapes.

"Yeah," I say, smiling. "Serena mentioned them." In a random text—and here I am.

"Liam came too, but wow." She juts her finger over her shoulder. "Those girls will never believe this!"

"We'll show them," I say.

She grins. "Tiffany's cool—she's the blonde—but Kari and Taylor are pure evil. Kari dates the quarterback. She thinks she knows everything about football and you... This is great for my street cred!" Her eyes glow, an earnest expression on her face.

Serena arrives and says a quick *hi* then hisses, "How did you know she attends here?"

"Chantal," I say in her ear. She smells like cherries, so damn good.

"But... Why did you come?"

"Impulse. Want me to leave?"

"I didn't invite you."

"I know. Sorry." *This is me, babe, trying to pursue you the only way I know how. Giving gifts. Making sure you get home. Helping your sister with her street cred.*

A group of girls in dance clothes encircle Romy. They lower their heads, whispering, sending me eager smiles. I catch a few words.

"...you know Dillon McQueen..."

"...so hot..."

"...why is he here..."

Serena glances over too. "Ugh. This is kind of a big deal. Now you have to go along and be the famous guy in the room who knows Romy."

"I won't embarrass you." I arch a brow.

She sighs. "Dance is what keeps Romy going. Some of the other girls have wealthy parents, and the transition hasn't been easy."

The dog licks my hand and I wince. "Can you take this thing?"

"The thing's name is Betty. Nana passed her off. You're stuck."

"You're mad I came."

"A little." Her forehead furrows.

I pause, my head tumbling. I don't know *how* to do this.

"Turo sent your Nana an orchid. Do you like those?" I never sent a girl flowers, except for my mother, but I'm willing. Anything.

"No." She watches as Nana moves to sit next to a kid with bleached hair.

"Is that the kid who snuck out her window?"

She puts her hands on her hips. "Chantal talks a lot."

I brush my lips against her temple, not able to stop it. Chantal also mentioned how worried Serena is about her sister fitting in. "She was drunk last night after I drove back to Caddy's to pick up Sawyer. I asked a lot of questions."

Romy approaches with the girls and one of them ventures forward, her face disbelieving. "So, uh, you came to watch Romy? *Really*?"

Is this the good friend or one of the not-nice girls? Either way...

"Yep. She's a cool kid. She almost dances as good as her sister."

"Hey!" Romy grouses.

"Can I have your autograph?" another one says.

"Please!" comes from another.

"Now look what you've done. They're going to mob you. Stop being so handsome," Serena mutters.

"Two minutes, girls! Time to get started!" announces one of the dance coaches on the sidelines.

I toss an arm around Romy in clear view of the others. "Go show 'em what you've got, sweetheart." She squeals, hugs me, and runs off.

Betty and I take in the lingering hip hop students. "Catch me afterward, girls, okay? Right now, I'm going to sit in the stands with my...girlfriend."

"Ooooooo," comes from the girls, and I wink at Serena.

She rolls her eyes in return. "You are deluded."

But she doesn't send me away. I follow her as we find a place on the bleachers next to Nancy and the boy.

As the tryouts begin, her leg is pressed against mine and she keeps sneaking little looks at me. She laughs under breath when I catch her gaze.

"Come on, you're glad I came, right?"

She pets the dog, currently in my lap. "Maybe."

Score.

Maybe, just maybe, she wants me around.

I'll take whatever she gives me.

Just...

Need me like I need you.

Let me in, Dandelion.

16

Serena

The sun is setting as I squat down to pull weeds out of the flower bed, a task I meant to do weeks ago. Mom took pride in her flowers, and look at them now: overrun with vines and grass. I huff out a breath and reach behind overgrown boxwood bushes to pull the Bermuda that's inched in. It's a clear attempt by the invasive grass to conquer new ground. If not for human intervention, half the world would be covered by Bermuda, the other by kudzu. "Grass Comes To Life And Overtakes Mississippi." That would make a great story.

"You missed a spot," a deep voice says.

Ass in the air, I let out a yelp while simultaneously hating that I'm wearing an ancient shirt tied at my midriff, cutoff shorts, and old gardening gloves. My hair is pulled back in a scarf like a fifties housewife.

I turn around and face Dillon. The last time I saw him was yesterday when he popped up at the tryouts. He's pressing hard. He's made it clear he wants me—any way he can get me.

And what do I think? I'm at a crossroads. One way is to run far away; the other is to sink into his arms and say *Put the D in me, football player.*

I gape at the camo pants and long-sleeved black shirt he's wearing. "Did Nana talk you into taking her squirrel hunting? It's not in season, she's terrifying with a gun, and squirrels are adorable. Did she promise you waffles?"

"Nah, I only hunt dangerous game, and you're part of it. Let's go." He pins me with stormy eyes, and I feel like one of those antelopes on the nature channel when she realizes the tiger has her in his sights.

"It's getting dark!"

"Goofball. You want to get to know me better for your article, and I want to spend time with you. I don't see a problem."

He wants to spend time with me. The statement makes me gooey inside. Resist!

I dust the dirt off my gloves. "I emailed you questions."

"Did you?" He grins. "I'll get around to those. Face-to-face is best. Put on some jeans and a dark sweatshirt, and you'll see a side of me you've never met."

Chapter 16 | 221

"It's eighty degrees—the last thing I want to wear is hot clothes."

"We'll strip them off later. You got any champagne?"

"Funny."

"Hurry, we're late. I'll help you pick out some clothes so you won't get hurt." He's already stalking away and heading up to my apartment.

"Hurt?" I call out after him.

He walks up my steps. "You look sexy in those shorts, but you can't wear them. Come on."

Ugh, the arrogance of him... So why am I smiling back at him?

I toss down my gloves and pruning tools as I glare back at the Bermuda. "We shall battle again soon, my friend."

I find him in my closet, face intent as he moves hangers around. He pulls out an old long-sleeved black shirt, frowns at the Four Dragons logo on the front, and shoves it back on the rack. "Why do you still keep his shirts?"

"They're just shirts." I forgot that one was even there.

"When I hear 'Sweet Serena', I want to hit something."

Okay... "Why?"

"He hurt you. This!" He holds up a black sweatshirt and waves it at me. He also finds a pair of black skinny jeans.

"Okay, cool, just make yourself at home," I say dryly. "My panty drawer is the top one. Help yourself—hey! I was being sarcastic!" I shout as he darts over and pulls it open. *Oh, it's like this, huh?* I jump on his back and wrap my arms around his neck, and he starts, surprised, then laughs as he grabs a black lace thong.

"Score!" He tosses me back and I crash down on my bed. He turns and twirls the panties for a moment then stuffs them in the front pocket of his jeans.

I shake my head. "I swear, if you don't give those back..."

"Nope. Mine. Get dressed, please. We have things to annihilate." He whistles and heads out to the den.

Five minutes later, I find myself bemused as I ride in his vehicle down a one-lane gravel lane outside of town. We're in deep farm country with no houses in sight. I've asked him questions about what is going on, but the man is a devil...

"Just so you know, I'm not killing anything. Not even a mouse."

"We won't be killing anything today. Just tagging."

Oh, the black clothes... "Paintball." Dread hits me like a brick wall. "Dillon, come on. I'll embarrass you."

"Nah." He takes his eyes off the road to give me a searching look. "Never."

"It's about time," Sawyer calls out a few minutes later

as we park at a clearing where several players stand around. We get out of the Escalade.

"Pool Shark!" Sawyer says when he sees me. "I have a killer idea. How about you participating in some skee-ball next week with the girls—"

I put my hands on my hips. "Pool was a one-off."

He laughs.

"You're late and you have all the equipment," Troy snips to Dillon as he jogs up. "We haven't won in *three years*. This time, we almost lost by forfeit." He flicks his eyes to me, surprised. "You brought a girl."

"Serena," I reply, arching a brow. "Right here."

He blinks. "I know. You're just the first girl to ever play with us."

Ah...

"Cool your jets, Texas. Had to pick up our best player," Dillon says.

I snort. "I'm here for comedic relief."

Dillon hands out equipment to our team—helmets, guns, vests—and Troy hands out green glow sticks for our necks. I eye the other team, who are also dressed in camo and black. Their leader passes out red glow sticks. Okay, green versus red. There are two teams. I can do this.

"Why do we need vests?" I ask.

"Cause it's gonna hurt like a bitch when you get hit," Sawyer tells me. "Suit up."

"Huddle!" Dillon yells, and we group around him. My vest feels restrictive and I tug at it while he looks at us individually, his eyes steely. Authority and confidence color his words. *This is the way he captains his team*, I think.

He claps his hands. "Alright, let's beat these guys. Pair up, you know the drill..."

No, wait, I don't...

He snaps out scenarios for our strategy with words like *bunker, battle pack, hopper, basecamp*... I get lost.

They whoop and fist-bump, and, of course, I miss Sawyer's high-five.

We walk to the other team and shake hands with the defensive players; most are brawny and thick and look as if they weigh twice what I do.

Trash-talking commences.

"Quarterback thinks he can roll in late...bunch of scared pussies..."

"Gonna aim for your face, Zane," Dillon shoots out.

"Trophy is ours!" calls Troy, adjusting his visor.

"I'm taking down the girl," someone cackles.

My eyes widen. "Can't I just watch, like from the sidelines?"

Dillon pats my helmet. "I'll take care of you."

"Uh-huh. I'm the only girl."

"Because I like you."

"I like you too, jersey chaser," a burly player says

before snapping his teeth at me. Linebacker. Jagger something. Big and mean.

"He's just messing with your head," Dillon murmurs as he hands me my paintball gun. "Don't hold it like it's a bomb. Come here." He stands next to me and positions the weapon in my hands, showing me the trigger and safety. "When you see a red glow stick, aim and shoot. You're good at pool, this'll be easy."

A bead of sweat drips down my back. "As long as I don't see blood…"

He grins. "Just breathe."

Fairy lights flicker on as if they were on a timer, illuminating paths deep into the woods.

"What are the rules?" I ask anxiously. "It kind of ran together in the huddle." In other words, I don't understand your jargon.

"The game is like a horror movie—kidding. It's awesome, and you'll get high on the adrenaline. See the paths? We'll run on those, hide in the woods, and take out the red team. Barricades make for great hiding places. Friendly fire counts, so if you shoot one of your own team, they're out. Each team has a base." He points at a small fort next to a fence and a green flag. "That's us. Their camp is on the other side of those woods with a red flag."

"The *dark* woods?"

"Yeah."

"And I have to *run* with a helmet, a gun, and a vest?"

"Yeah."

"I'm going to kill you."

He grins.

"Slowly. Maybe while you sleep. Or poison."

He looks delighted. "You like to win, right?"

"Hell yeah." Tension rolls off me.

"Badass girl—I knew you'd get it. The defense killed us last year, so we need your spunk. Two ways to win: either wipe out the players on the other side, or steal their flag and move it all the way back to our basecamp."

He rubs black face paint on himself then on me.

"Defense has gone to their base," Sawyer says to the group around us. I stare at his goggles. Fancy. He flashes me a smirk. "Out here they call me Bullseye because I never miss."

Dillon smirks. "Bullseye was the last man standing last year and almost made it back with their flag before he was shot. This year he's out for blood."

Sawyer raises his gun and makes a shout.

"What's up with the goggles?" I ask him.

He pulls them down over his eyes.

"Night vision. Army surplus."

"Where are my night vision goggles?" I ask Dillon.

He throws an arm around me. "The rest of us just run around in the dark. More fun that way."

So. Much. Fun.

I follow my team to our fort, counting nine of us as the

guys touch the flag for luck. I dash for it, sending a prayer up. *Lord, help me be decent at this.*

I hear a voice off in the woods scream, "Ten seconds!"

Dillon rolls his neck and looks at me. "Hang with me."

"Okay." I breathe out, easing closer. I'll be on him like a fly on a pie.

"Safeties off. All rounds are live!" Dillon calls as they tense, guns up.

I heave mine up, trying to mimic them.

My heart jumps in my chest. Five, four, three, two, one...

HOOOOOONK! An airhorn explodes around us, drowning out the crickets and frogs in the woods. The players split apart, darting down paths, obviously with a plan in their head.

Dillon, Sawyer, and I run down a trail between trees to a small barricade surrounded by bushes.

"Now what?" I whisper as I look around. I don't see any other players on either team.

"Wait—" Dillon starts.

A paintball smashes into the tree next to me, making me scream as it splatters glow-in-the-dark red paint. Three more hit the tree in rapid succession.

I shut my eyes, duck down, squeeze the trigger, and fire a single shot—directly into Bullseye's back.

He jumps up and turns around to try to see the green splotch on his vest.

"Seriously?" he says as he whips off his goggles.

"I am *so* sorry." I try to wipe the green paint away.

"You weren't supposed to kill me!" he wails.

I wince. "I got nervous."

Dillon grimaces. "Oops. Rest in peace, Bullseye." He flashes a mock salute.

"Can I be out and not him?" I whisper.

"Don't cry for me, Serena," Sawyer says as he hands me his goggles. "War is hell. Stay alive. It's up to you now. And I've got beer waiting for me back at the clearing." Louder, he yells, "I'm out!" Then he places his gun in the air with his green glow stick hanging from it as he walks out of the barricade.

More paint explodes on the tin roof on top of us.

"They have someone in the trees. We need to get better cover. Follow me," Dillon says. "Be quiet."

In the dark? Yeah, I'll get right on that.

I don't have time to put the goggles on, so I tuck them in the pocket of my vest.

He takes off running through the woods, and for half a second, I think of standing and making myself an easy shot to get out of this mess, but I crouch and take off after him. Not a quitter!

We run through the trees, leaving the fairy lights behind, then slow down and circle back next to a large wooden crate. I make every step he does, trying to not crunch on leaves.

Dillon puts a finger to his lips to signify being quiet —*I am!*—then points at me and then at our fort with the flag. I shake my head. *What?* Are we guarding it?

I interpret that we're going there next and he wants *me* to go first.

While I try to figure out the best rudimentary sign language to use to argue with him, he holds up three fingers and starts counting down to one.

Crap! On three, I take off running, paint exploding around me with every step. I hear a voice up in the trees yell out, "Dammit!" and the barrage stops.

I turn and see Zane climbing down the tree with Dillon under it. "Red out!" Zane grumbles to whoever is listening, gives Dillon a fist bump, and sprints through the woods.

My mouth gapes as I walk back to Dillon. "I was a decoy?"

"A great one. Once he started firing at you, I got a clean shot."

"I was bait! I could have been shot!"

He chuckles.

"Now what?"

"If they had someone sprint all the way here, they're probably swarming our fort at the basecamp. They did the same thing last year." Sweat drips down his face as we take cover behind a tree and he gazes around. "This way."

He weaves through the trees for what feels like forever

as he meanders, making his way to another dugout area near the edge of the tree line. How many hidey-holes are in these woods?

"In here," he calls as he ducks into the little structure.

"I don't think anyone's following us," I reply, my lungs tight from running. My walking and yoga haven't prepared me for this kind of cardio.

"They think their sniper can protect this flank, but we rushed him out of the gate. So while most of our group is on the east side, we'll come up the west and grab the flag. Problem is, we also can't protect our flag, so we can't stay here long. Make sense?"

I take off my helmet to breathe better. "How long does this go on?"

"Couple hours. There's a flurry of action at the beginning for spots, then both sides dig in for a bit and figure out where everyone is before moving into an attack formation."

"Like dating," I muse.

"Yeah." He smiles. "Ready to move?"

I nod and slide the goggles over my mask. The entire world turns green and I can see detail! Each point of light becomes a star.

"Whoa, these things are great," I say. "I can see everything."

"Maybe you won't shoot our side now."

"Smartass," I mutter.

We leave and start toward a path, heading to the other side of the woods. Dillon motions for me to get behind some bushes then slides in next to me and whispers, "Can you see anyone watching their flag?"

"Yes. Two big red things in the trees behind the really bright red thing."

"Okay. How high in the tree?"

"About ten feet."

Someone rushes toward us from the way we came, and I lift my paint gun. I'm ready! Dillon knocks it up into the air before I fire off a round.

"Flash!" announces a voice in the darkness.

"Bang!" replies Dillon. "That's one of ours," he tells me.

Troy kneels down below our cover with us.

Dillon gives him an arm pat. "On three, let's run a pinch play on the two guards. Serena, you stay here. Count to thirty Mississippi then start shooting at both of those trees. Keep your shots high to avoid us."

"Keep it high, right." *Goodbye, world. I'm about to die.*

"Just distract them. Once they're down, we can grab the flag and then have an easy time going back to our side to win the game." Dillon puts his mask against mine. "I'm counting on you."

"Roger." I hope that sounds official.

Dillon and Troy move off into the woods and everything gets quiet.

One Mississippi, two Mississippi...

When it's time, I ease up and fire toward the first red light in the tree.

"LEFT SIDE!" I hear a red tree person scream to his partner.

I keep firing and switch to the other tree. Dang it. Most of my shots are too high.

"I can't see the shooter!" yells one of them.

"Left bunker. Second is trying to sneak up behind us. Third below you. Alpha, Bravo, Gamma, engage! Engage! Engage! Hit the girl!"

A barrage of balls shoot toward me, splattering the wood, and I duck below cover.

I hear a rustling in the brush behind me and raise my gun.

"Flash!" a deep voice calls out.

"Boo!" I reply.

"You're supposed to say bang," Dillon says then drops down next to me as the balls continue to hit our cover.

"Is this the plan?"

"Uh, no. Things are basically FUBAR."

"Oh, yeah, I agree. We need tequila." I hear the guys from the trees rustle around. "Will they move in on us?"

"If they're smart and have the cover. We should go," he says.

"What about Troy?" I ask.

"Scouting."

"Flash," comes a voice from the bushes.

"Boo," I say back.

"It's bang." Troy leans down to our hiding place.

"I know. Just trying out a new word."

He smirks at me and looks at his leader. "There are three guys dug in outside our base. Let's get back, pronto."

"Take the dark path, the one with the lights out," replies Dillon. "Run on three."

I close my eyes.

"One, two…"

The guys run with me between them. We dash through thickets and I think I step on something squishy and smelly and big, like maybe a dead possum. Yells sound behind us as the other team closes in.

"Dude! I'm out of paint!" Troy gasps out.

We duck behind a barricade and I look down at my gun. "How do you check?"

Pop!

I glance up, mortified. Why do I suck at this? Troy glares at me then at the green paint on his foot.

"I'm so sorry!"

"Dammit. At least I'm at the graveyard." He lets out an exhalation, fist-bumps Dillon, and runs to a bench in the field where all the 'deceased' players must be.

Dillon counts the players, contemplating. "Troy makes six of ours out to three of Red Team. We've got Sinclair, and they have six players."

"It's the Alamo all over again," I say.

"Sinclair is hiding, so it's just him and you and me, but we aren't giving up. Let's take some red guys out."

How can he be so confident?

We dart in between trees and end up in a trench. He pops up and scans the horizon. "Incoming!" He ducks as the *pop* of paintballs detonates around us. He fires back, his shoulders rippling. "I got two. Yeah!"

Me? I killed a spider crawling up my arm. Normally, I'd be doing the spider dance, but I've screwed up twice already, so I contained my urge to jump up and run and scream. "So, is this, like, a date?"

He fires more paint. "Totally. Our second. Maybe third if you count the tryouts. Hate it?"

Surprise visits for Romy, now paintball. Is this his version of romance? The thought makes me smirk. He's different, and I don't hate it at all.

"I would have asked you to the movies, but wasn't, um, sure you'd agree. Usually, uh, I meet a girl at the bar and we like each other, and we see each other, ugh…" He looks away. Blows out a breath. "Here I go, spewing crap out of my mouth." He grimaces. "I'm just…kind of…spontaneous. It's been known to backfire."

"No pun intended."

He looks over the edge of the trench. "Dammit. Sinclair's in our fort with the flag. He's surrounded. We're going right up the middle to assist our man. Ready?"

"As I ever will be. What about the guys shooting at us?"

"Imagine Bigfoot behind you and run. I'll take care of them."

I swallow and nod.

"Go!" he yells, and we break into the clearing, dashing toward our basecamp.

"Behind us!" screams one of the red team.

Dillon fires at them and bellows, "Sinclair, help! Now!"

Owen rises out of his bunker and fires on the enemy to cover us. Looking over my shoulder, I watch as green paint splashes around but misses the targets.

"You got their flag?" Owen asks as we hunker down inside the fort.

Dillon growls. "If I did, you'd see it, rookie."

Owen wipes his face just as a red player slides in from the side and aims his gun at me. I freeze, a deer in the headlights as green paint hits the enemy on the side of his helmet. I wilt in relief.

"Red out," the player calls out before running off.

"Got 'em." Dillon grins. "They have three players left."

"You saved my life," I say.

"It's war. Do I get a kiss before I go back into action?" Dillon asks with a grin.

"No making out!" Owen grouses. "This is a man's game."

The fort has slots in the walls, and they utilize one to fire into the trees behind us.

"Serena, you see anything?" Dillon asks.

I peek over the edge for a second. "Three near the edge of the woods, moving fast."

"We're trapped," Owen mutters.

"Your attitude needs adjusting, rookie," Dillon asserts as he fires on the enemy and hits one. "They've got two men left!" he shouts.

A blob of enemy paint hits Owen on the arm. He curses and jerks up to standing. "I'm out!"

Dillon gets a determined look on his face as he watches Owen leave the fort. "Just you and me, Serena. Odds are against us, being pinned in and all."

"It's the *Titanic*."

"I'll go down with you." He pops an eyebrow. "On you too."

He is incorrigible! I elbow him.

A rustling reaches my ear and I peek up. "Incoming!" I say as the enemy creeps forward, ducking behind trees as they approach.

"Hold 'em off! Reloading!" Dillon mutters as he pulls a tube off his belt and pours it into his gun.

"You can do that?" I turn to him—and my gun goes *pop!*

Dillon drops to the ground and grabs his crotch.

"Dillon!" I drop to my knees. "Dammit! Why did you bring me? I'm terrible!"

He groans, his voice gasping. "You've got plenty of paint. Up to you...take them out..."

My hands are clammy as I clutch my gun. "No. No. No."

"They're down to the girl!" I hear one of the red team call to the other. There are two of them—against me.

"Please don't let them win..." he groans and whips off his helmet. His face is pale.

"I'm really sorry for your pain."

"Just kill them, Serena."

I take a deep breath and peek through the slot. Fate is on my side when one of them trips over a root and stumbles, not enough to make him fall, but enough to slow him down. *Pop!* I hit his chest and whoop!

The other one crouches and runs.

"What's going on?" Dillon wheezes.

I don't take my eyes off the enemy. "I got one. There's another one behind a barricade doohickey."

He laughs then grimaces as if it hurt. "Alright, you'll need to rush him. He won't expect it from you. He thinks you're weak."

"I am!"

"No, you're fierce."

"Just run at the gun?"

"Last chance. You run out of here, dodge his paint,

and pummel the hell out of his barricade, climb over the doohickey, and get to him."

"Run, dodge, climb, kill..." My heart pounds.

"Zigzag pattern. Ready. One, two, three!"

I jump out and run as fast as I ever have, straight to the enemy. I stumble and fight to keep my balance. Somehow I manage. My finger stays on my trigger, paint splattering everywhere as I flail myself on the wood of his barricade and crawl up.

He's waiting for me and fires a shot that goes wide.

"Say hello to my little friend!" I yell then paint him with green.

He stands and glowers at me. "Killed by a chick. Red. Out." He marches off, and I run back to the fort.

"I got him!" I dance around, high on adrenaline. This is the most fun I've had in forever!

I make it to the fort, see Dillon, and stop celebrating. "Are you okay?"

He's thrown a hand over his face, still lying on the ground. "Fresh as a daisy."

The airhorn blasts and footsteps sound as our guys rush to the clearing.

"Green wins by annihilation!" a voice calls.

"Offense takes it!"

Our team storms the basecamp, slapping me on the back. Everyone is covered in paint except for...me.

Owen throws an arm around me. "You're alright, even if you killed three of us."

Troy gives me a back slap. "Nice kill, Serena."

I beam.

Sawyer picks me up and swings me around, and I flail about. When I look up, Dillon has made it out of the fort and is watching us with an expression on his face I can't decipher. Maybe part satisfaction, part amazement?

Someone's handed him a cold beer and he's pressed it to his crotch. His team surrounds him, smacking him on the back and giving him a hard time about me shooting him. I watch, biting my lip as I realize how close he is to them. He mentioned that he doesn't see his parents often. His adopted father is on the West Coast and his mom is a socialite. What must that feel like, to rarely see them? After losing a sibling? I'm lucky to have a close-knit family, but not everyone does. Family isn't always about DNA or the people who raised you. It's about who's there when things go to hell. For him, it's his team. And he brought me here to be with them.

"Great date?" I ask as I walk over to him.

"Better than pulling weeds."

"I promise to make it up to you."

"What about my future children?"

"Fact: a serious groin injury makes you puke. I've read where some guys can't even get up off the ground."

"Sorry I'm not vomiting."

I bite my lip. "This *was* your idea."

"I need you to drive me home, cook dinner, and make ice packs. Do you have any frozen peas? Also, I might need a shoulder rub." He hobbles closer. "Will you take care of me?"

Oh, Dillon. My breath hitches. He meant it in jest, but I wonder if anyone really ever takes care of him?

"He's milking it!" Sawyer bellows. "Dude stuffs socks down there every day—today's no different."

"I did wear a cup to paintball, this is true, but it still hurts."

Sawyer hands Dillon a plastic, golden trophy of a woman with a bowling ball. She's scratched up and faded. "This should make you feel better," he tells Dillon.

When I ask Sawyer where it came from, he tells me it belonged to his granny. She loved bowling and won several championships. "That's why we had to get the trophy back this year."

Dillon, the color coming back to his face, holds it high. "Offense today, boys! LSU this weekend!"

Whoops sound from the players.

I hook my arm through Dillon's. "Come on, let's get you home."

~

Chapter 16 | 241

THE HOUSE IS quiet when my eyes open. It's two in the morning, and I lie here trying to figure out what woke me. Straightening my camisole and sleep shorts, I tiptoe into my den and take in the large man on my couch: currently sound asleep, one leg thrown down on the floor, an arm over his face. A deep breath comes from his chest. The quilt I gave him hours ago has slipped down, and my eyes track the contours of his pecs, the red roses there.

Last night, before we hit the city limits of Magnolia, Dillon changed his mind about going home and had me drive to my place instead of his. Sawyer and the guys were planning to have people over to celebrate the win, and Dillon didn't want the company.

He moves in his sleep, settling into the couch. One of his ice packs, now water, plops to the floor, and I pick it up. I felt absolutely terrible about injuring him, but he assured me his cup prevented a worse injury. However, he did insist I cook spaghetti and play *Five Nights at Freddy's* with him, a survival-horror video game he downloaded on my laptop. It's not bloody or gross but was engineered to scare the shit out of people. Set in a haunted pizza parlor like Chuck E Cheese, the evil animatronics (Freddy Fazbear, Bonnie the Bunny, Chica the Chicken, and Foxy the Pirate Fox) want to kill the player. They killed me a lot. Later, after some giggling, we found a movie to watch. I suggested *Pitch Perfect*—Chantal totally looks like the blonde chick. He begged for *Shaun of the Dead*, a campy zombie movie. I agreed.

Halfway through the movie, conked out on Aleve and exhaustion, he pulled me down to lie next to him. I thought he might kiss me again—I wanted him to—but he tossed a muscular arm around me then promptly fell asleep. For an hour, I lay there, enjoying the feel of his body, his rhythmic breaths, the scent of his skin. Finally, around midnight, I got him a quilt and a pillow and headed to bed.

"Serena," he murmurs. "Come here."

I start, not sure he's fully awake. Walking over to him, I sit lightly on the edge of the coffee table. "You feel better?"

"Mmmm, had a nightmare. The *Titanic* was sinking, and we were on it. I tried to save you, but Freddy and Bonnie showed up to eat me. So weird…" His eyes flutter open then close. His chest rises, his full lips parting.

"Good to know," I muse, "that I'm part of your nightmare."

I tug the quilt up, my fingers grazing his hand as a sigh comes from me. He's so heartbreakingly beautiful. With one last look, I stand up and force myself to walk away, trying to remember that beautiful things are hazardous to my heart…

17

Dillon

Tomorrow is game day, and I'm tense. This is our first big game against a ranked team.

"Morning, boys!" the quarterback coach calls out as Sawyer, Troy, and I pile out of the Escalade at the private airfield a few miles from campus.

"Holy fuck, that's a big plane," Sinclair mumbles as we walk up. He's got a queasy look on his face. "I've never flown before."

"Not even when you came to school?" I ask.

"Bus brought me." He rolls his shoulders, hitching up his duffle. "And before you ask, I'm *not* scared. You?"

"I figure since my bio dad and grandparents crashed in a jet, the odds of me dying on a plane are low."

He pales. "I forgot about that."

I get in line as the ramp comes down for us. Everyone

is dressed in slacks and button-up shirts, belts, and dress shoes. Coach likes a clean-cut image when we waltz into our hotel in enemy territory.

"Put your earphones in and meditate. You'll be fine. Good paintball this week."

He gives me a wary look. "Yeah, thanks for including me."

"Just waiting till you love me like everyone else."

"You are such an asshole."

I'm not listening to him as I hear Serena's voice behind me. The last time I saw her was when I woke up on her couch, peeked in her room, then left for my run. I wrote her a note thanking her for our *date*. Ha. We've texted on and off, but with the game looming, I crashed last night.

I turn and see her with Neil. I'm cool. Not gonna punch him. She said he's just a friend. Don't even know what *we* are... Just taking it slow. She needs baby steps.

I take my seat and dig out my headphones, waiting for her to walk past, jonesing to see her face.

An exhalation slides through my lips when she approaches, tension easing. She's wearing one of those tight little pencil skirts, black heels, and an orange Tigers shirt. My eyes snag on a navy ribbon around her neck that leads to something hidden under her blouse. Her hair is up in a high ponytail.

"Ballbuster!" Sawyer calls out to her.

"Everybody cover!" Troy chimes in. "Cod Killer is on the plane!" He slaps her on the arm, then reddens in embarrassment. "Uh, 'cod' is slang for a certain male appendage, you know, in case you didn't get it."

She smirks. "I got it, Troy."

"Hey," I say when she gets to my seat.

"Hey."

"I'm glad you're here."

"Me too."

We gaze at each other, and my blood hums.

"You look nice," she says.

"What's under your shirt?"

"My skin."

"Uh-huh. What else?"

"My bra."

"Come on. Is there a certain, um, charm under your shirt?"

"Please keep the line moving," comes from one of the assistants at the head of the plane.

She looks back at a scowling Neil then back to me. "Gotta go. I'm causing everyone to wait."

"Later." As soon as she's gone, I blow out a breath.

I mutter under my breath. Lame, fucking lame. Why did I ask about the charm?

"Who you talking to?" Sawyer asks, giving me side eye from the seat next to me.

"No one."

"Himself," Troy says from the seat across the aisle. "Get your head in the game, QB1. Your challenge can wait."

"Shut up and mind your own fucking business, Texas," I mutter, frowning.

The challenge isn't real to me, *she is*.

By the time we land and get to the Double Tree Hotel, it's after two, and we immediately change and head to the field for a scheduled practice. When we get back, we're sweaty, worn out, and ready for dinner in the hotel. After that, we'll have a few hours to ourselves, but curfew is at ten. Coach runs a tight ship, and I'm expected to be a role model, which means I tell some of the younger guys *Hell no* when they plan to hit a bar down the street, maybe a strip club. In my younger years, yeah, I would have been all over that, but now…my game starts at one tomorrow, and it's televised.

My dad is coming.

He's been on my mind this week and we've spoken a few times, working out a plan to see each other. He's flying in on his private plane, watching the game, and then we're going to grab dinner before we leave.

Brianna is also coming, and they're bringing Marley, their nine-month-old. The last time I saw them was in February when I flew to California to see her after she was born. I passed on meeting them in the Hamptons this summer, opting to stay in Magnolia with Sawyer. Seven months without seeing my dad...

"Your phone is ringing off the wall, man!" comes from Sawyer as I step out of the shower in our hotel room.

"Okay!" I quickly dry off, throw on shorts, and come out to the room I'm sharing with him. Snatching up my phone, I do a quick redial, and Dad answers. "Hey! You here yet?"

"Dillon, son, I'm sorry." His voice is gruff. "We can't come."

I clench the phone, disappointment crawling over me. "Why?"

"Marley's got a fever, probably just teething, but Brianna doesn't want to travel with her. She's fussy and can't rest, and it will be hell. Brianna isn't feeling great either. We're... She's pregnant."

My heart drops. Mom's getting married and Dad is having another baby? A long breath comes from my chest. Do I even matter at all anymore?

"Congrats," I push out.

"Took a look at your schedule," he continues as if everything is fine. "Maybe we can make the Alabama game in October."

My heart thumps, anger rushing like a wave. "Ah, I see. You don't have a nanny to babysit. Funny, I recall you jetting off whenever you felt like it when you were married to Mom, and you can't even come to a game? You didn't make the national championship—"

"Brianna was nine months pregnant—"

"I haven't seen you since February. I came to see *you*."

There's a long silence, just the sound of his breathing. I picture him at his house in Malibu, maybe looking out the windows at the blue of the Pacific. I hear Brianna talking in the background, the cry of a baby.

"Dillon…" He sighs. "I'm sorry. You're upset. I talked to your mom."

Oh? He wants to change the topic?

My jaw clenches. "Yeah. Guess you won't be at her wedding? Whenever it is. If it happens…"

"She sprung it on you, didn't she?" A gusty exhalation comes from him. "You must be feeling left out—"

"Nope, don't drag her into this to make yourself look better."

There's a heavy silence. "We live on opposite sides of the country, Dillon. I work every day. I have a baby. Look, I haven't given you the attention—"

His excuses cut me to the bone. My eyes shut and I see Myles diving off that cliff…

"We both know why you don't want to see me. You can't look at me without thinking about him," I say, hand tight on the phone. "Take care of your new family." I end the call and throw my cell across the bed.

"You alright?" Sawyer asks, and I shake my head as I shove my feet into my shoes, grab a shirt, and pull it on.

"Where you going? Dillon—"

"For a run."

"Wait and I'll go with you," he calls out as I slam the door and stalk down the hall.

My throat feels raw and tight as I jab the button for the lobby. My chest wants to explode. Angry and frustrated, I stare at myself in the mirrored walls of the elevator. I scrub my jaw as the door opens and Serena walks in, giving me a surprised look as she settles beside me.

"What's wrong?" she asks softly. Her hand touches my arm, and I close my eyes.

"My dad said he was coming and now he's not. Just... need to run and I'll be over it."

She's changed into a slinky red dress and stilettos, and her hair tumbles around her shoulders, the lighter colors making her eyes stand out. Her lashes are thick with mascara.

"Where are you going?"

"Neil asked me to have a drink with him and some of the press. We're going to talk football."

Uh-huh, I just bet.

The door slides open and she takes a step out to the lobby, but I grab her hand and pull her back in. My hand hovers over the floor selection panel on the wall. "What's your room number?" I ask.

She takes a deep breath, licks her lips. "714. But I told Neil—"

"Text him. You aren't going." I hit the button for the seventh floor and cage her in with my forearms against the wall. Adrenaline and anger and jealousy prick at me. I've tried to handle her at a gradual pace, but I want her so much it hurts. "You and me. Now." My nose runs up her neck, the smell of her intoxicating.

Her hands land tentatively on my chest. "Dillon..."

"Say yes, Serena, say yes. Please." My lips dip to hers, hovering, waiting.

Her lashes flutter as she tugs on my hair, fisting it and pulling my mouth to hers. The kiss is hard and savage. I haul her up with my hands on her ass. Her legs twine around my hips, her dress riding up. My hands knead her ass as she sucks on my tongue, a low sound coming from her throat. The steel pipe in my shorts hardens more.

She's a hot flame, a fire I can't walk away from.

The door opens and she pulls back, her chest rising rapidly. "Someone might see—"

"Don't give a fuck." I hold her against me, carrying her as we step out. "Which way?" I push out, drunk with desire.

"Turn right. Four doors down." She kisses my throat, peppering me with touches, sucking on the rapid pulse just beneath my skin. We make it to her door. "Key... purse. Let me down," she says breathlessly.

She fumbles around with me behind her, my hands on her hips, my face in her hair, immersing myself. My body throbs with need. My head buzzes with the smell of her. I've never done cocaine, but I wonder if she's my drug, if I'll get addicted. One kiss freshman year was enough to torment me for months. My lips suck on her neck and she leans back, nuzzling into me.

We fall into the room, and the door barely shuts before we're panting, facing each other. I hardly take in the space, seeing her rumpled bed, her laptop, her scattered clothes.

"It's been a long time for me," she says.

Satisfaction hits me and I rush my words. "Good. Do you have condoms? I don't. I can go to the drugstore across the—"

She takes a deep breath, turns, and digs around in a duffle in her closet. Turning, she holds up a box. "Never leave home without them, you know, after..."

My fingers slide the straps of her dress down. There's no bra as I reveal her nipples, dark pink, taut, and delicious. Clenching the fabric of her bodice, I drag the silky material up and down against her breasts, teasing her until they're pebbled and erect. My lips close over one, flicking then sucking it into my mouth.

She cries out, gasping as she arches. Her fingers dig into my scalp. She groans as I move to the other breast, testing the weight, my thumb circling her nipple and tugging.

"You can't deny this." I kiss her lips, deep and hard, my tongue searching her mouth, committing the feel, the taste of her to memory. Her hands find my hair as her hips rock against mine. Dark need rushes at me and I sway on my feet.

Is her passion as big as mine? As frightening?

I roll my erection against her and she whimpers.

Serena. You make me insane.

I can't get enough of her mouth. The sweet kiss we shared at Cadillac's isn't what I want. No, no—I want her dirty and ugly and hard. We collide, eating at each other, breaths mingling as I slant over her lips, trying to get deeper, wanting all her secrets. Sounds of pleasure and desire erupt from her throat. I drop her dress to her feet and she shoves at my shirt. I help her tug it off over my head and toss it on the floor.

We stare at each other, chests panting. She's perfect and beautiful and proud in her red lacey thong, and the sight of her hits like a fist to my gut. So long I've waited. Days. Nights. Years.

My fingers hook in her panties and I pull her back to me, our flesh sizzling.

"Serena..." I sweep her up and she's light as a feather as I drape her on the end of the bed. I scoot her down and kneel between her thighs. "I want to taste you."

Her body clenches, her legs quivering as I kiss her. Her hand touches my face, her thumb sliding between my lips, and I suck it, my tongue wrapping around her finger.

She pulls it away, her voice needy. "Don't make me wait." She arches her hips as I slide down her thong, revealing her mound, her slickness gleaming between her legs. A long gust of air comes from me. She's perfect...

"Drenched," I say hoarsely.

Dipping my head, I lick her from the bottom of her sex to her clit. She shouts my name as I bury my face in her scent, the folds of her skin, her tight channel. Hauling her closer, my hands lift her ass and I delve inside her, fucking her with my tongue. I devour her. She's all I want. Nothing else matters, not parents who don't need me or a brother who died.

One finger glides inside her, then another as I work it in and out. The shadow on my jaw abrades her thighs as I pant against her skin, breathing, just breathing. I haven't been with anyone in months and now *it's her*. I want to consume her, want her to come so hard she'll never forget me.

My tongue toys with her clit. I suck soft then hard as I fuck her with my fingers. A keening noise comes from her lips.

"Come, Serena," I say, my voice rough, soaked in need, dying to be inside her.

She writhes under me and tugs my hair. "Kiss me."

"Come first." I kiss her thigh then her clit, flicking.

She lifts her leg, her heels digging into my back as her body arches up, her pussy spasming against me, grasping and fluttering as she goes over the edge. Tremors vibrate through her, her hips twitching.

I climb up to her and we kiss, the taste of her still on my lips. Reaching over her head, I find the condom on the nightstand but can't rip it open. My hands shake. She takes it from me and uses her teeth, dazed eyes holding mine.

"Hurry," I growl.

She scoots up on the bed and beckons me with a curl of her fingers. "Come here."

Like a man dying of thirst, I crawl over her, my thighs straddling her as I rise up on my knees. Her breasts brush against me as she takes me in her mouth.

"Fuck!" I throw my head back, tearing my eyes off the image of her full lips wrapped around me. Hands on my ass, she tugs me closer, her hot mouth taking me in, her throat closing around me. I can't breathe.

Must look at her.

Her eyes gaze up at me, heavy with desire.

"Enough," I mutter through clenched teeth.

She gives me a slow smile as she gives my crown a final lick and slides the condom on.

She pushes me down to the bed and climbs on top of me. My hands caress her from her hips to her breasts, tweaking her rock-hard nipples between my fingers. "Ride me." It's a demand.

"Don't boss me around."

I growl and pull her down for a hard kiss. Her forehead presses to mine as I test her slick entrance, rubbing through her sex. She leans back and sets me inside her, inch by inch, until I'm gasping. Her heat wraps around me, her sheath tight and hot.

"Dandelion," I rasp. "Take all of me."

She starts for a moment at the nickname, then moves her hips and I sink home, shuddering.

"Faster, harder," I plead as she moves, rising up and down, her hips rolling like a dancer's.

Serena...

I need control. I flip her under me, and my first thrust is hard, my second harder. She gives it back just as wild, hands in my hair, her pelvis rising to meet mine. I kiss her as I fuck her, and she calls my name, feeding off my frenzy. I bite her shoulder and she bites me back, sharp and stinging, the sensation going straight to my cock.

"On your stomach," I gasp.

Without waiting for her, I turn her over and she gets on her knees. Gripping her ass, I groan as I pump inside her heat once again. I hover over her back, my lips latching onto hers as she cranes her neck to find me. Our tongues tangle in an erotic dance as I twist my hips and stroke into her.

She cries into my mouth, her hands fisting the covers.

"Roar when you come," I whisper as I reposition her ass, angling my body to hit the top of her, my pelvis slapping against her. My thumb rotates against her nub in sync with my thrusts. "Serena, Serena, Serena..."

Grunts reverberate around the room, the sounds of our sex filling my ears as sweat drips down my face.

She moans, the sounds indecipherable, and I groan with her, clutching her tighter.

"Dillon!" she yells as she shatters, clenching around me.

"So fucking good..." I shout as I join her, her name on my lips as I break apart, still thrusting as my arms wrap around her waist and hold her against me.

We pant for several moments, our bodies slick with sweat. I slide out, dispose of the condom, and plop back down on the bed next to her. She's still face down taking deep breaths. I trail my fingers over her shoulder and kiss the dimple at the base of her spine—the one I always knew was there. "That was amazing. Round two in ten minutes?"

She says something, the sound muffled by the bed. She turns over, a smile on her face. Her hair sticks out at the top and my lips twitch. "Again?" she asks.

My heart skips a beat when our eyes cling. My words are soft. "*Pour toujours.*"

"What does that mean?"

Forever.

"It means that we're gonna use the chair next time. You on top."

She laughs, the sound soft and husky, taking me right back to a starry night.

Finally, finally, Dandelion. *Mine.*

18

Serena

I'm late. Ugh. The bus left an hour ago, so I'll need to get an Uber to the stadium. Thankfully, Neil is still around when I arrive in the lobby. He's wearing a blue dress shirt and tailored gray slacks, his hair swept back, glasses on. A broad smile crosses his face as he takes in my navy skirt and white shell blouse.

"We missed you last night. Got to meet some of the ESPN guys," he says. "Your headache better?"

A blush steals up my cheeks. Headache. Right.

I banged Dillon McQueen.

A shiver races over me at the memory, his demands, that insatiable side of him. After the mattress acrobatics, round two was on the chair, my legs straddling his, his mouth sucking my neck as I rode him. Round three was in the shower, my back against the tile as water poured over us. His mouth clung to mine with every thrust of his hips.

The sex god left for his room at midnight, late for his curfew. Two hours with him...was it enough? No. He's sneaking inside me, making me crave dangerous things.

My hand touches the charm around my neck, tied with a ribbon and hidden by my shirt. *Good luck for the team*, I told myself when I put it on yesterday. It's not like I'm in love with him. That's crazy.

"Just tired from the flight."

Something he sees on my face makes him pause. "Are you involved with McQueen?"

I compose my features, but uneasiness makes me stiffen. There's no rule that says I can't. Yes, I'm interning for the *Gazette*, and that does put me in an odd position... Pushing my thoughts aside, I settle for the best answer. "No."

He exhales, searching my face. "Ah, good."

"Why would you ask?" Does my gaze linger too long on him in the stands? It can't be the articles. I'm simply reporting the game particulars, the touchdowns, the passes, the score, etc. It's the most boring writing I've done, but at least I'm learning the game.

"On the plane, when you walked past him, I thought I heard some talk..."

My attention sharpens. "What talk?"

He shrugs. "It's just that you're new and don't understand how rowdy players can get. In the past they took bets, usually offense versus defense."

"I remember something like that...they had a trophy and maybe a scoreboard?" It's a distant memory.

He nods. "They live and die by their traditions. When I played basketball, we did our own things."

"You think there's a bet about me?"

"I heard Troy ask Dillon about a challenge and you'd just talked to him—"

"And you think they meant me?" My tone is sharp, and he shrugs.

"I'm sure I was mistaken. Besides, you're smart enough to avoid a guy like him."

He *isn't* a bad person. Plus, Dillon wouldn't set me up as part of some contest, like the Theta thing.

"Serena! Serena!" comes two girly voices.

I look over Neil's shoulders as Chantal and Bambi waltz through the lobby. Decked out in tight jeans, cropped jerseys, styled hair, and full makeup, they look gorgeous. Tiger stickers adorn their cheeks, blue and orange pom-poms in their hands.

"Who are they?" Neil asks, caught in their thrall.

"My sisters," I murmur. "Didn't know I had them until recently." I smile at his confusion. "Thetas. They like me for some reason."

"We adore you!" calls Chantal, overhearing my comment. They smother me in hugs and squeals.

I rear back, some of the anxiousness Neil's words caused disappearing. I do a quick round of introductions while he wanders off to arrange an Uber for all of us.

They tell me about the seven-hour drive. "Thank God Ashley rode in a different car," Bambi grouses. "If I hear her playlist for her and Dillon one more time, I will shoot myself."

"So, Troy? What happened after I left Caddy's?" I've missed talking to her this week.

She flips a strand of blonde hair over her shoulder. "He's being weird."

"But..." I arch my brows.

"Maybe I'll give him another go." She shrugs.

I elbow Bambi. "And Sawyer?"

A blush steals up her face. "Um, about that. I asked him to the Fall Ball, so..."

"What she means is...Ashley wins the contest by default," Chantal says tersely. "She's babbling to anyone who'll listen about her big night with Dillon. It's all over Insta. Wouldn't be surprised if she took an ad out in your paper." She gives me an appraising glance. "What's wrong?"

I'm picturing Ashley in a gorgeous floor-length dress and Dillon in a tux at the formal. They're dancing, and he's holding her, her curves against his...

My hands tighten.

"What the heck is that on your neck?" interrupts

Bambi. She leans in, pulling at the silky tie thingy near the hollow of my throat. "Well, well, it's a big, juicy hickey. Call the paramedics, Chantal. Our girl's been busy!" She pokes me. "You need a blood transfusion?"

"Oh, a love bite! Show me! Move, I can't see, Bam," Chantal edges in, elbowing Bambi as they inspect the side of my neck.

"Keep it down," I mutter as I eye Neil.

Did he see it? Is that why he asked about Dillon?

Inwardly, I groan. Have to hide it from Romy...

"I dabbed makeup on it for fifteen minutes," I say ruefully.

They blink down at me.

I huff. "It's just a little bruise!"

"Maybe put some ice on it," Chantal says on a snicker.

"Was it WBBJ guy?" Bambi whispers, eyeing Neil a few feet away. "He's cute, like an accountant. Or a lawyer. Maybe a professor. I like them with less tweed and more brawn, but to each their own—"

"No."

"Was it some guy from the hotel bar? That's a fantasy of mine," Chantal muses.

I retie my shirt, adjusting the front of my blouse. "No!"

"So who?" Chantal presses as she reaches behind me.

"What are you doing?" I ask.

"Taking your hair down. The up-do is cute, but your

necktie is slipping and everyone'll see it. Your hair needs to be down. It's so gorgeous."

"It was Dillon," Bambi says, her eyes sharp. "He was all over you at Caddy's."

I touch the dandelion under my blouse. "No."

"Liar!" she calls, and I shush her.

"Stop yelling. Fine, fine, *it was*, but you can't tell anyone. It was a..."

"One-time thing?" Chantal finishes.

I shrug.

Her mouth twists. "Oh, honey, don't..." She trails off, looking to Bambi for support.

Bambi exhales, pink lips pursed. "He's a slippery one. Keep your heart locked away, feel me?"

"Did you do the deed?" Chantal asks. "Was he huge? He looks huge."

"Three times."

"Was it amazing?" Bambi gushes.

It was. "No comment."

"Meanie," she chirps.

I circle back to what Neil mentioned. "Have either of you heard about the guys doing bets?"

They frown in sync, and Chantal responds, "There *used* to be bets until Ryker got involved with a girl over one and it blew up in his face. He had to grovel his way back into her good graces. Why? Want me to investigate?"

Her eyes narrow. "I will kill Dillon McQueen if they've brought that tradition back."

Bambi shakes her head. "He'd never do that."

Neil calls out that the Uber has arrived.

"Come on, forget that. Let's get to the stadium," Bambi says, and I follow them outside. We laugh and chat about the game, but inside, a kernel of doubt drops and swirls. The Dillon I know *does* get hung up on superstition and traditions, but he's not the kind of guy who'd use me for his team. He's not the one-dimensional, shallow person I assumed he was. I push the idea out of my head and think of him in the elevator, his face devastated that his father wasn't coming.

19

Dillon

Boos rain down as we run off the field for halftime. Nothing makes a crowd angrier than a visiting team showing up and snagging a twenty-one-to-nothing lead in the first half.

"Who dat kicking LSU's ass!" Troy shouts.

"LSU who? Dillon is the man!" Sawyer replies. "It's because you won your challenge," he says to me under his breath, and I send him a sharp look. When I came in last night, he took one look at me and figured out where I'd been. Serena is *not* about the challenge.

Coach Alvarez rolls in, his eyes roving over each of us like an eagle. "Simmer down! We've got a second half to play, and you can bet the other locker room is working their ass off to figure out how to flip the script." He puffs out his barrel chest. "Good half."

We whoop.

"McQueen, excellent job. Keep chipping away at the small stuff, but don't get sloppy."

I nod.

"Break into your groups, listen to your coaches, and keep the fight on their side of the field, because who are we?" He puts a hand to his ear.

"WAYLON! TIGERS!" More whoops as Sawyer drops to the floor and does a body roll, pads and all.

We head off to team breakouts, and I suck down a Gatorade and sit next to Sinclair. He's quiet as Coach Allen breaks down our plays, my passes, the coverage we can expect for the second half. He finishes with some changes he wants to try, and I study the plays.

The noise from the LSU fans hits us like a wave in the ocean as we line up for the second half. My nerves are stretched as we run the ball on first and second down, picking up eight yards. All we need is two more for a first down.

"Hike!"

Moving fast, I turn to fake a handoff. The defensive end on the right side has beat Sawyer, so I aim downfield for the tight end and send a perfect pass.

The LSU safety comes out of nowhere and snatches the ball then steps out of bounds. Fuck! It's my first interception of the season.

Our defense takes the field, and one of them slaps me on the ass. "Chin up, McQueen."

My shoulders roll as I walk off the field and wait for Coach.

"What the hell, McQueen? Why are you forcing the ball downfield? We want first downs, not touchdowns. Play my game, not yours."

Alright, alright. "Yes, sir."

The crowd erupts as LSU scores on our defense on a trick play.

Our offense takes a nosedive. Not one Waylon player can catch my passes, and running the ball is getting us nowhere. It's third and long when I call a short, safe pass. The ball snaps and the LSU defenders blitz me. A hand grabs my jersey from behind and yanks me down. I double over backward and slam into the ground.

"I'll be here all day. All day!" the LSU player yells in my face.

"You alright? You landed on your leg," Sawyer says as we approach the sideline.

He's right, and my knee hurts with each step I take, but a player knows the difference between being injured and hurt. I'm fine.

Play by play, I pace the sidelines as our defense starts to struggle. Tension fills the stadium as LSU marches down the field. We grow tight-lipped on the bench, and shoulders sag as I try to rouse them, popping helmets and slapping backs.

LSU scores another touchdown.

Sawyer grimaces. "Our turn, man. Let's do this."

I lead the offense to the line and LSU shifts, switching and adjusting fast. I inhale a deep breath, easing it out through my mouth guard.

"Hike!"

The right defensive end from LSU beats my lineman and, shoves him into my face. Rolling out behind him, I see clear grass and run for the first down, but a hit from behind makes me stumble. Spinning out of the tackle, I grunt as I'm hit by a linebacker from the opposite side and the ball slips out of my hand. It floats in the air for what seems like eternity before another LSU player catches it at a full run.

A defender crashes on top of me. Then another. The crowd roars and I close my eyes. Touchdown. I've fumbled the ball and they've scored to tie the game.

"Too bad Ryker ain't here. He made it more fun," says the LSU lineman as he gives my leg a kick the refs don't see. Eighty-four. Douche.

"McQueen—my fault, man," says my offensive lineman. He hauls me up. "He beat me. Won't happen again."

I give him a pat and take a step toward the sideline. My knee twinges as I put weight on it, testing it. Nothing broken or sprained, but I have to limp off the field.

Trainers run up, help me to the bench, and push and pull on my knee.

"Just took a knock," I insist.

Coach Alvarez comes over and pulls off his headset. He doesn't look at me, but at the trainer.

"How is he?"

"Fine," I mutter.

The trainer nods. "He's okay. Nothing's torn. He may have strained some ligaments. We should put some weight on it before he goes back in."

I stand and pace the sideline. "No. I had worse in prep school."

"Keep checking him out. We'll go with Sinclair," Coach says into his headset and turns away.

What the...

I am fine!

No!

"Coach, I'm good!" I protest.

He lets out a gusty exhalation. "So you say. Walk it off for a few plays and we'll let Sinclair take a shot."

He leaves and I hunch over, pretending to test my knee as I suck air in.

This isn't happening.

Sinclair already has his helmet on, and I grab him by his jersey.

"Hands off, Grandpa."

"Don't be a little shit for five minutes!"

His eyes widen.

My jaw pops. Emotion claws at my throat, disappointment in myself, that I'm not enough for this team. "Watch that line. They're changing directions and pushing our own guys in my face. They're fast, better than the last teams we played. Watch DeMarco—eighty-four. He plays dirty."

His throat bobs. "Alright."

"You nervous?"

He nods and turns to go, and I snag his sleeve. "Remember the basics. Don't be a superstar. Play safe. Take control of your men and play—"

"Nothing fancy. Got it."

"You're learning." I slap his helmet. "Go. Score. Win."

The trainers have me running around the sidelines to keep my body ready to go, and my chest burns to get out there. By the time the clock has run down to the fourth quarter, my eyes keep darting to Coach. *I'm here, I'm ready.*

The clock is ticking down to three minutes when LSU scores a field goal, and I groan. 21 to 24. I tug at my hair. We can't lose!

My eyes flit up to the stands where Serena sits with the press. She's bent over her seat, her face stark and eyes wide. Our eyes meet for a moment and she holds her hands up in a praying motion. *Yeah.* I swallow thickly.

At a minute left, Coach calls a time out. My trainer

pulls him aside and gives an update on my situation. "*He's good*," I hear, and Coach motions for me to come over.

"I'm pumped," I say. "Put me in."

"No," he tells me quietly. "I make decisions for the team. I'm going with Sinclair. You've played a good game, but just take a breather."

A breather?

"I can win."

He ignores me and calls the team over. "McQueen's knee is still a problem. Sinclair's going in for the final drive and overtime if we need it."

Sawyer and Troy and a few others give me questioning looks, but I shake my head. I'm not going to disrespect Coach. He's letting me save face by saying I'm injured. He *wants* Sinclair.

I rouse the offense and yell, "We came to LSU to beat them. Their defense is kicking you in the teeth. Show them who we are!"

The team replies in unison as they run out onto the field.

I'm pacing the sidelines, pissed at Coach, angry with myself, and anxious that Sinclair isn't going to score. They're stuffing the run at every turn, and his passes are too short. He's not close enough for a field goal.

I clutch my helmet as the seconds pass. Ten, nine, eight—

The snap comes and Sinclair drops back; he throws a

tight spiral down the left side to Sawyer. Impossible to catch—but he does, jumping up and snatching it out of the air. He runs like a fucking gazelle.

Touchdown.

I yell in relief. Exhilaration erupts from our side as we rush the field. When I see Sinclair getting Gatorade dumped on him, part of me wants to punch him for taking what was mine. It feels like a lead weight in my stomach. But, we won. I can't deny that. Grinding my teeth, I battle down my insecurities and give him his due.

20

Serena

The flight home is quiet. I can't see Dillon from where I sit, but I remember his face when I boarded the plane. Hard like granite, inscrutable, yet he flashed a smile if anyone looked. He's pretending he isn't reeling from the game, but I sense he is. Our eyes met as I walked by him, me trying to see underneath. He took my hand, brushing his thumb over the top, but dropped the clasp when he saw the *Don't do that* on my face. Neil was right behind me, and the last thing I want is more questions about my love life.

We land at four, and by the time I get to my car, I'm dragging. I'm dressed in gray joggers and Converse, dreaming about a long nap. Maybe Nana has something left over from brunch.

I halt at my window, grimacing at my hair, which is

still hanging down in my face though I yearn to put it up in a ponytail. "That's what you get for letting him mark you," I mutter under my breath to my Highlander as I click the fob.

"Does the car ever answer back?"

I turn around. "In my head."

Dillon has stopped at my car. He tosses his duffle over his arm as Sawyer and Troy do a wave and head to the Escalade.

"Thank you for Friday. I needed that," he says gruffly once they're out of earshot. Heat fires in his irises as if remembering our night, and I barely hold myself back from launching my body at him, wrapping my legs around his waist, and kissing him. I want to soothe that helpless look he's been wearing since the end of the game.

But... *Thank you?*

Okay, hook-up—it's confirmed. I can deal. It's what I wanted!

I hum a response and open the back door, throwing in my overnight bag.

"Serena..." A hesitant looks flashes over his face. He heaves out a breath, and before he can say anything else about what happened between us, I jump in.

"How's your knee?"

His face clouds and he looks away. "Fine. I choked out there. I'm just not as good as Ryker."

"From what I've read, he's a lot to live up to."

"I'm not him. I've tried, I have, but..." He rakes a hand through his hair and vulnerability flashes on his face.

"Owen isn't going to steal your senior year." At the press conference after the game, Coach Alvarez announced Dillon's knee would be fine. "Coach said you'd start next week."

"Trust me, he can change his mind at any moment, just like everyone else."

"Like your dad?"

"Yeah." He rolls his neck, a contemplative expression on his face as he studies me. "So? What's up with you?"

"Me?"

"You've got your guard up. Big walls, lots of armor. You ashamed of me?"

Ah, the dropped hand. "You're Dillon McQueen, superstar. Please."

"Which you care nothing about." Worry tugs at his mouth. "Look, there's something we should talk about before we go further—"

"I'm starving, man," calls Sawyer as he leans against Dillon's car.

Dillon holds up a hand—*Wait a minute*—then takes a step toward me. His hand takes mine, and just when I think he might pull me to him and kiss me, he settles for brushing his fingers over the pulse on my wrist.

My body melts. Damn him for these romantic quirks. They're havoc on my heart.

"What should we talk about?"

Uneasiness flashes in his eyes and he flicks them to Sawyer, then back to me. "You free tomorrow night?"

"Romy needs me more since she made the hip hop team. Homework never ends. Plus, her practices run late, and she isn't allowed to drive yet. She is seventeen, but she wrecked my car, and honestly, she needs more lessons before I trust her—"

He drops his hand. "I've been chasing you, Serena. You want this?"

I know what he means by *this*. Sex. Just sex.

I swallow at the fear that swirls in my stomach.

Can I do this without getting burned?

I take a breath. "Alright. I need monogamy while we hook up. I won't be one of a string of girls. Once you get bored or I do, we'll end it."

He frowns and pulls back from me. "Not acceptable."

Cement drops on my chest, and I grapple to find the right words. All I can push out is, "I see."

He lets out a rough noise and looks up at the sky, back at me. "No, you don't *see*."

"Dillon..." My phone pings with a series of incoming texts then rings, and I snatch it out of my purse. "What?" I snap.

"Serena, baby, where are you? I'm at your place." Vane.

I sputter, "What? You can't just show up..." I dart my eyes to Dillon, tempering my tone. I turn to the side and lower my voice. "Don't do this to me."

"Give me five minutes, baby, *please*. That's all I'm asking. You owe me a conversation," he implores. "I gave you a no-contest divorce. I did what you wanted. I haven't seen your face in eighteen months. Am I asking so much?"

I curse. Vane can be a dog with a bone, especially if he's driven all the way from Memphis. Just rip the Band-Aid off and get it over with.

"Who is it?" Dillon asks, frowning.

I shake my head at him and tell Vane, "I'll give you five minutes, but not at my house. Nana..."—*might find the shotgun and shoot you*—"won't like it."

"Alright," he says softly, hope in his voice. "The park, the one with the big trees. You remember it?"

"Fine. Okay." I click off.

"That was Vane," Dillon says, and it's not a question.

My eyes avoid his. "He wants to talk."

"You still *talk* to him?" His tone is incredulous. "Fuck that."

"Not by choice. He calls me a lot. I—we didn't have closure, I guess."

A deep breath rises in his chest, and he lets it out slowly. His jaw pops. "Let me go with you."

"Dillon. No. I don't want drama or you—"

"Punching him?"

I rear back. "*No*. It's complicated. We have a history—"

"And you still love him."

I frown. "*Not* like that. He won't give up until he sees me. I know him. He's been on tour and he..." My words trail off. There's so much more I could say: *We've been through hell together, I was with him for years*, or that yeah, maybe *I need to see him*. "You don't get it because you've never been with someone for a long time."

Hurt flares in his eyes as a long breath leaves his chest. He scoffs. "Right. I'm too young to know how screwed up relationships can get. Doesn't matter that my own parents couldn't even stand to be in the same room together while I was growing up. Doesn't matter that my mom flits from guy to guy, that my dad dumped me. No, that doesn't count. I don't know jack. You're the only one who knows what it feels like to be hurt." He sticks his hands in his pockets and takes a step away from me. "I'm a womanizer. I'm not *good enough*. Hell, you don't even like football. You want to fuck me and move on."

"Dillon, I didn't word that right..." I search for more words, but I'm so unsure of where we stand. What are we?

He clearly said *I want to fuck you* at yoga.

How else am I supposed to take those words?

Last night was incredible, and yeah, I want him again —but it's terrifying.

I went skydiving once. Jumping out of the plane was

exhilarating, freefalling with the blue sky above and the green grass beneath. It felt like flying as I stared adventure straight in the eye, and it was breathtaking. Spending time with Dillon is like that, only instead of a smooth landing, I'm terrified I'm going to crash and burn.

"Dillon—"

"See you around," he mutters.

Before I can say another word, he stalks away from me.

~

I PUSH Dillon out of my head and focus on the meeting with Vane.

When I pull into the park, he's already there, leaning against a red Ferrari. My gaze sweeps over him as I get out of my car. Wearing ripped jeans and a tight black distressed shirt, he looks like the rocker he is. His hair is longer, past his shoulders, the black curls sprinkled with copper highlights. There's a new tattoo, a Day of the Dead skull, on his bicep.

Seeing his beauty is like a slap in the face, yet I know what's underneath his pretty package.

I wait for the weak feeling that comes when I catch sight of him on TV or hear his music, but...

"Nice car," I say lightly. *Play this cool, Serena.*

"Money is mighty fine." He smiles as he straightens

his lean frame and fast-walks to me. Before I can stop him, he gives me a hug. "Baby girl." He buries his face in my hair. He still smells like pine trees and man. Then, he kisses me before I can turn my cheek, his lips soft. He laughs and gazes down at me with his velvet brown eyes. "Fuck, it's good to see you."

"Don't do that," I say, untangling myself from his arms.

"Alright, alright. My bad." He takes my hand, pulling me over to a concrete table under the trees. "Remember this spot? You texted me to meet you here, then told me you were pregnant—"

"And you asked me to marry you." I sit down, my legs fidgeting. We sat at this very table and talked for four hours that day. I loved him, but underneath I was unsure that he was as committed as I was. He held my hands and painted a glorious picture of us with a family. He told me how perfect it would be. He promised he'd be a good husband.

I believed him.

He drinks me in, amazement on his face, and I shift around, feeling twitchy. He, of course, is relaxed and easy—because he's gotten what he wants.

"How are you?" I ask.

He pushes hair out of his face. "I miss you like crazy. Every time I sing your song, I wanna cry, baby."

"Vane...don't..."

He shrugs, looking away from me. "Right. It's been a hard year. The tour killed, but it's a lot of work. Traveling, the schedule, the cramped bus with the guys... It was getting to me. I need to feel free, ya know?"

"Hmm."

"We've got a new manager and a contract with Ecko. They've got big plans for us. The fame is cool, but I need space to work on new music. So, I'm back. For you." His eyes come back to me. "You never gave me a chance to explain or see you, baby. You sent those divorce papers, and I signed them. I wronged you, I cut you deep, but what you saw, that girl—I didn't even know who she was."

Words I've heard before on the phone.

"That just makes it worse." My words are flat. "She wasn't the only one, right? All those pretty girls in the VIP room must have been tempting."

He brushes at a skull ring on his finger, not meeting my eyes. "I was lonely, baby. It's the lifestyle, Serena, but it won't happen again. If I'd known you were coming to Nashville—"

Anger rushes in like a tidal wave, but my words are soft. "You would have arranged to not be getting your dick sucked? I miscarried. I wanted to see you. And boy, did I ever."

"*Baby, I'm sorry,*" he implores.

I study his face, the lines of tension, his twisted mouth.

"We can work on it," he says in a rush. "Come to Memphis with me, move your stuff into my place, and when the tour starts, come with us. I'll never be out of your sight. Come on, we've been through some shit, Serena, but we still love each other. We made a baby."

"The condom broke. It wasn't on purpose."

"You wanted our baby."

Grief hits me in the face as I grind out my words. "I did, so much. Stop manipulating me with it. It hurts, Vane!"

He grimaces and pulls at his hair. "I made a mistake, and you taught me a good lesson, but you can't just throw it all away. *Baby girl.* We belong together."

A sound of disbelief comes from me. I taught him a lesson? Divorcing him wasn't a game I played. He cheated on me! He thinks if I babysit him, he won't do it again? I'm not his mother.

My hands fidget and I temper my tone. "I care about you as a person, Vane, but I have a life here. Grad school, remember? Romy needs me. I can't just leave her. I don't want to. I spent too much time with you, away from her, and she got in some trouble."

"Bring her."

"No."

"You can write anywhere. Give me a chance. All you need is me. We *were* happy."

I sit back and stare at him. Were we? Or was I always

jumping when he snapped his fingers, supporting him, putting my family on hold? Romy did drugs. My grades suffered. I barely graduated with a decent GPA. He's always put himself first, his music, his career. He hasn't once asked how *I* am.

As if he senses my train of thought, he says, "I took you for granted, but I'll rebuild our trust." His throat bobs. "Where's the girl who fell in love with me in one night?"

That girl was needy and naïve. She was looking for something to fill the void left by the death of her parents. I'm older now. Smarter. "She's not me."

He jerks up from the table and paces around, hands clenched.

I rise with him. "I came out of respect for what we had, and because I knew you needed to hear it from me in person. I'm done," I say softly. "Move on, Vane. Write your beautiful music and become a superstar."

"I don't want to." His voice is dejected as his shoulders slump. "No one gets me like you. You're real, baby. I could write an entire album with songs just about you."

I sigh. "Maybe it's all about fate, about *when* you meet someone. The timing wasn't right for us—"

He holds my eyes. "You loved me once—"

"I deserve better," I say sharply.

A bird chirps in a tree, a car horn sounds somewhere in the distance, and the world turns as he lets my words sink in. He paces back and forth as the silence settles around us.

Whether he accepts it or not, I have. "Your five minutes are up." I stand and he rushes over to me, his eyes shiny.

He takes my hands. "You're really not coming back to me?"

Oh, Vane. Never in a million years. "No."

We stare at each other for a long time. He lets out a long breath, his hands cupping my face. "Baby girl. Whoever he is—because I know there's someone—I hope he deserves you."

21

Serena

Welcome to Theta's Man of Mystery! is splashed across a plastic banner hanging over the library door. Underneath is scrawled *Talk to a Stranger and Fall in Love.* Little hearts dance around the words.

I scoff as I halt, digging my heels in. "No way, girls. Better yet, *hell* no. Don't care if I go through a pack of batteries in a week—my bullet is better than some kind of what, speed dating thing?"

"What's a bullet?" Bambi asks, pulling me by the arm, undeterred.

"Vibrator. Tiny and *very* effective," Chantal replies to Bambi, latching onto my other side.

"Oh," Bambi murmurs thoughtfully. "Are they on Amazon?"

"Yes," Chantal says. "They come in all colors. Mine is purple."

"Forget the bullet, girls. Am I a prisoner?" I ask dryly.

"Yes," they chorus.

"Okay, so let's see if I have this right: you waited for me after yoga, said you had something I had to see, then you woman-handle me into walking into a trap to meet mystery men? No."

Bambi smiles, waving her hands at me. "So dramatic. It's a new event to raise money for a local women's shelter. Where's your Theta sense of sisterhood? Your love for helping others? Don't you want to contribute to the community? More importantly, where's your intrinsic drive to mate with a hottie?"

"Dead," I chirp. I had sex with Dillon; I might be good for another eighteen months.

She titters. "We have some sexy applicants. Not surprised—we *are* the best sorority." She turns and, as a trio, we do our secret handshake. In the glass reflection of the door, I see the goofy grin on my face.

"And you just might meet someone nice," Chantal adds.

"I'm in leggings and flip-flops! Worse, I'm sweaty. Also, it's dark—"

"It's eight in the evening. God, you're old," Chantal says as she elbows me.

"Come on, Serena. You're bored and lonely." Bambi

pulls my hair out of my ponytail and arranges it around my shoulders. "They can't see you anyway. It's like that show *The Dating Game*, only we made it better. This event is about getting to know someone—without seeing them. You might meet Mr. Right."

"I'm not lonely." I haven't seen or talked to Dillon in four days, and I miss him. I keep expecting him to pop up wherever I am, and he hasn't. A long sigh slides through my lips.

"As far as I'm aware—and I would know since I'm part of the committee—no football players signed up, so you don't have to worry about *you know who* being here, if you were," Chantal says.

"I wasn't."

Bambi pulls out a tiny glass bottle and spritzes me. I bat it away, even though it does smell nice.

"Settle down, it's just some Louis Vuitton perfume. Free sample in the mail. Score."

"We did help you write your article for the LSU game," Chantal reminds me, a gleam in her eyes.

I heave out a breath. "Fine, but I'm only staying for half an hour. That's it. After that—"

They squeal.

"I'm a firm believer in love at first sight. My dad fell for my mom in a heartbeat," Bambi gushes.

"My parents hate each other, but don't listen to me,"

Chantal says with a grin. "Honestly, we just need more participants."

I don't believe her as I take in the line of guys and girls waltzing into the library, most of them dressed for going to the club...

Screw it. I *have* been lonely.

Monday night, I consumed a pint of ice cream as I rewatched *Shaun of the Dead*. On Tuesday, I outlined a fluff story called "How To Suck at Paintball But Win"—kind of on the nose, but I'll fix it later. Then earlier today, I almost texted him when I thought I saw him inside the student center.

"Let's rock this," I grouse.

Another squeal.

The young girl at the entrance to the main lobby glances up at the officers on either side of me. She almost does a curtsey. Ah, I recall those days of pledging.

"We've brought fresh meat," Chantal says to the pledge.

The girl at the podium takes my name, cell number, and email then passes me a piece of paper that resembles some kind of scorecard and tips on dating.

"Ticket, please, or if you don't have one, it's a hundred dollars," the pledge says.

I gasp, nearly running out the door.

"No need for that. She's a sister," Chantal pronounces, as if I'm the queen of England.

The girl smiles at me brightly. "Welcome! Please proceed upstairs to Room 100. They'll make announcements there and explain the rules."

"Rules?"

Bambi pats me. "When you frown, it makes lines on your forehead."

I give her my fake smile.

"Creepy. And don't squint. Try again."

"We can't all look like Mila Kunis—"

"Funny," she says as we walk up the stairs and enter the spacious room, taking seats in the back.

"One of the Kappa guys is explaining how it works," Chantal murmurs. "You made us late."

"I didn't intend to come!" I whisper ferociously. "Where's Ashley?"

"Oh, she's behind the scenes getting everything organized," Bambi says.

The guy on stage is dressed in slacks and a lavender Ralph Lauren shirt. He says his name is Kevin and goes into a spiel about how their fraternity has partnered with the Thetas to benefit the Magnolia Women's Shelter, giving details about the importance of the facility and the cost of maintenance. I listen while scanning the crowd. There are about twenty-five girls, none of them familiar. The guys must be in a separate room.

"...women will be assigned small rooms, one of the study carrels, on the third floor. If you've never been to the top floor, just take the stairs right outside the door here. The men will rotate rooms. You'll have seven minutes to get to know each other—*seven minutes in heaven*, I like to say. Heh." Kevin smirks. "After that, a buzzer will sound and the men will move to the next room."

A hand in the front goes up. "What if we want to leave with our dates and go somewhere private?" It's a girl in a Chi-O jersey.

He smiles. "Leave at your discretion, but we'd prefer that you stay and meet everyone. We've got a great group, and you might find more than one match."

She stands up and looks around. "Are there any football players present, specifically Dillon McQueen?"

"Please, girl, sit your ass down," Chantal grumbles under her breath. "Gah, I hate that I was as desperate as she was to hang with them. I'm *still* doing it."

"You love the game," I insist.

I focus on Kevin as he replies to the girl. "The guys are in another room, getting their instructions. It wouldn't be any fun if we all knew who was here, would it?"

More murmuring comes from the crowd, the excitement rising. Another girl stands and asks a question, her blonde hair billowing in loose waves down her back, her halter dress tight and clingy. There's a cute pink cloche on her head.

"Alexa, play 'Raspberry Beret' by Prince," I murmur.

"Who are you talking to?" Chantal hisses.

"Myself. It happens." I blow at a piece of hair in my face then sniff my armpits. Deodorant still works. No date clothes, but hey, I smell like cucumber.

Kevin continues with, "Each female has been assigned an ID number and a scorecard for her mystery man. Simply turn that in at the end of the event, and our computers will tally up your best matches along with photos of the men you liked. Will he be what you thought? Will he like you?" He grins, a hint of slyness on his face. "That's up for you to decide—after you both receive your match's phone number."

Great. If there are the same number of guys and each one gets seven minutes, this event is going to last almost three hours. I twitch in my chair. Yeah…so? What else do I have to do? Romy is situated for the night.

After the introduction is done, we head up to the third floor, and I'm assigned a room at the end of the hall near the stairwell, tucked between nonfiction shelves. Seems appropriate that I skim them and grab *How To Unf*ck Yourself*. If the dates get boring, I can always do some self-improving.

Bambi and Chantal have wandered off to do their duties for the event, and it's a pledge that leads me inside the room. It's on the small side, about six by six, a desk with a partition in the middle.

"That's so you can't see faces," the girl tells me as I

settle into the seat. She instructs me to tuck my feet in since they would be visible if I didn't, and I scoff.

"You think he'll recognize me by shoes?"

She shrugs, unconcerned. "Use the tip sheet for questions, and there's a buzzer if you need help—"

"Help?"

"If he comes on too strong—or if you do."

"Don't lunge for the mystery man, got it."

"Have fun," she calls as she slips out the door, and I exhale, glaring at the flimsy plywood in front of me. Will we even be able to hear each other through this thing?

I glance at the tip sheet. *What's your favorite color? What type of music do you enjoy?* and so on. Meh. I mark them out and pencil in a few of my own. I read through the directions again.

A bell rings, people move out in the hall, and my door opens. Heavy breathing and a cough are the first things I notice, and I almost peek around to see if he needs me to resuscitate him.

"Are you okay?" I ask as he takes his seat. Looking down, I note the skinny jeans and leather flip-flops. His big toe is remarkably tiny.

He clears his throat, then another racking cough comes from his chest. "Just a cold. I think I have a fever."

I don't recognize the voice, although I didn't expect to. "Oh. Well, uh, I hate to be uptight before we even get started, but my nana has a heart condition and COPD, and my sister has asthma, so if you don't mind, please scoot your chair back."

"Seriously? There's wood in front of us."

"Yes."

He huffs and scoots back. When I ask him *Would you rather live in a universe set in* The Office *or* Game of Thrones? his reply is *TV is destroying young minds*. No, no it isn't. I give up and let him talk about his crappy roommate who steals his clean underwear. Apparently, not seeing your date's face encourages people to vent.

Another guy arrives, and after he tells me he likes his women to call him Sexy Daddy in bed, I zone out. Is this all I've missed in a year and a half of being without a man? I text Romy to see how her homework is progressing. She sends me screenshots of math problems and I text back directions. Multitasking.

By the time the seventh date leaves—yes, I'm counting—I'm bored out of my head and ready to jump across the partition and dash for my car.

The next guy walks in and sits as I put my phone away.

"Hey." His voice is low and deep, like silk over steel, and I'm instantly at attention, prickles of awareness skating down my spine.

"Hey," I reply.

There's a beat of silence, and it goes on too long. I shift

in my chair as I glance down at his shoes: orange Converse. Nah, no way.

I clear my throat. "Um, first off, I'm in grad school. What year are you?"

His leg moves, stretching out. "Senior." His tone has changed, more alert. "What's your favorite color?"

I sigh. "Do we really have to do those?"

"What color?" he insists.

"Blue? I've never thought about it. Yours?"

"Topaz."

"So yellow?"

"You say tomato, I say Bloody Mary."

"Funny. I like those. Do you put bacon in your Bloody Mary?"

"With cheese and peppers. Give me all the spices."

I relax back in the chair. "Ever eat the celery?"

"Most vile thing to land on my tongue."

I laugh under my breath. "Fun fact: celery stalks can reach over three feet."

Another long pause. Then, "I'm picturing one coming to life and grabbing me with stringy arms."

"Me too. Terrifying, right?"

"Hmm. Almost as scary as running through the woods in the dark."

My breath hitches, and I swallow as nerves hit. I can't think of a single original question, so I resort to the list. "Um, let's see...biggest fear?"

The silence builds. I squirm. It's him, it is... Does he know it's me? Bambi and Chantal either didn't know he was here or told a whopper of a lie.

"Hello?" I inquire.

"Creatures with wings, I guess. Birds, chickens. They freak me out. When I was a kid, my brother got pecked by a cardinal. Scared the heck out of me." He lets out a small laugh.

"But...they're so...nonviolent?"

He scoffs. "Ever see a hawk eat a cute chipmunk? I have."

"I see. What are you looking for in a girl you date?"

My lungs squeeze as he shifts closer, his other leg stretching out. I can almost picture how tall he is, trying to get comfortable in the small chair. "Someone different from everyone else."

"How?"

"She won't care about my talent."

"What's your talent?"

A pause. "Lacrosse."

My breath snags. "I, um, hear it's a complicated game."

He hesitates. "Yeah, there's a...stick with a net on the end."

Oh, really... "I believe it's called a *pocket*."

"Like I said, you say tomato—"

"I say salsa."

He laughs. "Anyway, my girl, I'll want to give her things, gifts, maybe a shirt with *my* name on it—is that stupid?"

"No," I whisper.

"She'll care about people, especially her family. She'll be fiery, a little terror at times. She'll like my friends. She'll listen to me when I tell her my secrets."

"You have secrets?"

"I keep things close. She'll be the kind of girl who likes yoga. Fun fact: yoga is good for loosening your pelvic muscles—in surprising ways."

"Yeah?"

"What about you? Who's your perfect date?"

You.

I bite my lip as my mind fills with images of Dillon running with me through the woods, using me as a decoy, laughing when I shot Bullseye, laughing again when I shot Troy, not getting pissy when I shot him. "He's the kind of guy who doesn't give up on me, even when I'm not sure which way to turn."

My head goes back to our last conversation at the airport. "I want him to leave his ego at the door and not care that I have a whole set of baggage. I've been through a bad relationship, and I've learned hard lessons. Caring for someone, putting yourself out there... It's like a beautiful butterfly in your hand. If you hold really still and *try* to do everything right, it might stay, but you're going to flinch, and when you do, it might fly away." I stare down at my hands. "I sacrificed pieces of myself for him, gave up friends, family, goals. I can't do that again."

Tension tumbles into the room, the sound of his breaths low, yet I'm tuned in, counting them. I hear him ease forward, closer to the partition. *"Je promets d'être bon avec toi."*

I promise to be good to you.

"Serena…" His voice is rough.

The room feels hot, and I inhale. "You scare me, Dillon."

He pauses as if searching for the right words. "What if you stop being afraid of how it ends and enjoy the ride? Nothing is certain. Life is fleeting. I lost a brother, a biological father, grandparents. It changes a person, and you get it. People see me as some kind of, I don't know, hotshot guy, but deep down there's only a few things I want: football, my dad's approval, and someone authentic. We had sex. Okay, acknowledged. It was amazing, so what the hell are we doing now?"

My fists curl at his fevered words. I take a deep breath, processing.

"Are you over Vane?"

"I'm not in love with him anymore. I had to see him, Dillon. It's like the ending of a book. It's finished."

He pauses. "You must have figured out that I'm not

interested in just hooking up, Serena. I guess...I snapped when he called."

Long seconds pass as my heart hammers.

"What are you thinking?" he asks.

A long sigh comes from my chest. "I wish..." I close my eyes, praying for bravery. "I wish you'd come over here and kiss me."

He snaps out of his seat and appears in front of me. With careful hands, he pulls me up to face him.

22

Serena

What happens when two people confess secrets then sit across from each other in a restaurant and look each other in the eyes? You'd think shyness or at least a few hesitant looks, but we do neither. He sits next to me in the booth and holds my hand inside Sugar's, a popular gathering place near campus. We can't stop staring at each other. A plate of cheese fries on the table is being ignored.

Dipping my head, I laugh.

His thumb caresses my hand. "What's so funny?"

"Those Thetas' faces when we ran for the stairwell. That Chi-O who heard your voice and came out of her room and ran at you."

He looks away uncertainly. "That bugs you."

I smile wryly. "You were with me, so I think I'll live. Her calling me a slut—well, that's just plain old mean and wrong for her as well. If you'd let me explain to her what that word does to women, it could have been a great teaching moment, but no, you had to swing me up on your back and run—"

"Wanted you to myself."

"And here we are...in a crowded restaurant."

"Your stomach was growling," he protests, laughing as a sheepish expression appears. "Besides, we need an official date besides Cadillac's, paintball, and hotel sex."

"You forgot the tryouts. Did Chantal and Bambi bring you to the event?"

"Yep."

"Those little devils. Did you know I was there?"

"Yeah."

"And your dates?"

"I can't recall a word they said. Was looking for you."

Satisfaction swirls inside me as I pick up a fry and stick it in my mouth while he watches. I give him one and he eats it out of my hand, his tongue sliding against my finger. Being close to him, like this, in a way with walls down, is liberating. Long after he's eaten the fry, my hand lingers on his face, touching the sharp jawline, his full lips, the way his eyebrows arch. I'm in Dillon overload.

"I still have questions for you," he murmurs. "Why is

there a light in the fridge if we shouldn't eat at night?" He grins. "I made up my own questions to mess with them."

"Me too!" I laugh, and he watches me with an intensity I'm getting used to.

"How 'bout this: would you rather be completely hairless or as hairy as a gorilla?" he asks.

I sputter. "Sweater back, so gross. Hairless."

"Son of a nutcracker, I figured since you had a thing for Bigfoot..."

He swoops in and kisses me.

"Y'all are disgusting," is the phrase that brings our eyes off each other. We turn, and Chantal, Bambi, Sawyer, and Troy are standing next to our table. It's Chantal who's spoken, but there's amusement in her voice. They plop down across from us, Sawyer grabbing chairs to pull up for him and Troy.

Dillon groans. "How did you find us?"

Bambi gives him a *Don't you wish you knew* look then smiles. "We drove around until we saw your Escalade."

"My sorority sisters won't leave me alone," I tell Dillon. "Apparently, they're setting me up on dates now."

He throws an arm around me. "You don't seem sad about it."

I whisper in his ear as the others order from the waitress. "I have five bottles of cheap champagne in my fridge. Don't know why I bought them except I keep anticipating you popping the cork, pouring it over me and licking it off..."

He gives me a smoldering glance. "You ready to go?"

"Alright!" Chantal says with a clap before I can reply. "Who's up for some poppin' duet singing?"

Groans and protests come from the guys.

She ignores them and struts to the stage, looking over her shoulder. "It's karaoke night, and it must not be missed. Dillon and Serena, y'all do 'Shallow' by Lady Gaga and Bradley Cooper or 'Islands in the Stream' by Dolly and Kenny. Which will it be?"

I jump up. "If I'm gonna sing, it's my pick! How about—"

Dillon's eyes widen. "Oh, God, no, Serena. I'm not getting up there. I can't sing. Anything but that. Please."

He rises anyway, his hand linking with mine.

"You're gonna die of embarrassment, especially considering your ex," he grouses.

Sawyer calls out, "He can hold a ball but not a tune!"

Dillon flips them off, and I jump into his arms, ignoring the catcalls from our friends. "I don't care how you sing—it's that you're willing to do it with me. I need you, Dillon, to sing a song with me. Will you?"

His arms flex as he holds me. "Pick something easy."

"Hmmm. How about an Elton John and Kiki Dee duet?"

"'Don't Go Breaking My Heart?'" He pops an eyebrow. "Is that a subliminal message?"

"Mmmm."

I'm ready for this crazy thing with him. I'm along for the rollercoaster ride, and I know the end waits for me. It might hurt, but for right now, I'm hanging on for dear life.

"Let's enjoy this," I say, repeating his earlier words, keeping my fear buried deep.

23

Serena

Rustling sounds bring me awake as I pop my head out of the covers. I tend to sleep burrowed down deep. Dillon has gotten out of bed and is pulling his jeans on. His back's to me as he peeks out my window, and a slow smile curls my lips. Last night we ended up back at my place after hanging out at Sugar's. We walked in the door, got the important parts of us undressed, and had unrefined, furious sex on the couch. I couldn't get him inside me fast enough, and he was the same, his groan when he slid in loud enough to wake the dead. When we finally did get our clothes off, he spread me out on the kitchen table and took me slow and careful, dragging out his strokes, his hands gripping my hips as I went over the edge and saw stars. We eventually made it to my bed.

It just made sense for him to stay the night. *Of course.* Too fast? At this point, I refuse to think about it.

He slips his shirt on and I sigh at the loss of the view.

"It's five in the morning," I murmur, and he looks over his shoulder.

"Did I wake you? I was trying to be quiet."

"Running with Owen?"

"Yeah, and I don't want your nana to see me leaving." He runs his hands through his hair, straightening his bedhead. I like him like this. I like everything about him. His intelligence, his complexity, his sense of humor, his words last night...

I scoot up to the headboard, the camisole strap slipping down my shoulder. "Coffee?"

"Nah, go back to sleep. It's too early."

"I'm not sleepy." I feel alive and exhilarated. I pick up his pillow and take a long breath in.

A smile twitches his lips as he bends over the bed and gives me a kiss. "You like my pheromones."

"Vanilla and man—what's not to like?" He nuzzles my neck, and my fingers start undoing his jeans. "Is it creepy that I want to roll you in sugar, dip you in chocolate, cover you in whipped cream, and devour you? I swear I'm not a cannibal."

"Attraction at first sniff. You smell like cherries."

"Shampoo, thank you for entrancing the football player."

He kisses me fast and hard. "You have no idea." He pauses. "Did you kiss anyone your freshman year at the bonfire?"

I pull his jaw to me. "The legend again? You're the only man I've kissed at a bonfire."

My hands have managed to push his jeans down, and I stroke his thick shaft. His crown is mushroom-shaped, a pearl of white at the tip. Rising up, I take him in my mouth.

He groans, his hands in my hair. "Serena..."

"No run?" I say as my tongue licks up his hard length.

"No run," he says gruffly as he pulls me up and kisses me.

I ease away and stand up, whipping my cami and thong off. I let my panties dangle on my finger as I throw him a glance over my shoulder. "I'm going to shower."

"Now?" His heated eyes stroke over me.

"Hmmm."

He jumps off the bed and stalks toward me. He whips his shirt off. "Not without me."

I giggle. "So macho."

"This body is all yours, Dandelion." He sweeps me up and into his arms and carries me to the bathroom.

∽

Dear Asking for a Friend,

Recently I reconnected with an old flame from college. We were the perfect couple. People said we "belonged together", and I fell deeply in love. After we graduated, he moved to Seattle for a job. We tried long distance, but it didn't work, and he broke up with me.

Now, he's back in town and begging me for another chance, but I'm torn. I never got over him, but how can I trust that this time it's for real? Please help. I don't want another broken heart.

Torn in Magnolia

Dear TIM,

Truth? There are no perfect couples or relationships. Heck, I'm still upset over Brad Pitt and Jennifer Aniston's divorce—then Justin Theroux. Tears. Why can't she find love?

The fear of risking our hearts is scary. (Alexa, play "Love Hurts" by Joan Jett.) Yet, it's this humble writer's opinion that by pushing him away, you might miss out on something wonderful. Perhaps the timing is right. Give yourself an opportunity to discover if this is real. I say, roll the dice and take a chance.

~Asking For a Friend

. . .

I HIT SEND ON the column and stretch my back as I rise from the chair in the campus library. I smile. I'm rolling the dice with Dillon—

The thought is cut short when my phone rings and several students turn to glare at me.

I snatch it up, keeping my voice low. "Serena Jensen."

"Ah, Miss Jensen, this is Headmaster Roberts at Magnolia Prep."

His voice is official and stern, and I stiffen. "I see. How can I help?"

"Yes, well, I need you to come in today. Right now if possible. I have Romy in my office. She's been suspended for two weeks."

"For what?" I yell, startling students. I'm already shoving my laptop into my bag.

"I'd prefer to discuss it in person."

I exhale. "I'll be there in fifteen minutes."

Moving through the tables, I take the stairs and dart outside, my mind swirling with what she could have done. My cell pings with another text, and I check it as I walk to my car.

Hey. I'm done early today. Where are you?

I bite my lip. Dillon. It's been two weeks of us together, nights of bingeing TV shows and video games and sex. Every time he walks in my apartment, I melt into his arms. His kisses are addictive. The sex is mind-blowing. The way he spoons me afterward and traces little hearts on my back makes me weak in the knees. I'm walking a tightrope with him, teetering as I try to keep my heart locked away.

But Romy... Crap! I send him a text explaining what's going on and that I'll see him later. He tries to call me back when I'm driving, but I focus on traffic and getting to the school.

I park and enter Magnolia Prep, noting the fancy artwork on the walls, the elegant wallpaper in the office, the plush leather chairs. It's a far cry from my public school education. "Should be at twenty grand a year," I mutter.

The secretary buzzes the headmaster, and he opens his door to usher me inside, face unsmiling. Romy sits in a chair, eyes red as if she's been crying.

Mr. Roberts and I greet each other with pleasantries, which are insincere on both sides. He's in his sixties, rather cold, and not as personable as you'd expect from someone in a job dealing with students. I thought so the first time I met him. He takes in my boots and curls his lip.

Whatever.

I take my seat just as the headmaster moves behind his desk.

The door opens and Dillon walks in.

My mouth opens.

He moves toward the headmaster and takes his outstretched hand in a firm grasp. "Dillon McQueen, sir."

The headmaster rears back. "I know who you are. You've been here several times for assemblies. Just didn't expect you to walk in—"

"I'm Serena's boyfriend. Thought I should be here." He unleashes a lethal fake smile for him, then gives me a kiss on the cheek. He tugs on Romy's hair and takes a seat.

"I see," Mr. Roberts says.

The headmaster sits, clears his throat, and proceeds to explain how Romy was caught skipping classes and smoking an e-cigarette in the theatre room. He slyly mentions her past infraction with marijuana at the public school then pompously outlines their tobacco policy. "It's not allowed indoors or out at our esteemed institution. Besides the suspension, she won't be able to compete in her dance competitions during that time," he says as he wraps up and folds his hands on the desk.

My chest rises. I watched Romy on and off while he talked, her eyes pleading with me, and now she blurts out, "Serena, I swear, I was not smoking! I skipped class, okay, I did that. But someone left the drama room when the bell rang, and the e-thing was just sitting there on the chair, and I—"

"It was in your hand, Miss Jensen," the headmaster says. "The drama teacher wrote it down on the incident report—"

"Let her finish," I say quietly, but not meekly. I know when Romy is lying. She gets twitchy and her eyes won't hold mine. Right now she's looking straight at me.

"Serena, you know how much hip hop means to me." Her head dips. "And I know how expensive this place is and how hard you work…" She stops, her eyes filling with tears. "I didn't do it."

"I believe you," I murmur. Yes, we went through a tough time getting her adjusted to Magnolia Prep, but she knows this school is her last option.

Relief floods her face. She turns back to the headmaster and puts her hands together in a praying expression. "Sir, I skipped calculus, that is true, but I wasn't smoking. My nana quit because of COPD. I know about the evils of tobacco."

Good, Romy, good.

"Then who *was* vaping?" he asks, a glower on his face.

Dillon leans forward. "Kids who tattle get labeled and bullied. This is a gray area, and while I understand your concern about tobacco products on school grounds, she's telling you it wasn't hers. Case closed in my eyes."

"Mr. McQueen, I'm a fan of yours, very much so, but I fail to see how your input matters."

"It matters," Romy snipes.

"Romy…" I warn.

Dillon straightens his shoulders, his eyes hard. "I just want Romy to get a fair shake."

This *is* a gray area, but she can't get suspended. Her grades will suffer. Her college applications... I exhale. "Romy, do you know who the e-cigarette belonged to?"

Romy crosses her arms. "I'm no snitch, but I also don't know who left it. Yes, I picked it up and looked at it. Did I put my mouth on someone else's nasty germs? No. Gross! There is no reason to suspend me!"

"Lower your voice," I tell her.

"Is there proof?" Dillon asks. "Perhaps video from a security camera?"

Romy nods eagerly. "Yeah!"

"Unfortunately, no, not in that section of the theatre," the headmaster says. "But in her past, she's been known—"

"You're basing her guilt on an incident that occurred at another school—over a year ago," I say. "Mr. Roberts, my sister may not have the best grades, but she is honest. She owns up to her mistakes. It wasn't hers. Therefore, the only consequence she should face is the fact that she skipped a class, which I would imagine happens frequently with teenagers. Don't you agree?"

He frowns as he squints at Romy's magenta-streaked hair. "Your sister has a history with drugs."

Why can't he let that go? Everybody makes mistakes!

"But your board gave her a second chance, and we appreciate that. That said, a headmaster who declares someone guilty without proof, well, that's extremely unfair," I say.

"Life is often unfair, Miss Jensen," is his curt reply. "Perhaps you're too young to realize that."

He wants to patronize *me*? I lost both parents on the same day! I know how life can suck. My hands clench, annoyance ratcheting up. What would a mom do? How do I handle this? My instinct is to jump over his desk and shake him, but...

"Are you aware I write for the *Gazette*?"

Dillon nods, catching on. "She's a great reporter. She uncovered a secret leather cult at the Piggly Wiggly."

I told him how I imagined him that night in the Pig.

"PETA was involved," I add. "I would, of course, be reluctant to write anything troublesome about this fine, prestigious school. However, the owner of the paper is Warren Bryson, an old family friend. One mention of this, and I may not be able to stop him from asking me to investigate other incidents here."

If the headmaster believes I'd write him in a bad light, he's damn right I would, but I'm not sure Warren would publish it. We aren't that tight. I'm grasping at straws, but keep my face flat as I stare at Mr. Roberts. My eyes say *Just try me. I may be young and small, but I will come at you like a mama bear if you mess with Romy.*

The headmaster sputters, and before he can answer, I

stand up and clear my throat. "Go to class, Romy. I've got this."

She hesitates, giving me a harried, worried look, then scurries out of the room, her skirt swishing as she shuts the door.

Dillon stands with me. "Anything else, Headmaster?"

He blinks, darting his eyes from me to Dillon. He opens his mouth, shuts it. "Fine. I'll compromise. Five days of detention after school. She'll have to sit out this week's competition."

I'll take it.

"Thank you," I say to the headmaster as Dillon opens the door for me.

We don't speak until we're outside on the sidewalk.

"We work well together," he murmurs. "By the way, you're badass. The way you told Romy to go to class, the way you tossed in the reporter thing—"

"Why did you come?" My head spins, reeling from the confrontation and the fact that he showed up to help. I shouldn't be surprised since he came to the tryouts, but this feels different.

"Because I care, Serena."

My heart skips a beat. I lick my lips as my eyes dart over to him, taking in his chiseled jawline, those broad shoulders, his searching eyes.

"Where's your car?" I ask, my voice low.

His breathing deepens. "You thinking what I'm thinking?"

"Hmm."

"In the back of the lot. My windows are tinted super dark. Like pitch black. No one can see a thing. It's probably illegal for them to be that dark."

"Lead the way." My legs move faster, following him.

We reach his car and I fidget as he pops the locks. I jump in the passenger side and unbutton my shirt with fingers that shake. My skirt is off in five seconds. I leave my underwear and boots on, impatiently watching as he whips his shirt off and unbuttons his pants. He doesn't get them down fast enough, and I pull at them, jerking his underwear and shoes off and tossing them to the floor. He undoes the laces on my boots and throws them over his head.

We don't speak, our breaths fast. He crawls to the back and pulls me to him. I straddle his hips as he unsnaps my bra and sucks a nipple into his mouth, lashing it with flicks of his tongue then moving to the other. I roll my hips against his hard length, and he hisses.

"I want you so bad..." he says breathily. He kisses me long and hard, his fingers digging into my hips as my body clenches. "Think we'll get suspended?"

"Might get arrested."

"You're a rebel," he murmurs.

"You like it."

"Fuck me, I do. Serena..." he groans and kisses me like a man who needs me to breathe. "You slay me."

"Let's do this fast."

"Not too fast."

"Make me come, football player."

"My pleasure." He rips my thong into pieces and I nearly combust right there. We fumble with a condom, barely get it on, and he sinks inside me. We pause for a second, both of us exhaling. He holds my eyes, slides out, and fucks me hard, using his hands to pull me up and down. He pants, his chest heaving as sweat dusts his skin. I can't breathe as he bites my shoulder then presses a delicate kiss there.

His fingers dig into my scalp to get closer, but we can't be any closer. I'm consumed with every nuance, his deep thrusts, my name on his lips, the flutter of his lashes. I take his mouth and suck on his tongue.

He palms my breasts, his fingers rolling my erect nipples. I moan, my head dropping back as my hips swivel to meet his, rubbing my clit against his pelvis. Incomparable passion roars like a lion in my veins.

He wraps his arms around me as we fuck. "Never. Get. Enough," is wrenched from the depths of his throat as he yanks on my hair, pulling me to him for a scorching kiss.

This. Him. Us.

Is it crazy that I want everything?

24

Dillon

Several days later, I park in front of Serena's apartment. I'm exhausted and rattled from our away game Saturday against Ole Miss, which we barely won. I missed her in the stadium. Since the LSU game, the *Gazette* requested she only report home games.

Serena.

I twist my hands around the steering wheel as tension rolls over me. I think about her at the oddest times, when I'm in class, in the library, the locker room. I dig her quirkiness, her smirks, her complexity, the way she takes care of Romy, her banging body...

I'm wrapped up in her, taking each day as it comes. When I'm with her, I'm on top of the world, but when I'm not, worry creeps in. Like now.

The challenge... I worry it's going to drive a wedge

between us if she finds out. A long exhalation leaves my chest. She might even break up with me. Fear lances through me as I scrub my jaw. I can't lose her; I just found her.

I kick the worry down and head to the front door of the house. Nancy meets me wearing jorts, an AC/DC shirt, flip-flops, and a straw hat with pink roses and ribbons that hang down the back. A button is pinned on the front and reads *Don't Hula Hoop Without A Bra*.

"About time you got here! Who shows up late for a day trip with the granny—for her birthday? Go inside and get my beer."

I laugh as I wave the dozen pink roses in my hand. "I brought flowers. Happy Birthday!"

She clutches them, taking a big sniff. "Good boy."

"How's Turo?"

A sigh of disappointment comes from her. "Not coming. He delivered my gift last night. Did I tell you he's Italian? When he says *mozzarella*, I melt. Oh, that's funny."

I dig her family. Nana is a hoot and Romy is great. Julian hasn't spent time with me yet, so that's still up for debate.

She hands me back the flowers. "Put them in a vase for me? They're under the sink. I need to go check my hat again. Don't forget my beer. It's in the kitchen in the good cooler."

"Where are we going?" I ask as we walk inside the house.

"How do you feel about ostriches?" she calls over her shoulder as she disappears down the hall.

I answer even though she's gone. "Birds, in general, are vicious monsters—"

"Dude, you're scared! Yeah, Serena let it slip," Romy says gleefully as she joins me in the foyer. She's wearing jeans and a Magnolia Prep green shirt. She gives me a fist bump.

"Dillon McQueen is a warrior. He fears nothing," I say. "Also, birds are evil."

Nancy comes out from what I assume is her bedroom. "I need you to drive. Is it okay if I bring Betty? Buster hates birds like you, so he's staying home."

A dog in my sweet ride? I just cleaned it. "Where are we going, again?"

A gleam grows in her eyes. "Safari park."

"In Mississippi?" My voice is incredulous.

"Yep. Some elk, buffalo, camels, llamas. Can Betty come? It is my birthday and you're dating my granddaughter—the best one."

"Hey!" Romy says. "Right here!"

"You're my favorite too," Nancy says and pats her head.

I smile. "What's dog hair when llamas are scratching my car?"

"Knew it. Keeper," she says then sashays past me and out the door.

I make my way through the house, taking everything in. The furniture is faded but cared for, the counters spotless, the wooden floor shiny. I grab the 'good' cooler, a ragged Styrofoam container that looks like it's more duct tape than foam. Inside are bottles of Bud Light and ice. "Nancy, I need to introduce you to Fat Tire," I muse on a laugh.

"She bought that cooler twenty years ago and treats it like a baby. Something about a man, a concert, and an enlightening afternoon." A chuckle comes from Serena as she comes down the stairs.

My chest unloosens as I take her in, some of that worry evaporating.

She's wearing a pair of orange harem pants and a cropped top. Her hair is down, the copper shining, and I resist the urge to kiss her senseless.

"Heard we're going to see some animals today," I say.

"Surprise. Like it?"

I huff out a laugh. "I deserve that."

"You really don't mind driving? We can take my car, but I don't trust it on long trips. Nana's needs new tires, so—"

"I don't mind," I say.

We walk out together as I carry the cooler and place it in the back, hoping it doesn't disintegrate.

"Not back there, up here," Nancy calls. "I need easy access."

"Alright." I put it in the middle of the back seat next to her, and she protectively puts a seat belt around it.

We drive for an hour and a half, passing wooded areas and rolling hills dotted with cattle and farmhouses. I didn't even know this place existed, but now I notice the signs for the *Best Safari Experience in Mississippi*. The park entrance looms, and I drive under a wooden sign with two llamas on it, maneuvering my Escalade behind a van packed with little kids.

I pull into a barn, and a woman in overalls and a cowboy hat approaches us. "How many and how much feed?"

"Uh, four people, and we brought our own. Stockyard feed," Serena says from the passenger seat next to me. She holds up an empty bag of animal food.

The lady squints at it. "Ah, that's a good brand. You wouldn't believe what kind of mess a bunch of bison can make after someone gives them a couple bushels of strawberries. That's thirty-six dollars. Please stay on the marked path and in your vehicle at all times."

My eyes flare. "People actually get out?"

The lady rubs the top of her hat. "Crazy people. Alright, then. Have fun. We're not responsible for scratches or animal bodily fluids on your car. It was entirely your decision."

I huff out a laugh. "Thanks."

Nancy hoots as they all roll down their windows, distributing white buckets of feed to the girls. Betty barks, her paws on the door as she gets a whiff of other animals in the vicinity.

"Where's my bucket?" I ask.

Nancy takes a sip of her beer. "You concentrate on not driving through a llama. Plus, you're gonna be scared when you see the ostriches. It's okay. We all have fears. I'm terrified of moths. I know, I know, they're the midnight butterfly, but look at their faces really close—demon eyes."

We pull past the first gate and a group of llamas surrounds my SUV, bumping into the sides and braying. One sticks its head in my window.

Nancy chortles and hands me a bucket. "Take this. He likes you."

"Yeah, he wants to eat my finger," I say as yellow teeth nip at my hand.

My llama deserts me when I run out of food and darts for Nancy.

Moving on, we pass deer and buffalo who flick their tails as they doze in the sun. Driving forward at a snail's pace, we arrive at the camels.

"Nope." I roll my window up when one looms. It's got to be twenty feet tall.

Serena lets one eat out of her bucket. He sticks his

head in all the way to the gearshift, eyeing me, and I inch away. "This dude has demon eyes, Nana," I say. Funny, I didn't mean to call her that.

"Moths, honey, *moths*. Tiny but brutal."

It sniffs my neck, I shoo it away, and when it sticks its tongue out, I groan. "Somebody needs to hose these animals down."

"If his jaws bulge up, duck," Nana chirps. "Sometimes they puke."

"What?" I call.

Romy makes a choked noise and I look back. Her phone is up and she's videoing.

"Don't you put that on Insta," I protest, shoving her phone down.

She wipes her eyes, shoulders trembling with giggles. "Oh, Dillon, don't be a baby. What if it goes viral? You'd be famous."

"Already famous."

"'Football Player Mauled By Rogue Camel,'" Serena declares.

I wave at the animal to move. "Get out of my car!"

"Alexa, play 'Welcome to the Jungle'," Nana chirps.

"There's no Alexa," I say, shaking my head, barely keeping up. "It's Bluetooth. Your Bon Jovi playlist is on. As requested."

"Just something we say, honey. Don't fret." She pets the dog and smiles at me. "You're doing good, so good.

Vane would have bailed after I asked him to drive. He never was any fun."

"Nana…" Serena warns.

We finally move on, and by the time we circle to the ostriches, I'm determined to prove my manliness and leave my window down. *Hell yeah, I'm better than Vane.* I eye the creatures carefully. *I am not scared of you.*

"Fun fact: ostriches have three stomachs," Serena muses, her eyes finding mine. "They run up to seventy miles an hour."

"Fun fact: contrary to popular belief, they do not bury their heads in the sand," Romy adds, proving she has a lot of her sister in her. "Probably came about because they tend to hunker and lie low for their prey. Their feathers tend to blend in with the sandy ground cover."

"Prey?" I inquire.

"Football players," Romy announces.

Nana coos, "Such adorable animals."

"Are you all crazy?" I exclaim on a laugh.

"We prefer original, honey. And yes, we love all nature's creatures—until we eat them." Nana gives me a smirk just as an ostrich peeks in her window. It's one of the smaller ones, about five feet tall. "Hey there, handsome. You're a young one." She smooches at him as he gobbles at her bucket of feed. "Who's a good boy? Who's a good boy? You are, sweet birdie, and of course, I'd never eat you—"

She yelps when he nips at one of the floral accouterments on her hat then snatches it off her head. Betty barks, body quivering as she lunges toward the window. Her nails scrape at my door and Nana hollers, pulling Betty back in the car before she goes over. Frightened by the lunge or the dog, the ostrich darts a few feet away—hat in its beak.

In her haste, Nana's knees bump the cupholder, and Bud Light overturns and pours out on the floor. "Oh, my beer—sorry, Dillon!" She shakes her head, in a tizzy, then calls out the window, "Bring my hat back!"

"Nana! You can't get out of the car!" Serena yells when Nana tries to open her door. Thankfully, the child safety locks keep her in.

"Romy gave me the pin for my birthday! It's a sweet memento, and I reckon I need all of those I can get at my age..." She swallows, a despondent look on her face.

"Alexa, play 'Crazy Train' by Ozzy," Romy says, watching the ostrich as it prances with the hat, waving it in the air.

Well, hell.

I look at the ostrich. He's only a few feet away, and his friends are on the other side of the car...

"I'll get it," I announce as I open the door and get out.

"Dillon!" Serena cries, reaching for me as I slam it closed. "Be careful!" she calls out the window then shoves her bucket at me. "Use this to distract him!"

I am *not* afraid of this bird, not his teeth or the rippling muscles of his carriage. He's just a linebacker. *Divert and grab. Watch for the blitz attack.*

"Easy," I say, stretching out my hand. I rattle the food around. He swings his head at me, gives me a beady look, and walks forward.

I yelp and back against the car. He stops, his long neck pivoting from me to Nana.

"Hey, little buddy, look at the nice chunky bits of brown. Come on, don't you want a taste?" I barely manage to say.

Of you, his eyes reply.

"He wants the hat," Nana says with a sigh. "It's the pink. He wants the pink."

Romy giggles.

People in the car behind us are yelling for me to get back in the car, and I tune them out. "Hand over the hat, buddy."

He cocks his head, coming closer. Three more steps and I can reach—

His beak releases the hat to the road as he pecks at the bucket.

"Good, good. Alright, that's right, keep eating..."

My body tenses as I kneel and swipe the hat with sweaty hands. In a rush, I fling the door open, jump inside, and slam it.

Cheers sound in the Escalade.

"You're my hero!" Nana says as she pulls the hat out of my hand and plops it back on her head.

"I'm envisioning a cape, maybe a bird on your chest. Bird Whisperer? Ostrich Man? No?" Serena asks me.

I turn to look at the girls, seeing Nana as she smooches on Betty, Romy with her phone, still videoing—and Serena.

She laughs, and it feels as if there's no one in the car but us. That thread between us tightens. The world stops, then restarts.

Anxiety crawls under my skin, warning me that I'm going to screw this up.

With a deep sigh, I tear my eyes away from her and focus on the road.

~

"WHY HERE?" Serena asks me as she spreads the blanket out on the ground. She sits and crosses her legs, her face upturned. She's wearing one of my practice shirts and a pair of frayed shorts.

I sit next to her and grab her feet, slipping them out of her flip-flops. "Why do you think?" After the safari park, we escaped to her apartment and took a shower together. Then I suggested an excursion of my own.

"Mmmm, that feels good." She leans her head back as my thumbs dig into the arch of her foot.

"This is where we met," she says up to the darkening sky.

I tilt my head to the meadow where the students congregated in front of the band. "You were dancing to the left, over there. I stood on the sidelines and watched."

She crawls over to me and lays her head in my lap. Our eyes cling, and we grow quiet, taking in the cool October breeze. Peace. Calm.

"What are you thinking about?"

I run my fingers through her hair. "Myles. He loved the outdoors. Boy Scout. He wanted to be a geologist."

She touches my leather cuff. "This is his?"

I start in surprise as I glance down at the quartz embedded in the material. "No, but I bought it with him in mind."

"You loved him very much."

I look off into the trees. "We were total opposites. He was quiet and reserved. I was the extrovert. Once, the nanny took us to the doctor for our checkups. He goes in the waiting room, sits in the play area, and builds a castle with blocks. She never needed to reprimand him, tell him to sit down, or be polite. Me? I ran through that place like a tornado, tore down his castle, made some little girl cry, then had a pee accident in my shorts and announced it to everyone.

"He used to wear these red cowboy boots when he was little, kept them right next to his bed. At prep school, the year before he died, we had opposite day for Homecoming. I went as him: dress shirt, glasses, khakis, and a pocket protector. He dressed in my jersey. It swallowed him, but the pride on his face..."

I fan her hair out with my fingers.

"The day he drowned..." The words get caught in my throat as I struggle to keep the emotion in check. "He shouldn't have been there, not with the crowd I hung out with, but he followed me around, and I couldn't deny him anything. When he didn't come up out of the water..." *I wanted to die.* "I dove in after him. He was a good swimmer, but he hit his head on a rock. I dragged him up to the shore, did CPR, but he..."—*was gone*—"never came back. I felt as if I should have died next to him." My breath catches.

"Oh, Dillon. That must have been horrible."

"My dad...he...he...I don't know. He couldn't stand to be around—" I stop, sucking in air. "My dad and I are screwed up."

Her lips brush my hand. "Grief makes people do crazy things. I hope you work things out with him."

"I showed up at Waylon with all this buried grief and anger. Why my brother? Why didn't I watch him better? Did I mess up the CPR? I shoved it down with football and parties." I hesitate. "Serena, I've been with a lot of girls..." I stop. "You're different. You know that, right?"

She eases up and straddles me, her knees outside my legs. "Thank you," she says.

I tug her closer until I can see the white glints in her honey-colored eyes. "For what?"

"For today with the safari park. Nana can be…"

"Ridiculous? But cute?"

She smirks. "And for telling me about Myles. A person isn't completely gone when we talk about them. He's still with you when you kiss your hands before you take the field. I understand, I see you—"

Overwhelmed, I kiss her, cutting off her words, my tongue finding hers. We start off slow and sweet as my fingers pull her shirt up and off. Her bra is black lace, her skin like satin. My fingers play with the charm around her neck. Seeing it fires off emotions in my chest. "I want to make love to you, Dandelion. Here."

She stills and her breath hitches as she stares at me. I don't know how long we gaze at each other. Crickets chirp in the woods. An owl hoots. The sun falls below the horizon, the last glints of the orange and pink lights making the night ethereal and otherworldly. How is it possible that our planet continues to spin with billions of people, yet it feels as if we are alone in this moment?

Something rich and complicated flares to life. Oh, it's always been there, but now I can barely breath. The air itself sizzles, and my chest hitches. My soul, my heart, the very essence of me... It's connected to her, a fragile string that's never been broken, not even by three years.

I said *make love*. "Are you freaking out?" I'm tense and swallow.

A gust of air comes from her. "This is happening fast."

"You want to run from us?" Please don't.

She shuts her eyes, then opens them. "Kiss me."

I kiss her. Again and again, lingering, drugging kisses, my hand in her hair, hers in mine. We make love in the meadow where we met and it feels like nothing in the world could ever come between us.

25

Serena

See you tonight is the text that comes from Dillon as I scurry around the bedroom two weeks later. In a fit of annoyance, I toss the phone on my bed and dart for my closet. Torn between his team's superstition and me, he dreads the Fall Ball with Ashley, but the night is here, and there's a knot of anxiety in my gut. I keep reminding myself that this is a commitment he agreed to in May before I even met him. So why am I stomping around my apartment?

My head goes back to last night when he cooked chili for me and Romy and Nana. Later, after we were alone, he wanted to make sure I was okay with the dance. Trying to be mature, I told him I was.

The university catering service asked me to work the formal, and I can't turn down the extra money. Snatching my black skirt and a white button-up shirt out of my closet, I dress. After getting my hair up in a knot and makeup on my face, I slide my boots onto my feet.

My reflection in the mirror is harried. I shut my eyes and remember the meadow, the tender way he touched me, with reverence, as if every single caress counted. The deeper he sinks into my heart, the more I think about him, the more I need him, the more I...

My eyes fly open. *Love him.*

My heart drops.

I love his spontaneity, his stark masculinity, the way he understands grief. My hands cling to the sink, deep breaths coming from my chest. My eyes close. He's dug deep roots in my soul little by little. Like the dandelion, he grew in hard soil, finding the path to my heart.

Romy bounces into my room wearing a black skirt and a white polo. The only positive is I begged Zena to add Romy to the list of servers.

"I'm ready for my first catering job!" Her hair swings around her shoulders. "Mo money, mo money!"

I push aside thoughts of Dillon. "Want me to put your hair up?"

She scrunches her nose. "Can't I wear it down?"

"Do sorority girls want to find hair in their chicken?"

She gags.

"Exactly. Come in the bathroom."

My phone rings and I snatch it up. "What?"

"Dandelion." Dillon's deep tone washes over me. Normally the nickname makes me melt, but now... "You didn't reply to my text."

"I'm getting ready. Aren't you? Don't you have to go pick up your date?" I check the clock and see he should already be on his way.

There's a long silence on the other side. "It's part of the tradition, yes. We're riding with Sawyer and Troy. They're waiting on me now." He pauses, lowering his voice. "You okay?"

"Super. Got to go. See you soon." I click off before he can reply and glare at my cell.

Romy arches her brow. "Trouble?"

I don't reply as we head to the bathroom. I busy myself brushing her hair and pulling it up in a high ponytail.

Her hand grabs mine. "Hey. Stop whatever you're thinking. Dillon isn't going to do anything with that girl."

I pause, meeting her gaze in the mirror, then stare at myself. My makeup is heavier than usual, bronze eyeshadow, my lashes long and thick, but nothing can hide the fear in my eyes. It's not about Ashley entirely. It's just... Falling in love with a man as charismatic as Dillon wasn't part of my plan.

"Trust your choices," Romy adds.

"And him?"

Her small shoulders shrug. "Has he done anything to make you think you can't?"

Not yet, a voice says in my head.

～

THE SOUNDS of a DJ spinning music drifts into the kitchen as I fill a tea pitcher and hand it off to a runner. So far I've managed to hide out in the back and help with prep. No way am I stepping out there to see them together. Anger simmers—at her, at him, at the team, at *myself* for being annoyed. This should be a no brainer. I shouldn't be jealous over this. This night is a job to him.

Like those groupies were to Vane?

"Two servers didn't show! These college kids…" Zena mutters as she ties her apron around her waist. "Serena, take these salads out." She points at a tray of food.

Romy pops up next to me. "I'll do it, Zena."

She frowns. "No, you're on the floor filling glasses. Don't forget the lemons. Serena has more experience. She'll take the salads."

Romy gives me a sympathetic glance. "Don't let that red-haired bitch get to you," she says when Zena walks off.

I give her a wan smirk. "Don't use that word."

"Okay." She rolls her eyes. "*Hussy*. Better?"

No. With a sigh, I pick up the tray of eight salads, put

them on my shoulder, and push through the swinging doors of the banquet hall. The centerpiece of the room is a wall decorated with black and gold balloons formed into an arch. A backdrop of the campus with the Theta Greek letters is plastered on the wall. They're taking couple photos, and Dillon and Ashley pose for the photographer. Wearing a strapless red dress that should clash with her upswept hair but doesn't, she looks like she belongs in a magazine. He's wearing a gray suit that has to be tailored, the fit tight as it clings to his broad shoulders. Her hand is hooked in his elbow, her face tilted up to his.

The image of them slams into me.

His worried eyes find mine.

Dandelion, they say.

Sucking in a breath, I turn away and drop salads off at an eight-top table then head back in for another tray.

When I come out, the only table that doesn't have salads is theirs. *You got this.* Chantal sits next to Troy and Bambi is next to Sawyer, their heads tilted together in conversation. Dillon looks up as I approach, and I feel the weight of his gaze. My spine straightens, and I give myself a pep talk. *A hundred bucks for this job.* Plus, with Romy's part, we've got her competition fees covered this month.

Bambi and Chantal give me cautious looks, and I force a smile. "Your salads," I say, placing them around the table.

"Yummy!" Bambi says. She's wearing a slinky gold dress and her hair is in beach waves.

Moving to Ashley's left, I ease her plate down. Her green eyes narrow as she sniffs. "Blue cheese? I thought we decided on raspberry vinaigrette when we made the menu. Girls? Am I right?" Her gaze sweeps to the others.

Her mouth twisting, Chantal replies, "It's a wedge salad. Traditionally, it calls for blue cheese."

I give her a mental high-five.

"Oh, it does, but I find blue cheese so…unsavory," Ashley insists as she looks at me. Her lashes flutter. "Would you run back and check, Serena? I'm sure the catering team must have forgotten to offer us a selection."

How about I just dump it in your lap? I smile tightly. "Of course. Anyone else?"

They say no. My hands shake as I set down Dillon's salad, starting at the scent of his cologne. It's new and foreign and rattles me. Where's his signature smell? Did he put on something different for her?

He says my name and tries to take my hand, but I tug it away, flip around and leave.

"What's wrong?" Romy hisses as I fumble around in the fridge then check the counters in the small kitchen.

"Nothing," I mutter. "You see any other salad dressings?"

"Let me take their table. Zena has me on the floor with food now."

I shake my head. "No."

"Why are you torturing yourself?" She puts her hands on her hips.

Maybe I *need* to see them together. I pause. I didn't have to accept this job tonight. I could have skipped it and picked one up in a week or so.

I *wanted* to see them together.

Because...

Do I want him to screw up? Am I self-sabotaging? Maybe. My throat tightens.

By the time I return, Ashley's tapping her fingers on the table.

"No raspberry vinaigrette, sorry. I brought what we had: French and oil and vinegar." I plunk them down.

"How disappointing."

"Get over it, Ashley," Chantal grouses.

Ashley's fork falls to the carpet, and her stiletto knocks it under the table. "Oops. I can't reach it. Can you get that for me, Serena?" She looks up and smiles at me.

"I've got it," Dillon says as he bends down and snatches it. He stands from his chair and gives the fork to me. He clenches my hand. "Look at me, Serena—"

I push away from him, my voice cool. "Excuse me, let me get a new one."

"And extra lemons for my tea," Ashley calls to my back.

I hear Dillon arguing with her as I march off.

Romy waits at the door in the kitchen. She's been working the other side of the room, delivering the entrees. She pulls the tray out of my hands. "Your face is red, sis. I'm taking over before you jump on the table and pull her hair out. You work my tables and I'll get yours."

"No."

She stomps her foot. "What are you trying to prove? She's trying to get a rise out of you! Alexa, play 'You Need To Calm Down'."

But I *have* to do this.

When I bring out the chicken and roasted vegetables, Ashley complains hers is cold and asks for a new plate, her water glass needs more ice, her rolls require more butter, and when I bring out the chocolate soufflé, she whines that hers has fallen and can I see if the chef has one that is adequate.

Dillon sits stiff and tense, his jaw popping as I turn around to get a new soufflé. I hear a chair scraping the floor and footsteps behind me. He's followed me and grabs my elbow. "Jesus, Serena. I'm sorry—"

"Please go back to your table. I'm busy."

He gets a panicked look on his face. "Serena. No. Stop. Don't push me away—"

I pull away from him and walk into the kitchen.

My heart thumps so loud I'm sure it's going to pop out of my chest. Somewhere between the salad and the soufflé, I've become a teetering domino, just waiting to fall.

"Most of the hard work is done," Romy says, her eyes narrowed as she sees me. "Why don't you take a break?"

I nod jerkily. "Good idea." I pull off my apron, hand it over to her, and leave the hall. Without a destination in mind, I take the stairs and walk until I'm out of the student center and outside on the sidewalk. The October air is crisp, alive with the feel of autumn. I suck in air, trying to calm down.

Relationships fail when people bring their insecurities to the table and project them as their partner's flaws. I know this. Overthinking poisons. *So, don't do it!* I tell myself. Have a little faith in the guy. Stop twisting scenarios in your head. So what if he doesn't smell right? Troy probably spritzed him with something. Ashley is provoking you and you're letting her. He never wanted to be the prize in the stupid contest.

Feeling better, I reapply my lipstick and head back inside.

I reach the hallway that leads to the banquet hall but stop when I hear my name, easing back behind the corner. Peeking around, I see Dillon, Troy, and Sawyer.

"Chantal is barely talking to me," Troy grumbles. "She only asked me because she needed a date."

"Where did Serena get off to?" Dillon asks. "She's upset."

I back away and hide, my chest rising. I shouldn't be

eavesdropping, but I never was one to pass up an opportunity...

"Romy said she came out here. Do you think she left?" Dillon asks.

Troy says, "What's up with you and her? You've done your challenge with her. You checked it off—"

"Our toughest team is Bama, though. He needs to hang in until then," Sawyer adds.

I start. *Hang in for Bama?*

A roaring sound fills my ears as the ramifications of what they're discussing slams into me. No way. It can't...

Their voices lower, a flurry of words darting between them. A sick feeling growing in my stomach as I strain to hear, only catching bits and pieces.

"...you rode the unicorn from freshman year..." says Troy.

"...one that got away..." comes from Sawyer.

"Leave it alone..." growls Dillon, the rest of his words tapering off as I hear them open the doors of the banquet hall and head back inside.

Mortification fills me as I put the words together. Is this the bet thing Neil mentioned? A variation of it?

"That was enlightening," Ashley's voice says from behind me.

I whip around, my face hot. She must have come from the restrooms.

She adjusts the gold necklace around her throat.

"Funny, I wondered what he saw in you. You're short term, Serena. Once he's done with this challenge thing, which I confess is news to me, he'll end it."

Betrayal claws at me as images tumble through my head. Fixing my car, paintball, the charm, the tryouts... He planned those things? I was the one who got away, so he set out to win me? Nausea roils. My hands clutch my stomach.

"Oh, my. You are upset." She shrugs. "Didn't you know that Dillon will do *anything* for his team? Even you."

She *is* a bitch.

Leaving her behind me—*she's so not worth my time*—I go back in the room, and a hand grabs mine.

"Serena." It's Dillon, his eyes searching my face. Worry brackets his mouth. "There you are. Look, I came and ate the meal. It should be good enough—hey, are you okay?"

I'm barely listening. I pull my hand out of his. "No."

"You're upset about Ashley. I had words with her. She's terrible—"

"Stop," I say, my voice calm. I'm shoving everything down, locking it away.

"Dandelion—"

"Don't call me that," I say louder and feel the murmurs of conversation lull as people notice us. I don't see Chantal and Bambi walking toward us, but I feel their presence when they arrive on either side of me.

"What's going on?" Chantal says, darting her eyes between us.

I break my gaze with Dillon to look at them. "You didn't know about the challenge?"

"What?" Bambi asks.

"No," Chantal retorts, crossing her arms. "Explain."

Thank God they aren't part of this.

"The way I understood the conversation in the hallway, I was Dillon's mission," I say as I turn to him and hold his eyes. "Let me guess, to work me out of your system so you're focused on the game?"

Doesn't he know *who* I am? This is reprehensible. Stupid college boy games.

Chantal pokes him in the chest with a long pink fingernail. "Is that true?"

Bambi joins her. "Fix this now and tell Serena you'd never do that."

He hasn't moved or spoken, blue-green eyes on me.

"Wait, Serena," Sawyer says in a rush as he joins us. I assume he's heard us. His hands are up in a placating manner. "I suggested the challenge after he saw you at the Pig—"

Bambi gasps. "Sawyer—"

"And I accepted," Dillon says in a low voice. "Let me explain—"

The dominoes fall, crashing into each other. "Oh, I've heard enough tonight."

I dart for the kitchen.

Romy meets me as I grab my purse and keys from the hooks in the kitchen. "Get your stuff. We're leaving."

"Leaving?" Zena rushes over. "The dance is still going. There's still cleanup in the kitchen, and we'll need to push the tables aside and clean the floor—"

We're in a hidden hallway that leads to the back exit when I hear someone bursting into the kitchen. "Serena, wait! Dammit!" A clattering sound reaches our ears, and I imagine Dillon's stumbled into one of the tables set up by the catering service. Low voices sound as someone asks him what he wants.

Zena sighs. "The football player from yoga?"

Please, my gaze tells her. *I can't let him get close to me. Not right now.*

I grab Romy's hand, seeing she's already retrieved her backpack. I look back at Zena. "I'm sorry we have to leave you. Just dock us, whatever. I'll explain it later."

"Go." She motions to the back entrance and we slip away.

26

Serena

Dillon bangs on my door. He's been here for the past ten minutes. I barely had time to get Romy in the house and get into my apartment before I saw the flash of his headlights in the driveway.

"Go away." My throat is tight, tears itching to fall.

"I know exactly what this seems like, but that isn't what—we—are." His voice is coarse. "I'm sorry you had to overhear it like that. Please just talk to me."

I whip the door open. His hair is a mess, his jacket gone, his shirt unbuttoned at the cuffs and rolled up. He makes a move to step inside, but I cut him off. "You're not coming in. Say what you need to, Dillon."

His eyes shut then open. He licks his lips, emotions

flitting over his face, ones I can't define. "At the bonfire, Serena..." He inhales a deep breath and scrubs his face.

"What?"

"You were so beautiful."

"All your women are." I have to be tough, hard.

His hands clench as if he's steeling himself. "Stop, please. I'm trying...trying to say this right, and I don't know what I'm doing." He exhales. "I saw you at the bonfire and it was more than just how you looked, okay? It was like déjà vu, like I already knew you. I loved how you danced. Your feisty attitude. It sounds crazy, okay, it's ridiculous, but after I kissed you, I dreamed about you afterward, I couldn't get you out of my head..."

He dips his head, and when he rises up, his eyes cling to mine. "Serena, I fell in love with you over a kiss."

There's a stunned silence. My head tries to process his declaration.

He rushes his words. "I looked for you for months, asked people if they remembered you, searched for you at every party, every class. I didn't look at another girl for months, hoping to find you. In my head, I had this idea... That I'd find you and we'd be together."

My chest tightens. Part of me wants to cling to the idea that he's been carrying a torch, but the other side of me aches at what I overheard. "Then you took something good and made it ugly."

Agony ripples over his face. "Serena—"

"I've heard about your bets."

Frustration flashes and he rushes his words. "No, the team doesn't do those. It's just Sawyer and Troy trying to amp me up. They only know we had sex because I didn't come back to the hotel room until late at LSU. Sawyer took one look at me and guessed. I haven't talked about us to them. I'm not like that—"

"You agreed to it." The thought slices like a knife and I clutch my chest. "I'm not one of your silly contests."

He winces. A long breath comes from him. "I know you're not. I'm sorry. The challenge is wrong, it's demeaning, and it wasn't the reason I pursued you. Sawyer kept asking, and I agreed to appease him, but it was never in my head." He fidgets, his jaw popping. "I know what you're doing. You're running scenarios in your mind, all the times we've been together, all the things I've said, but I never faked with you. I was real; we are real. Don't turn what we have into something sordid—"

"You already did that," I say, shaking my head. "You *promised* you'd be good to me. If that was true, then you should have *told* Sawyer and Troy how you really felt about me. But you didn't, obviously. You lied to me. You hurt me." My voice breaks.

His head dips. "You're right. I should have told them. I just...don't talk to them about feelings—"

"You let this challenge idea linger, and I became a contest for your friends. Neil had to drop hints and then I find out at the dance—with Ashley standing there." My hands clench. "Can't you see how all this looks to me? How it makes me feel?"

He groans and rakes a hand through his hair. "I do, and I'm sorry for all of that, Serena. I tried to tell you about it at the airport after the hotel. Then Vane called and things went haywire between us. After we got back together, I didn't want to rock the boat." He pauses, his voice rough as he leans toward me. "Please believe me when I say you were never a challenge to me."

Seconds tick by as his eyes hold mine. I see the sincerity in the depths, the emotion he's baring. Do I believe he dated me just for laughs? No. Now that the initial shock is over, I know Dillon wouldn't set me up as a challenge, not on purpose. I can see him agreeing with Sawyer to placate him. He was scared of my reaction, and I get that, I do. I tend to react and avoid emotional confrontations. I divorced Vane without ever seeing his face.

I swallow thickly. "I believe you didn't set out to win me for a challenge."

Relief floods his face. "Thank God."

I fell in love with you over a kiss.

Maybe Dillon does love me, *maybe he does*, but Vane loved me in his own way. I said I was ready to take a chance on Dillon, but my trust is like bits of torn paper on the floor.

"But, I'm not sure"—my heart squeezes—"where this leaves us now." I pause, the words like jagged rocks in my throat. "Over, I guess. I can't see you again."

"What's going on?" comes Julian's voice. He's wearing his police uniform as he shoulders past Dillon, pushing him to the side as he comes in and stands next to me. "Romy texted me. Are you okay?" His eyes search my face.

No. My hands clench. I'm barely holding it together.

I look at Dillon, pushing the words out. "You need to go."

There's silence, the air thickening with tension.

"No," he says, eyes glued to my face. "Let's talk this out. I can't accept that we're over."

"She asked you to leave," Julian says with a frown, his body tensing.

I grab my brother's arm. The last thing I want is for my brother to tangle with Dillon. "He's leaving."

Dillon shakes his head and looks at me, desperation there. "Please, Serena. I fucked up, I did, okay, *I fucked up*, but I can't leave you—"

His words are a fist to my gut. "Stop. You sound like Vane," I gasp and shake my head.

Julian stiffens and puts an arm around me then turns to Dillon. "I don't know what you've done, but she can't handle your bullshit right now. You two need space."

"Don't run away from this, Serena," Dillon says, his chest heaving as he holds my eyes.

Oh, Dillon. Running is the only way I know how to survive a broken heart.

I turn away from the door, and Julian slams it closed.

~

My brother leaves an hour later. He attempts to get me to tell him what happened, but my brain won't go there. I'm despondent, the tears falling. I want to pack Dillon away, stuff him in a box, and set it in the darkest part of my closet. Like I did with Vane.

How is it possible that the thought of never seeing Dillon again hurts more than Vane cheating on me?

I crawl in bed and try to sleep. My head replays the meadow when Dillon asked to make love to me, and I weep again. I fell for him that night, only realizing it today.

In a bid to distract myself at one in the morning, I get out of bed and pop open my laptop. There's an email from Warren asking for the article on Dillon. He wanted it midseason and here we are. I grab a bottle of the champagne in the fridge, pop the cork, and turn it up for a long drink. My heart aches as I grab the notes I've been taking over these past weeks with him.

. . .

Chapter 26

IN THE WORDS of Dillon McQueen, "My team is my family." This quarterback arrived on the scene at Waylon and bided his time to start for the Tigers. Under the tutelage of Ryker Voss, he dedicated himself to football, playing running back with stats to rival anyone in the SEC. Year by year, he waited for his chance to lead. Amidst the excitement of new recruits, his leadership and talent have been up for debate. This writer sees the heart of a fighter, fueled by hard work and loyalty to the team...

BY SIX IN THE MORNING, I've drained the bottle and sway in my seat. With bleary eyes, I email the piece to Warren along with a brief message that I want to be removed from the football games, reminding him that George is due back. I won't step into that stadium again.

27

Dillon

I flip the channels on the TV. I'm not really watching, my head full of cotton from a horrible night of sleep. I rub my temples.

It's been over a week since the formal, and Serena won't answer my texts or accept my calls. Meanwhile, we lost to South Carolina, where I threw two interceptions in the last quarter. Sinclair never even got the chance to go in. I fucked it up that fast. At this point, Coach hasn't said who's starting this weekend against Alabama.

The front door opens and I stand up. I keep hoping for Serena to show up. I've tried with her. I've gone to her house. Her car is there, but no one answers. She's cutting me from her life, and I can't keep chasing her. I have a little pride left. A lonely feeling crawls over me.

Exhaustion hits me when I see who it is, and my shoulders dip.

"What do you want?" I snap at Ashley in a raspy voice. She's the last person I want to see.

She smiles brightly. "Just checking in on you. Heard you guys were back from South Carolina. Bad loss, but you'll bounce back, Babycakes."

"Don't act like you care about me. The Theta thing is finished. I played my part for the team. In case you didn't notice when I left you at the dance, I'm done with you."

She pauses, her eyes narrowed. "You can't still be upset over that girl—"

"Shut up, Ashley. I've wanted *that* girl for three years," I snap. My head throbs and I clutch it. I had her and I screwed it up.

She holds her hands up. "I can see you're upset. I can grab us dinner—"

"No."

"Dillon..." she cajoles.

I keep my voice calm though I'm itching to lash out. She acted horribly at the dinner, and I haven't forgotten it. "Get out."

"I'm the Theta president. You're being rude."

I'm being pretty damn nice considering...

I sit back on the couch, shut my eyes, and say, "Don't let the door hit you on the way out, Madame President. Oh, and don't come back."

She leaves in a huff, and a few minutes later someone else walks in and sits next to me on the couch. "Grand Central," I mutter as Sinclair fidgets. He's taken to hanging out in the afternoons after practice.

"Yo, D, put on that LSU game. Tell me where I screwed up."

Myles used to call me D. I toy with the leather cuff on my wrist, ghosting my fingers over the quartz.

I just...

My chest twists.

Loving a girl, being at her *mercy*, is new to me.

"Alright, I'll cue it up. You just talk," he says when I don't say anything. "I miss us running. I can beat your ass now. Been going on my own."

I grunt. I missed every day last week. "Good."

The TV rolls the game, and I wince when I see me getting tackled, then the fumble.

He elbows me. "Shouldn't have waited in the pocket so long."

"Yeah." My tone is lackluster.

He exhales and stands up in front of me, blocking the TV. "I'm gonna give it to you straight: you suck right now. You've thrown some shitty passes, the press is eating you alive, and our rank has dropped five spots. Twitter is calling you the worst quarterback in Waylon history."

Anger shoots through me and I rear back. "Who said that?"

He gives me a smile. "Me."

"Dick." I go back to playing with my cuff.

"I didn't really say it on Twitter. I'm telling you to your face."

I huff out a laugh. "It might be true."

He paces into the kitchen, opens the fridge, and comes back with a Fat Tire. My stomach drops. Serena swiping all the beer then giving it back to me, realizing who she was...

"Make yourself at home," I murmur.

He shrugs and eases back down beside me.

Sawyer comes out of his room, notes the game on the screen, and plops down in the recliner. I can feel him looking at me, the uneasy weight in his gaze. I talked to him and Troy about what happened. They know everything.

He exhales. "Dillon, dude, I'm sorry, again. I didn't realize..." *how much you loved her.* He sighs. "My granny is turning over in her grave over this. What else can I do? I went to her house to apologize, but she didn't come to the door. I left her a note and said I was sorry. I said that challenges are belittling to women and called myself a pig. I swore I would never run my mouth again about your relationship with her. I said I'd take a class in the women's studies department next semester. I suck. Have you heard from her?"

My eyes cut to him. "She's made her mind up." She doesn't give second chances.

Just...

Just get me through this season.

Get me out of this town.

"Dude? The game." Sinclair elbows me.

"Yeah." I scrub my face and lean in, pointing to the screen as Sinclair takes the field for me at LSU. "Alright, see that defensive guy, he's reading you like a book. You twitch your right shoulder when you get ready to…"

~

By Friday afternoon, the week has caught up with me. Between midterms and practice, I'm in a shit mood and can't fight down the exhaustion that haunts me.

I'm rolling my neck in the lobby of the library, about to go out the door when a flash of copper hair on the second floor catches my eye. My heart drops as I dart for the stairs and take them two at a time.

"Hey!" a guy says as I jostle past him.

"Sorry!" I call out.

It's Serena, just ahead with her back to me—and she's with a guy. Anger flashes. Who is she with? They turn the corner into the shelves and I follow, my chest tight.

"Serena!" I say as I make the corner and see them kissing.

She jerks out of his arms and glares at me. "Who?"

"Whoa, sorry." I reel back. She doesn't look anything like Serena. Her hair is shorter, the highlights duller. Her eyes aren't champagne-colored. She's too tall.

"You mind?" the guy asks.

I feel winded with relief as I flip around. "I thought you were someone else," I mutter as I walk away.

Monday I thought I saw her outside the stadium after practice, Tuesday it was on the quad, Wednesday it was a car that looked like hers, and Thursday I waited for her to go to yoga but she never showed.

I don't recall driving home, but I arrive, pulling in behind a white Mercedes sedan I don't recognize. Sawyer meets me on the porch. "Your dad is here."

I stop at the bottom of the steps. *Now?*

"Why?" The car must be a rental.

His eyes search my face, an apologetic look there. "He gave me a call, you know, since you haven't answered his. Your birthday is coming..." He keeps talking and I zone out, a huff leaving my chest. With everything pressing on me, I pushed my birthday to the back burner. I spent my last birthday with the team, not my dad.

I mentally prepare myself, squaring my shoulders as I walk into the house.

He's sitting next to Brianna on our couch. Marley bounces on her knee as they coo down at her.

"Dillon," he says in a gruff voice as he stands. Wearing

khakis and a dress shirt, he's not as tall as I am, his frame trim and wiry. His hair is dark brown and styled in a businessman cut. "You look well. I like your place. Much better than the dorms."

He's *in* my house. My eyes run over his face, seeing the extra lines added since February. His expression is hopeful, and I glance away.

"Surprise!" Brianna says rather uncertainly as she stands with Marley. "We flew in on the jet. We would have called, but..." Her eyes dart back to Dad. "Wes wanted to surprise you for your birthday."

My words are flat. "Guess the baby isn't teething this weekend?"

"No." Dad gives me an awkward hug, his fingers grasping my shoulders. He pulls back, looking hesitant. "We're staying at the Hilton in town, so we won't crowd your space. Planning on being here when you play tomorrow. We've already gotten our seats. Marley's going to her first football game to see her brother..."

Brother. The word hurts, and I suck in a breath.

Brianna thrusts Marley into my arms, and I blink.

"Aw, she's smiling at you," Brianna says.

"Probably gas," Dad jokes.

She's adorable, big cheeks and curly brown hair the color of his. I shift around uncomfortably.

"Here, put her on your hip," Brianna says, moving her

around on my frame. "She's much bigger since you saw her in February."

"Yeah."

Marley spits up then giggles as Brianna wipes the milk on her bib. I take in the orange and navy shirt she's wearing with the Waylon logo on it. They must have ordered it online or made a run to the student center store, I guess.

I swallow, feeling weird, as if this is happening to someone else. I don't recall holding her in February. Maybe because she was too little, or maybe I didn't want to. "She's cute," I say, the words feeling ripped from my chest.

Sawyer slides in, clearly trying to smooth over my familial issues. "They haven't eaten yet and I ordered pizza."

"Pepperoni for the guys and veggie for Brianna," Dad adds with a smile. It looks a little forced. Yeah, yeah, I feel that too.

We manage a strange, stilted meal. Dad asks me questions about Mom, and I tell him she's texted a few times to update me on the wedding plans. He tells me about a new hotel they're building in London, about the day Marley crawled for the first time...

Brianna feeds Marley baby food with a dainty spoon, something orange.

"What is that?" I ask, searching for topics. It feels as if I'm in a parallel universe, but I'm trying to roll with it.

"Sweet potatoes. They're her favorite. Wes said they were your fav too," Brianna replies.

As if to show her agreement, Marley giggles, her nose scrunching up, and a bubble of orange goo comes out of her mouth. I'm struck by the pale blue color of her eyes.

"She looks like Myles," Dad murmurs next to me.

A ball of emotion clogs up my throat. Suddenly, it's too much, this shitty week, him surprising me, him gazing at Marley...

"Yeah, she does." I wipe my face and stand. "Excuse me, I need..."—*a minute*—"...a walk."

I dart for the door and step outside. The late October air is crisp, and I drag in a deep breath as Dad jogs up next to me. "Let me join you."

"Alright." We don't look at each other, our paces in sync as we walk. When we get to the end of my block, I can't stand it any longer. "Why are you here?"

He sticks his hands in his pockets. "It's your birthday tomorrow, and I wanted to see you. You weren't answering my calls. Maybe you had the right not to."

"I see." I really don't.

He flashes a careful, searching look at me. "Dillon, we need to talk. I left your mother at a terrible time, right after Myles—"

"You left me." My stomach churns as I stop to turn

and look at him. I feel off-centered and disoriented, as if I'm unraveling. Part of it is the loss of Serena, the way my game is falling apart, and I can't stop the spiral. I'm stuck in a black pit, itching to crawl out, but I can't find the energy.

His blue eyes meet mine and a nod comes from him, almost hesitant. "You think I blamed you, and I did. I blamed everyone—myself, you, your mom, the postman, the grocer, the water, the rocks, the air itself. I sank down into an awful place and I forgot about the people—you—who depended on me. Then, I met Brianna. I didn't plan on meeting someone new and starting a family, and I'm sorry I hurt you."

I shrug. "You're not even my real dad."

"Dillon..." He opens his mouth, looking for words. He exhales. "Son, I raised you from the age of two. You are mine in my heart."

"I thought I was," I say softly.

Regret is etched in his voice when he replies, "Grief ate me alive until I didn't have anything left. I wanted out of that house, away from everything that reminded me of him. You're going to have a new sibling next year. I want us to..." His voice catches. "Be a family. I want you to forgive me for leaving, for not being the father you deserve."

A long pause stretches. My teeth grit to keep from blurting out that I love him, that I missed him, that I want to know Marley, that I want him in my life so fucking bad. I want to see him in the summer. I want to hold my sister without feeling left out.

I look away from his face and at the setting sun.

His words are ones I've longed to hear, but...

I picture Myles's ghost next to me, telling me to give Dad a chance.

He's my father, bio or not. He was there for me when Mom never was. We were close.

Dad speaks, a hoarse quality to his voice. "When I watch you tomorrow, when you kiss your hands, when you put Myles in your heart, save a little room for me?"

I shut my eyes, my throat tight. His words settle deep, taking root. I let out an exhalation. "Yeah."

28

Serena

"What's that?" Romy asks as she bends over my shoulder.

Sitting at my desk, I push the sewing machine to the side and flick out her skirt. "I hemmed your uniform. It was frayed on the side." I'm doing anything to keep me busy. If I stay on a task, then maybe I won't think about him.

"I meant the gift on your desk." She points down at the black box.

Oh. I stare at it. It's been lying there for a week. "Just something I got for Dillon's birthday, but—"

"Ooooo! What is it?" She tries to snatch it, and I grab it back, holding it to my chest.

"Nothing." I push the skirt into her hands. "Mind your

own business and go try this on—" I stop as Nana enters. "No bingo tonight?" I ask.

She plops down on the couch and waves me off. "I'm staying in. Thought I'd check on you."

There have been lots of evenings when she checks on me. I know what they see. I'm grieving. My face is haunted, my eyes sad.

Romy dances around me and sits next to Nana. "Serena bought Dillon a birthday gift..."

I sigh. "I'm going to return it. I bought it before—"

"Anyone home?" Julian pokes his head in and holds up a six-pack of Bud Light. "Thought I'd check on my girls." He grins broadly.

"And you brought sustenance!" Nana chortles as he twists open a bottle and hands it to her.

I take one—*might as well*—and we all clink our bottles together, Romy with a soda.

A few minutes later, Liam knocks and comes in.

"Oh, goody, Tree Boy is here. I say we do a Friday night movie," Nana says, her arm curling around me on the couch.

Well.

It's obvious they planned this, a whole *Let's keep Serena company* brigade. I give them the fake smile.

"Creepy, sis," Romy chirps, then she says, "I want *Pride and Prejudice*—"

"No," Julian calls. "We've watched that one ten times!"

"Now it's going to be eleven!" Romy says as she pokes him. "Suck it up."

"Fine, but I'm calling dibs on the next one. *Fast and Furious*," Julian mutters.

"Go get snacks from the house," Nana declares, shooing them. "I'll need my guacamole and chips. Liam, did I tell you Turo's Italian?"

He bobs his head. "Yes, ma'am. Very nice."

I manage a smile.

"Come with me, kids," Julian says to Liam and Romy. "Let's grab the snacks."

Liam shifts a wary gaze to Julian. "Can I take a look at your bike?"

Julian narrows his eyes. "Don't put smudges on it, and don't even think about sitting on it."

"Yes, sir."

Romy grins and grabs Liam's hand as they follow him out the door.

"Serena..." Nana pats my hand. "Let's talk. I've kept my mouth shut, but, dear, you miss him terribly. You've had time to process, but you look like ten miles of bad road."

"Nana..."

"You try so hard to be good, to be a role model for Romy, to provide for her, and you're the kind of girl who'd never break a promise, but people do. Romy screwed up when she got in with a bad crowd and did wacky weed.

You put your life on hold for Vane. Julian goes through women like water. I tend to say things I shouldn't. And Dillon made a mistake. He didn't correct his friends when he should have and you had to hear it in a horrible way. Men, in general, tend to not talk about deep things. Perhaps this incident is a hurdle, yes, but how you deal with it is what matters. You love him, and his face is happier than a pig in sunshine when he looks at you." She hesitates. "Don't judge him by another man's scorecard. You're scared because of Vane, but all I get from Dillon is a boy who needs you. He's younger than you, yeah, yeah, but his soul is aligned to yours."

"He's..." Tears spring up behind my eyes and I blink rapidly. My hand hits my chest. "He isn't Vane, I know it, but..." *I don't want to be hurt anymore.*

The others come back in, and I turn away, swallowing. They find seats and I snuggle under a blanket as Darcy and Elizabeth battle it out for love.

The question is, what am I willing to do for love?

29

Dillon

"This was on the porch." Sawyer tosses me a package and I catch it. It's in a brown manila envelope with an orange and blue ribbon around it. My name is scrawled across the front.

I sit back down on the bed, shoving my duffle for the game to the side. "Who left it?" My dad and Brianna have already given me their gift, a set of diamond cufflinks. Dad suggested I wear them for the NFL draft in April. He wants to go with me to New York and bring the family.

He shrugs. "Beats me. We got ten minutes before we're due at the stadium."

"Right."

When he's out of my room, I tear open the package, my chest tightening at the note.

. . .

DILLON,

I got this before. It felt wrong not to give it to you. I wish for you everything. Kisses in meadows. A sky full of stars. All the wonderful things destiny has in store for you. Happy Birthday.

Serena

POPPING OPEN THE BOX, I pick up the sterling silver football charm. I shut my eyes, thinking about where she is right now. She sent it, and it has to mean *something*.

Later, when I run onto the field for the game, I kiss both my hands, tug the charm out of my jersey, and brush my fingers over it, for her. My eyes rove the stands, searching, hoping, but she isn't in the press area, nor do I feel the weight of her gaze anywhere in the stadium. She isn't here. Disappointment flares, but I'm not surprised.

My eyes land on my dad. He waves a foam finger at me while Marley bounces on Brianna's knee. We sat up last night reminiscing about childhood memories and going through videos I had of Myles on my phone. No family is perfect, but, perhaps, ours can be united. Problems exist, yes, but the blame we both shared is lighter. Grief is horrible. In the space of one heartbeat, I can picture my brother going over that cliff. Dad can't change how he dealt with Myles's death, how he cocooned himself, pushing the world away, just as I can't change that I didn't stop him from jumping, but we can forge ahead and make a new path for ourselves.

"Yo! We've got a team to destroy!" calls Sawyer as he slaps me on the ass and runs past me.

I take in the formidable Alabama defense, huge linebackers with mean faces as they run onto the field.

"Teamwork, D," Sinclair says as I put my helmet on. "Show 'em who's the best quarterback!"

I cock an eyebrow at him. "You're encouraging me?"

A smirk spreads on his face. "Be the thermostat, not the thermometer, yo."

"So you do listen."

"Kill that defense, D." He tosses a football in the air. "If you can't, I'll take over, 'cause I'm awesome, but I think you've got this. They're ranked four and it's a mountain of a team to climb, and your focus has been shit, true, but now's the time to set it straight."

I look up at the press section, taking in the television cameras, the ESPN guys, the scouts on the sidelines. Coach said I was starting, but to be prepared for Sinclair to come in. That familiar pressure sits on my chest, but this time, *this time*, it's not as heavy. The critics may be right—I may always be second best—and so be it. Failure might come, but I'll never accept it; I'll keep training and working and pushing myself. I'll never be Ryker, and that's okay. I am talented. I know how to lead. I care about the people I play with. Any NFL team would be lucky to have me.

I look at my dad again. He's here, he loves me, and it's enough.

"Let's roll the Tide out of our stadium!" I shout, and we take the field.

30

Serena

A tall, ripped man wearing snug jeans walks into the Piggly Wiggly Saturday night.

He walks in alone, no entourage in sight. Well, except for the cashier who squeals and leaves her customers hanging as she runs over to him, arms flailing. He signs the paper she thrusts in his face. His usual wicked smile is missing, but she doesn't notice, swooning as she walks away, clutching the paper to her chest.

He's wearing a Waylon hat. It creates a slice of diagonal shadow on his chiseled face, giving me a partial view of one bladed cheekbone and the side of a full, pouty mouth. Dark stubble covers his diamond-cut jawline, and a pair of expensive silver-mirrored aviators shields his gaze. He wipes them off and tucks them in the neck of a faded blue lucky Tigers shirt.

Stomach jumping, I turn before he sees me, my head down as I move to another aisle. I touch my face, hands trembling. No makeup to speak of, but at least my hair is down. My pants are camo, and my shirt—well, it isn't a Four Dragons one. I threw them all out.

Somehow I find myself in front of the cookies. My head tumbles around, my skin prickling when I feel him behind me.

He's close to me, the heat from his body emanating through the air around us. It crackles with tension, the sound of his breathing a symphony to my heart.

His voice, when it comes, is husky, layered with emotion. "Someone told me once that it takes fifty-nine minutes to bake an Oreo."

I keep my eyes forward. "Sounds like an interesting individual."

"She's incredible." A long breath comes from him. "She doesn't need me the way I need her. She's never going to forgive me because that means making herself vulnerable." He shifts, coming closer to me, and when his hands land on my shoulders, my lashes flutter. "I've thought of a hundred ways to make some kind of grand romantic gesture, even begging her, but this girl...ah, she's seen guys beg before, and it doesn't work. She kicked a rock star to the curb. She's a goddess with armor. Tough as nails." He pauses and drops his hands. "She thinks I'm a shallow asshole."

My hands clench. He isn't that. Never.

"Please. Just look at me, Serena."

I turn and face him. The beauty of him takes my breath. He's gorgeous, with his chiseled face and towering body, all rippling muscle. His eyes, framed by thickly curled lashes, hold mine. His full lips part, devastation growing on his face as he hungrily takes me in. He's a man whose edges have been ripped apart.

"How did you know I was here?"

"Romy. I went to your house." He pauses, swallowing. "You're wearing my shirt."

I nod. "I watched you beat 'Bama by fourteen points on the TV. Had to show my school spirit. You played the whole game—congrats."

His chest expands. "Wish you'd been there. My dad came. We're working on things."

My heart swells. "Oh, Dillon. That's great."

"I miss you so much," he whispers as he shakes his head and looks away for a moment. He bites his bottom lip and fidgets as if he wants to touch me. "I'm sorry I hurt you. I, um, don't know what else to say. I've never been here, never felt this, like I had a taste of something real and it was yanked away."

My throat dries. That's exactly how I feel. "Yeah."

A hesitant expression crosses his face. "I fell in love with you at the bonfire, but I *loved you* with my whole heart in the meadow. I loved the girl I'd gotten to know, the girl with the quirks, the one who loves her family. You own me, Serena."

He swallows. "This feeling… It isn't the infatuation from freshman year, but real and so big that it blows me away. I should have told you that day, but I didn't know if you'd, I don't know, freak out."

A determined glint flares in his gaze. "When I gave you that dandelion… I bought that charm two years ago at some arts festival at Waylon. I took one look at it, picked it up, and knew someday I'd give it to you. You were always my goal, yeah, *to get you forever.*"

His words resonate inside me, unfurling inside my heart.

He sighs. "I don't deserve you, but life keeps bringing us together. Call it fate or some legend, hell, I don't care, but there it is. Once, I told you I'd be down on my knees for you, and I am." He kneels, right there next to a container of peanuts. He stares up at me.

I gasp. "Dillon…don't…"

"I promise to never hurt you, to always be there, to tell my friends how in love with you I am, the whole world…" He pauses, his face uncertain. "Just tell me how to fix us, how to get you back."

My lashes blink rapidly, holding back the tears welling up inside me. I want him, I need him, *I love him.*

More than my young, misguided devotion for Vane.

More than anything.

A long exhalation leaves my chest and clarity settles deeper inside me. Yes, I needed our time apart, but the moment I sent him his gift, I knew I could never let him go. The truth is, people are never free of baggage, but sometimes you have to take a chance and jump in feet first. I want this with him. I want him tracing hearts on my back, loving me. And I see *who* he is. Kind, intelligent, funny, loyal, and...*mine*.

"Oh my God! Are you asking her to marry you?" screeches the cashier girl.

I huff out a laugh as I wipe a tear from my eye. "You better get up. She's getting her phone out."

He rises, eyes never leaving mine as he stands. His forehead touches mine. "The night of the bonfire my heart picked you, and I'd do it again, a million times. Is there any way you could *need* me the way I need you?"

I brush my fingers over his face, my hand curling around his neck. There's a small bump under his shirt, and I tug out the ribbon and see the charm around his neck. My eyes meet his and my chest hitches. Emotions tug at me, hope for a future with this warrior. "I love you so much," I whisper.

Amazement washes over his face. His mouth parts. "Serena...Dandelion..." He kisses me, his lips slanting over mine, our mouths devouring each other. He tastes like home. He feels solid and real, the kind of love that grows in your heart and digs deep roots. When I was seventeen, my dandelion meant second chances in the face of adversity, and this with Dillon? He's worth all the chances.

He hitches me up until my legs are around his waist. Without breaking our connection, he walks us down the aisle and through the store.

I laugh into his chest. "Aren't we going to buy anything?"

"I've got what I came for," he murmurs, elation in his voice. "You."

I dip my head to his chest and inhale his scent. "Happy Birthday," I say. "You're only two years younger than me now."

He clutches me tight as we step outside. "I want everything with you. I'm going to love you so good it's going to freak you out, a lot. I've waited a long time for you, and I might go overboard..." A smile curls his lips as I laugh.

He stops at his Escalade and puts my back against his door. I kiss him slowly, relearning the way he feels. A car drives by and someone whistles. We laugh and pull apart.

His hand cups my cheek. "You need a ride, mystery girl?" he asks, taking me back to the night at the Pig.

"Sure, Damon."

"You're slipping. You've already used that one."

"Dillon McQueen, I know you," I say softly. "You have my heart."

"I will never break it, Dandelion."

"I know." I see the truth in his eyes, the solemn expression on his face.

He goes in for a quick kiss. "We're going back to your place, and I'm going to show you some new moves."

"Promise?"

"*Toujours*. Always. Tell me you love me again."

I gaze into his stormy eyes. "I love you, football player."

EPILOGUE

Dillon

A few years later...

I leave my agent's office and pull out of the parking lot in downtown Denver and hit the highway, pointing Serena's white Range Rover to our place in the Rocky Mountains outside Breckinridge, Colorado. We have a spacious penthouse in the city, but during the off-season we like the peace that comes with crisp air and majestic mountain views. The historic town is perfect, quaint restaurants, locally owned galleries, yoga and dance studios, small bars where musicians play, and snow skiing in the winter.

After I clear the traffic of the city, I pull over at the grocery store. I put on my aviators and grab an old cowboy hat. I want to get in and get out without being recognized.

After the Waylon Tigers won the Sugar Bowl, I was drafted to the Broncos that following April. We weren't national champs again, but I played some of my best football that year. Sinclair did too.

Once in Denver, I was named the backup, but after the starter suffered a shoulder injury and retired, I stepped up and filled those shoes. This past year we won the AFC West conference and maybe next year, the Super Bowl. I'm at the top of my game and honing my skills as a leader.

Inside the store, I keep my head dipped and move through the aisles, grabbing steaks for dinner, beer, arthritis cream for Nana, cookies for Serena.

A text comes in from Romy. **Thanks for letting me hang out at this kickass house, bro. BTW, I need tampons and Aleve. A real man wouldn't have any qualms about purchasing them.** She adds several laughing/crying emojis. **FYI, ditch the steaks. Serena made other plans.**

Is she cooking? I mentioned the steaks before I drove into the city, but maybe she's changed her mind, which is weird. She doesn't like to cook. Usually I make our meals at the cabin, mostly on the grill.

Romy doesn't reply.

Serena and I were engaged in May after we graduated, then married a year later after my first season in Denver. Contrary to my dream, I didn't ask her at a football game. I wanted it to be private. I asked her in the meadow as we lay on a blanket with the stars above us. My hands shook as I opened the black box and presented the three-carat diamond to her. My dad helped me pick it out when we were in New York for the draft.

I was nervous as hell. Was the ring too flashy? Was she ready? Was I rushing? I tend to do that, I do, but when I know something, *I know*. She was my dream since freshman year, and yeah, I wanted a ring on it.

I stayed up late the night before practicing the proposal. I'd already asked Julian and Romy and Nana if I could have her hand, and I knew she loved me, but what if she said no?

She gaped at me when I kneeled at her feet and went for it... *Will you, um, you know, be my mine forever? Will you take on this world with me? I want to be your family. I want to wake up every day and see you next to me...*

Yes, yes, yes, she told me, jumping up and down.

She picked out our penthouse in Denver and moved in right before summer camp. With her graduate degree done, she spent her time writing her short stories and selling them to various magazines and online publishers. Last year, she picked up teaching dance part time.

I bought Nana a condo on the floor below us. At first,

she protested at the gift, but with my promise of great grandkids in the future and with Romy enrolling in Colorado University, she came around. *You're a keeper*, she told me. Julian moved into their house in Magnolia, and we see him on the holidays.

Our wedding took place in a chapel in Denver, and we kept it small. Marley was our flower girl, Dad was my best man, and Romy was Serena's maid of honor. My mom broke off her engagement and showed up with a new man in tow.

Simply put, it was the happiest day of my freaking life.

She took a chance on me, and I'm going to make damn sure she never regrets it.

An hour later, I pull in the driveway of our three-story, eight-thousand-square-foot A-frame house at the base of the mountains. There are two balconies at the back plus a glassed-in porch with a fireplace to enjoy the cold days. The best feature of the property is a fast-running mountain stream behind the house. Most mornings, we sit on the balcony, drink coffee, and talk.

I walk in the door and the place is quiet. Romy appears in the hallway, and I toss her the bag with her things in them. Her hair is cut chin length, a wheat-colored blonde this year. She gives me a fist bump and a blinding smile. "Thanks. Did it freak you out?"

I pop an eyebrow. "I'm a married man. Your sister has similar requests. And nothing bothers Dillon McQueen."

She rolls her eyes and tells me about her latest boyfriend and asks if he can drop by for the weekend. I tell her to check with Serena.

"Where is she?" I ask.

"Kitchen."

Huh. I don't smell anything burning, so maybe dinner can be salvaged.

I head that way, eager to see her.

I walk in the kitchen and see her washing a dish at the sink, her copper and honey-colored hair spilling down her back. She's wearing skinny jeans and a red, flowy blouse. I ease up behind her, stealthy, and wrap my arms around her waist. "Serena." I smell her scent and exhale, letting the day wash away.

She leans back against me, resting her head on my shoulder. My hand settles over the baby bump on her waist. Our little one is due in four months. Using my face, I push her hair aside and kiss her tattoo. "How's he doing?"

She sways against me as we move together to unheard music. It's always like this with us. I can't get enough of her, her smirks, her kindness, her fierceness, her beauty, the way she loves *me*. "She's good. Kicked today when I did yoga."

"Hmm, an athlete. You're torturing me by not getting a sonogram."

She turns around and drapes her arms around my neck. "I thought you liked surprises."

"Only when I'm in charge." For her birthday last year, I surprised her with a trip to Paris. On a random weekend this past March, I flew in Bambi and Chantal and they had a girls' weekend while I hung out with Sawyer and Troy. Sawyer plays for Seattle now and Troy coaches high school football in Boston.

She laughs, champagne-colored eyes sparkling. "Um, surprise."

"What do you mean? Are we going out to eat? I saw a new Chinese place on Main Street." I give her a slow kiss, dragging it out, immersing myself in her.

"No, the caterers are coming any minute. We're having a party."

I kiss the tip of her nose. "Did Nana invite people to the cabin?" She invited her book club last month. Five old ladies showed up—surprise—and we hung out with them all weekend, mostly keeping them fed and showing them around town.

"Let's just say it's an early birthday party for you. October is right in the middle of football, so..."

I'm confused. "There's no cars in the driveway."

"Because I'm that good. Every guestroom in the house is filled."

Okay...

"Come with me," she says mysteriously as she takes

my hand and leads me out to the balcony that overlooks our backyard. It's dusk, a little cool, the sun setting behind the Rockies. Below us, scattered around a roaring fire pit, people mingle.

My heart squeezes. I never imagined the family I have, but there they are, my dad and Brianna and their two girls. I see Nana running a makeshift bar, beer and wine set up on a table. Emotion tugs at me when I see the guys who were my non-blood family at Waylon. With everyone playing professionally, getting engaged or married, it's hard to meet up—except on the field against each other.

I take them in, Maverick and Delaney, Ryker and Penelope, Blaze and Charisma, Sawyer and Bambi, Troy and Chantal.

Blaze, his arm looped around a smiling Charisma, looks up and sees us. He's the starting wide receiver for the New York Jets. "Yo, about time you got here! This party has started, man. Get your ass down here and stoke this fire. It's going out."

Damn, I missed him.

"I love you, Serena," I murmur softly.

She leans against me. "You like it?"

"I'm the luckiest man in the world."

She takes my hand and we walk down the steps and meet them.

Maverick, a killer player for the Titans in Nashville, slaps me on the back and congratulates me on a good season. I comment on the defensive records he's broken in football. The man is incredible.

Serena, Bambi, Delaney, Penelope, Chantal, and Charisma drift over to the stream where we strung up fairy lights next to the water. They grab drinks from Nana along the way. I smile as Nana starts talking. She's probably regaling them with stories of her latest boyfriend Antonio.

Ryker, the starting quarterback for the New York Giants, gives me a bear hug. "Good to see you, man. This place is amazing. We need a ski trip out here."

"Come anytime you want."

Blaze gives me an arm punch. "How's the season looking this fall?"

"Good. Gonna beat you."

He laughs and gives me a hard time about a sack I took against the Jets' defense last year.

Sawyer and Blaze compare their stats while Ryker and I discuss summer camp. Maverick talks about winning the Super Bowl and flashes his gold ring. We laugh about the bonfires at Waylon, the girls that captured our hearts. Whether the legend is true or not...

Before long we've eaten some fancy tacos and downed some beers and are sitting in chairs around the fire while the girls laugh nearby. Dad and Brianna have taken the girls to bed and Nana has retired to watch TV. Someone, probably Romy, has turned on the speakers, and music plays in the background.

"Girl on Fire" by Alicia Keys comes on and I can't help but smile around my beer. Serena was listening to it the night she saw me in the Pig. It's her theme song, and man, it fits her. *She looks like a girl, but she's a flame.* My flame.

I glance over at her, and as if she senses me, she turns her head and our eyes cling. Contentment and satisfaction unfurl inside me.

Dandelion, my eyes say. *Thank you for loving me, needing me, trusting me. I promise to love you until my dying breath.*

She knows my heart is true.

She smiles and blows me a kiss.

~

Dear Reader,

Thank you for reading *I Promise You*! I hope you enjoyed Dillon and Serena's love story! A charmer and a bit of a player (Alexa, play "Womanizer"), Dillon needed a kickass girl, and I couldn't WAIT to write Serena into his world. Nana and Romy; Sawyer, Troy, and Owen; Chantal and Bambi: I loved them so much. Tentatively, I'm saying this is the last of the Waylon University books although I may do a spin-off someday.

. . .

REVIEWS ARE like gold to authors, and I read each and every one. If you have a few moments, please consider leaving a rating or a review for I Promise You.

A SPECIAL NOTE! Please Read!

BELOW I HAVE a short excerpt of *Dear Ava*, an epic, powerful romance that brought me to my knees when I wrote it. There is a trigger warning for sexual assault. It's there so you aren't surprised, and I think that's important. No, the assault does not happen *on* the page, but she does recall it, and the incident becomes the driving force for the heroine. I wanted you to be aware of this before you scroll to the end of your kindle. It's my most highly rated book with over 1600 reviews on Amazon.

XOXO, *Ilsa Madden-Mills*

P.S. PLEASE JOIN my FB readers group, Unicorn Girls, to get the latest scoop as well as talk about books, wine, and Netflix:

. . .

https://www.facebook.com/groups/ilsasunicorngirls/

Sign up below for my newsletter to receive a FREE Briarwood Academy novella plus get insider info and exclusive giveaways!

http://www.ilsamaddenmills.com/contact

ABOUT: DEAR AVA

Dear Ava

#1 Amazon Charts and WSJ bestselling author Ilsa Madden-Mills delivers a gripping, enemies-to-lovers, secret admirer, high school romance.

The rich and popular Sharks rule at prestigious, ivy-covered Camden Prep. Once upon a time, I wanted to be part of their world—until they destroyed me.

The last thing I expected was an anonymous love letter from one of them.

Please. I hate every one of those rich jerks for what they did to me. The question is, which Shark is my secret admirer?

Knox, the scarred quarterback. Dane, his twin brother. Or Chance, the ex who dumped me...

Dear Ava, your eyes are the color of the Caribbean Sea. Wait. That's stupid. What I really mean is, you look at me and I feel something REAL.

It's been ten months since you were here, but I can't forget you. I've missed seeing you walk down the hall. I've missed you cheering at my football games. I've missed the smell of your hair.

And then everything fell apart the night of the kegger.

Don't hate me because I'm a Shark. I just want to make you mine. Still.

★★★★★ "*A gut punch right in the feels. These characters wreck you. It's a deep storyline, with such* **tender, beautiful, unbelievably perfect romance.** *Gah. I. Am. Wowed. Five Stars!*" Angie, Angie's Dreamy Reads

Recommended for ages 18 and over.
Trigger warning for sexual assault.

Dear Ava

Wall Street Journal Bestselling Author
ILSA MADDEN-MILLS

Copyright © 2020 by Ilsa Madden-Mills

Chapter 1
Ava
Junior Year

My hair covers my face and I shove it away, my heart pounding as my eyes flare open in the dark. The air is cold, an early winter nipping on the heels of fall.

Where am I?

Straining to recall, I distinctly remember the road that brought me to these trees, a narrow, rutted lane, can barely even call it a road, really just a path used by tractors, ATV vehicles, and cars with good front-wheel drive.

No matter the road you take, it doesn't matter if it's beautiful or ugly, hard or smooth, paved or pitted with ruts—it's your road to take. What matters is how it ends.

One of the nuns told me that once, but I can't recall

why—wait, *God* my head hurts as if someone took a sledgehammer and whacked me.

Blinking, I try to focus, mentally willing the pain to stop.

Where am I?

A keening sound breaks into the night, and I jerk, realizing it's me making that noise. Shivering at the eerie sound, I stop, sucking in air then hissing with the effort it takes as I attempt to sit up. I decide against it when agony reverberates through my lower body. There's a gnawing there—

Screw it. Just let me lie here.

I'm in tall grass, that I do know, and I breathe slowly, orienting myself as I stare up at the starry sky and look for answers. The moon is full and bright, illuminating the high pine trees towering over me, their branches rustling as the wind blows, like ghostly hands rubbing their fingers together. Watching the creepy movement reminds me of a horrid Grimm fairytale where a young girl ventures out into the enchanted forest to pick flowers, only to be gobbled up by a monster.

I close my eyes.

Open them again.

This isn't an enchanted forest, but it's definitely the woods.

How did I get here?

Twisting my head, I see the embers of a low bonfire

glowing several yards away in a mostly open meadow. Images dance in my head—me at the fire, laughing, dancing, drinking—

I inhale a sharp breath as another memory pierces, and I kick it down. *Just not ready.*

My hands clench the dirt and damp leaves underneath me. My clothes are dirty. At least I didn't wear my red and white cheer outfit. No, I had time to change into a mini skirt and a new blue tank top with scalloped lace at the top, "the perfect match for my eyes," Piper had said even as she told me not to—what? What did she tell me not to do?

More pain spirals in my head, and I wince, swallowing convulsively to pull moisture into my dry mouth.

I focus on that meadow.

Before I was in the woods, there was a party there, the Friday night kegger after the football game. Yes. At one point, people and music and cars encircled this meadow. Guys still in jerseys, some in jeans and preppy shirts, pretty girls decked out in expensive clothes I can't afford, jewelry and shoes I'll never have...

It's empty now.

I lick dry, chapped lips when my stomach swirls. Bile curls in my gut. I'm not sure how my addled brain knows poison lies somewhere within me, but it does, and my body wants to eject it.

But it's hard to move, and I'm exhausted, and if I could just close my eyes and drift...

Something howls off in the distance, a dog or a coyote.

Definitely not a wolf, I remind myself. This is rural Tennessee, not Alaska.

My body twitches in disagreement. *Doesn't matter! Leave this awful place!*

But, I'm so tired and weak and maybe if I just go back to sleep and wake up again, this will all just be a bad dream—

Those ghostly fingers in the trees brush again and I snap to awareness, forcing my eyes to stay open.

I sit up and prop my back against the tree behind me. A collection of pictures tiptoe through my mind: Jolena and me getting ready for the party at her place and my nervousness at being surrounded by the opulence of her mansion, then us arriving at the field party in her black Range Rover. We chugged shots of Fireball before we got out to join everyone. She offered, her ruby lips smiling, and I took it anxiously, needing the bravery for my first kegger. These people weren't like me, didn't *really* know me, except as Chance's girl. They're the Sharks at Camden Prep, rich and popular and pretty much assholes except for Chance. They rule the school. They decide who comes to the parties. They decide if you're good enough.

My fingers press on my forehead.

Knox Grayson, QB1 and the leader of the Sharks, was the first person I saw when we walked up to the fire, his arm curled around...Tawny? Yeah. With the golden brown hair like sunlight. She's not just pretty; she's beautiful, wrapped in wealth and superiority—*ah, crap, forget her.* She doesn't even know my name. It's an image of him, of Knox, that lingers...the long, ugly scar that runs down from his right temple, through the hollow of his cheek, slicing into his upper lip. The devil. Hades. I call him that in my head sometimes before I shove him out of my thoughts and lock him away tight. My subconscious has always known to flee when I pass him in the hall, to run like the hot winds of hell are at my back.

He watched me walk up with Jolena, an intimidating glint in his narrowed gaze.

What are you doing here? his face said with a curl of those twisted lips.

His little looks—oh, how can I call them little? They've always been big looks, sweeping and brushing over me then dismissive, reducing me down to nothing but the air he breathes, the very dust motes that float around our hallowed school.

But...tonight—*God, it's still the same night, right?*—I forged ahead, swallowing my misgivings about him because Chance appeared in front of me. Beautiful, sweet Chance. My heart, which feels sluggish and weak, beats quicker. He's a Shark, in that inner circle, but he *likes* me.

He's been mine since this summer, little touches and slow kisses. We're building up to more, so much more. A leftover wisp of joy caresses me as I recall him twirling me around, kissing me on the cheek, and asking me to sing. After much cajoling and another shot of Fireball, I stood in the bed of someone's truck and belted out "Skyscraper" by Demi Lovato. Cheers rang out. Even Jolena smiled, and I don't even think she really likes me. I felt...elated.

Things get fuzzy after that.

Stumbling around inside my head, I wince at the images I see. Chance is there, but he isn't glad to see me anymore—which is weird because he invited me. He begged me to come. He made other promises too, but suddenly I see him right up in my face, jawline clenched, eyes blazing.

What...what did I do to him?

Doesn't he know I've put him on a pedestal and thought he might be different? I didn't want to fall so fast. I don't love much. I don't. To allow love in makes one vulnerable and it—

Forget him.

What is *wrong* with my body?

A lone tear wets my face and I wipe it away fiercely, surprised by the emotion.

Stop it, Ava.

You're just in the woods, and God knows you've slept in worst places.

Still, another drop of moisture sneaks out, and I swallow down the lump of emotion in my throat.

This is just me being drunk. That's all.

Nothing terrible has happened. Nothing at all.

I...I drank too much. That's it.

I suck in air as more faces from the party zoom in and out of my head, their features vague, funhouse images playing out, a horrible fair ride gone wrong. I see Knox leaving with Tawny. I watch Chance with another girl and my heart cracks. I see Jolena whispering to the other girls on the squad while they stare daggers at me.

What did I do?

Faster and faster and faster the events tumble around until I feel sick and lean over and vomit.

When I was ten, I managed to escape Mama at a fair, which wasn't really an escape because she didn't care what I did as long as I eventually came back. She slipped inside one of those rusty trailers on the outskirts where the workers lived. That night, she followed a man with thinning oily hair, a bushy beard, and a red bulbous nose. He pushed money into her hands and they wobbled off to disappear into that tiny metal house while I dashed for the rides, zeroing in on the Zipper. *Most Exhilarating Ride at the Fair* the blinking red lights said, but once the lady clamped that bar down and hurtled me into the sky, I screamed, my hands white-knuckled and clenched, certain the next spin into the heavens would be my last and I'd come crashing down, my guts flowing over twisted metal when the thing hit the earth.

But, I didn't cry. Not one time. Even when I went back to that trailer and snuck inside and Mama was on her knees in front of the man. His pants were at his ankles as her hands cupped his privates. Her eyes flashed at me then up at him. A long moment passed, seeming to stretch into eternity, then she motioned for me. *Come here, Ava.*

He zipped his pants and lurched toward me, and I flew out that door and ran and ran and ran. He chased me while I flew past the Zipper, past the corn dog stand, past the goldfish game, and right out the exit. I didn't see Mama for two days.

Focus, please Ava, time is passing and you're not right in the head and your body is wrong, just stop thinking about Mama and get yourself up and go go go go go go go go go go go...

With a huge breath, I push myself up more. God, I hurt everywhere. I touch my face, checking for injuries, but there's no swelling or blood. My arms are fine, goose bumps rising in the chilly air. I rub down my chest, squinting in the darkness. My shirt is shoved up to my throat, exposing my plain white bra, issued to me by the nuns at Sisters of Charity. The cups have been maneuvered down, and I adjust it with careful, slow movements, putting my breasts back inside.

My legs are jelly but still there, and I huff out a laugh as if expecting fatal injuries. No Zipper death yet.

Wait... I let out a primal sound, as if my body knows, only it's taking my brain a minute to catch up. My skirt is bunched up around my hips, my pelvic area bare. No plain white underwear from the nuns. Dimly, I process the leaves and twigs from the woods digging into my bottom. My hands flail uselessly over my skin as if the scrap of material might magically appear.

Oh, Ava, oh Ava, you know what this is—how could you be this naïve...

Craning my neck, I lean forward and take in small, purple-looking bruises on my inner thighs. I touch myself, there, and groan at the pain from the swollen tissue. My heart picks up more, flying inside my chest. Blackness dances in front of my face.

"No, no, no..." I say then vomit off to the side, again.

More memories—*are they real?*—slam into my mind.

Me heading off to the line of trees. I had to pee. Was Jolena with me? No. I shake my head as an image of someone else pops up, male, looming over me, leading me away. He took my hand and told me he had something to tell me, and for some reason I followed him—

I touch my mouth.

He kissed me hard.

He yanked my hair and shoved me down to the ground.

Clarity and realization take over the cloudy memories, cutting like a sharp knife. I don't remember details, most of it totally blank, but a monster was with me in these woods.

I hear Piper's voice in my head. *Don't trust them, Ava. You might be a cheerleader today, but no one gets inside their group.*

But...I just wanted to be close enough to be with Chance.

I wanted to live in his world.

Where is he now?

My thoughts drift, and I don't know how long I sit in the grass, grappling with what happened one second then wailing again the next as the reality of it settles around me.

Clinging to a tree, I try to stand but slide back to the ground.

Long minutes pass, and I'm aware of the moon as it moves through the trees. Just a little more time and I can walk.

I have to.

Someone needs me out there. I brush my fingers over the cheap, gold-plated locket around my neck, touching the flimsy chain. He's small and tiny and if he doesn't have me and if I don't get up, what will happen then?

That thought gives me strength, just enough to crawl away from the trees and across the open meadow. Past that meadow is that old road, and beyond that is a real highway where I can flag someone down—

I hear the soft rumble of a vehicle as headlights flash in front of me, a car swinging into the field. A brief elation rises in me then crashes and burns.

What if it's *him*?

My anxiety ratchets up, panic beating at me, and my muscles burn as I attempt to crawl back the way I came.

I'm good at hiding.

Always have been.

The bright glow of the lights blinds me, and my head swings wildly around, looking for somewhere to go.

Run, run, run...

Shuffling sounds break the stillness, a car door slamming, a voice calling out.

Fear courses through me and I cover my face, ashamed to be so defenseless. Me. ME.

Broad shoulders stand over me, and he speaks, and I blink up. I can't see him with the beams of light from his car in my eyes.

More talk from him. I can't respond. I retch instead.

He walks toward me. Bends down. Strong arms come down and sweep me up. Shifting around in his embrace, I try to fight, but it's nothing but a flinch, no struggle, no girl from the inner city who knows how to fight. I'm empty, my body unable to resist him putting me in his car, snapping the seat belt around me. He speaks, maybe my name, asking me questions, but I can't think straight. I can't do...anything.

He pulls away from the field, the car moving fast, so fast, and my head lolls to the side on the seat, staring at my captor.

Who is he?

Do I know him?

I squint, catching a glint of chiseled jawline and furrowed brow. His head turns and his steely gaze locks with mine. I think I see anger, and just when I think I know him, just when it's on the tip of my tongue—there's nothing but darkness as I slip away and sink back into oblivion.

End Excerpt

~

If you want to continue to read, head to the Amazon store to get the entire full-length standalone novel Dear Ava. You can also checkout all of my other books on the *Also by* page.

ALSO BY ILSA MADDEN-MILLS

All books are standalone stories with brand new couples and are currently FREE in Kindle Unlimited.

Briarwood Academy Series

Very Bad Things

Very Wicked Beginnings

Very Wicked Things

Very Twisted Things

Briarwood Academy Series

Dirty English

Filthy English

Spider

Fake Fiancée

I Dare You

I Bet You

I Hate You

I Promise You

Boyfriend Bargain

Dear Ava

Not My Romeo

Not My Match (Coming 2021)

<u>The Last Guy (w/Tia Louise)</u>

<u>The Right Stud (w/Tia Louise)</u>

ABOUT THE AUTHOR

Wall Street Journal, *New York Times*, and *USA Today* bestselling author Ilsa Madden-Mills writes about strong heroines and sexy alpha males that sometimes you just want to slap. A former high school English teacher and elementary librarian, she adores all things *Pride and Prejudice*; Mr. Darcy is her ultimate hero. She loves unicorns, frothy coffee beverages, vampire books, and any book featuring sword-wielding females.

*Please join her FB readers group, Unicorn Girls, to get the latest scoop as well as talk about books, wine, and Netflix:

https://www.facebook.com/groups/ilsasunicorngirls/

You can also find Ilsa at these places:

Website:
http://www.ilsamaddenmills.com
News Letter:

http://www.ilsamaddenmills.com/contact

Book + Main:

https://bookandmainbites.com/ilsamaddenmills

Printed in Great Britain
by Amazon